The Christmas Fayre on Holly Field

Lilac Mills lives on a Welsh mountain with her very patient husband and incredibly sweet dog, where she grows veggies (if the slugs don't get them), bakes (badly) and loves making things out of glitter and glue (a mess, usually). She's been an avid reader ever since she got her hands on a copy of *Noddy Goes to Toytown* when she was five, and she once tried to read everything in her local library starting with A and working her way through the alphabet. She loves long, hot summer days and cold winter ones snuggled in front of the fire, but whatever the weather she's usually writing or thinking about writing, with heartwarming romance and happy-ever-afters always on her mind.

LILAC MILLS

The Christmas Fayre on Holly Field

CANELO

First published in the United Kingdom in 2023 by

Canelo
Unit 9, 5th Floor
Cargo Works, 1-2 Hatfields
London SE1 9PG
United Kingdom

A CIP catalogue record for this book is available from the British Library.

Print ISBN 978 1 80032 882 2
Ebook ISBN 978 1 80032 881 5

This book is a work of fiction. Names, characters, businesses, organizations, places and events are either the product of the author's imagination or are used fictitiously. Any resemblance to actual persons, living or dead, events or locales is entirely coincidental.

Cover design by Rose Cooper

Cover images © Shutterstock

Look for more great books at www.canelo.co

Printed and bound in Great Britain by Clays Ltd, Elcograf S.p.A.

1

Chapter 1

The madness has started already, Harriet Parry thought, as she pushed her shopping trolley into the supermarket and saw the stacked tubs of Quality Street and Roses chocolates.

For pity's sake, the kids had only just gone back to school after the summer holidays! The store still had school uniforms and protractor sets on display, and yet there they were, trying to force Christmas down shoppers' necks.

It wasn't that Harriet disliked Christmas; it was more a question of dreading it. This would be the second Christmas she would be facing on her own, just her and the children. Last year had been pretty awful, but this year she had the added bonus of knowing what to expect.

Scowling, she marched up and down the aisles, scouring the shelves for buy-one-get-one-free offers and any reduced items. If she was lucky, she might grab a bargain or two and find some meat that had been marked down because the sell-by date was up. Declan's meanness and inability to pay maintenance on time often meant that meals containing meat were a rare treat. She tried to tell herself that it was better for her family's health and for the environment to eat a vegetarian diet, but damn and blast, she'd sell her right arm for a roast beef dinner.

With the shopping finally done, she stowed the bags in the boot of her little hatchback and drove home in a cloud of irritation and disgruntlement. She hated doing the monthly shop: not because she disliked grocery shopping as such, but because she was confronted by temptation at every turn, and she could cry when she saw yet another tantalising treat that she couldn't afford. Still, it was done now, and she could put it out of her mind for another month. In between supermarket visits, she would shop locally in Foxmore, and sometimes she would manage to bag a bargain from the bakery if they had any leftover bread, rolls or cakes that they wanted to get rid of at the end of the day. And when she needed milk or fresh produce, she would pop into the convenience store, although often there wasn't a great deal that was convenient about it.

As usual, Etta, their three-year-old dachshund, launched herself at Harriet as soon as she opened the door, and Harriet spent a few minutes fussing the dog. Although Etta was supposed to be the kids' dog, she was Harriet's fur baby, acquired when Declan had vetoed having another child, arguing that two was more than enough. In hindsight, Harriet realised it had been for the best – because a year later he had walked out on her.

Harriet hadn't been home more than five minutes, and was still putting the shopping away, when the front door slammed open and her children barrelled through it. She winced, guessing that the dent in the wall from the door handle had probably deepened by another millimetre or two. Yet one more job that needed doing, but wouldn't get done anytime soon. She tried her best, but DIY had been Declan's forte. If she ever attempted any repairs, she usually made the situation worse.

Deciding to ignore it (these things added character to a house, didn't they?), she greeted her hungry children, batting away eager hands as they delved into the bags to see what she'd bought.

'What's for tea? I'm starving!'

'You're always starving,' Harriet told her son.

Bobby was nine and growing fast, which meant he was perpetually hungry. She hoped she wouldn't have to replace his school shoes before Christmas because she hadn't long bought him a new pair, but she knew she was fighting a losing battle. He grew faster than a weed in a flower bed.

Sara presented her with a different set of problems, because her daughter thought she was eighteen, not eleven. She had only started at the comprehensive school three weeks ago, and Harriet could see the child changing before her very eyes. It was terrifying.

Sara grabbed a cheesy snack, unwrapped it and stuffed it in her mouth, chewing vigorously. Bobby's prize was a reduced yoghurt and he darted off to his room to eat it, leaving his school bag and coat in a heap on the kitchen floor.

With an overly dramatic sigh, Harriet bent to pick them up and popped them on the table. She would go through his bag later. She should really call him down and tell him off, but as she had managed to dodge the what's-for-tea question, she let it go. Her lentil and bean version of shepherd's pie wasn't their favourite, but it was healthy and filling, and they'd eat it or lump it.

'I've got to take five pounds to school tomorrow,' Sara said, having finished her cheese and eyeing the remaining yoghurts. 'Ma-a-am,' she whined, 'Bobby's eaten the strawberry one.'

'So he has.' Harriet refused to be drawn. If Sara hadn't gone for the cheese first, she could have had the strawberry yoghurt instead. 'Five pounds? What for?' Her heart sank, but she tried not to show it.

'School trip.'

'Where and when?'

Sara shrugged. 'Dunno. It's to do with STEM.'

'STEM?'

'Science, Technology, Engineering and Maths. There's a letter in my bag that you have to sign.'

'Oh, right.' She supposed five pounds wasn't so bad. She found her purse and counted out some coins. But when she read the letter, her heart sank again. The five pounds was only the deposit. Another eighteen pounds was required a week before the trip took place.

Wordlessly, she signed the permission slip and dropped the coins into an envelope.

3

'Oh, and can I have some makeup?' her daughter asked casually, as she shoved the money into her school bag.

'No, you're too young to wear makeup.'

'Darlene does.'

'I don't care.'

'And everyone else does.'

'Not listening,' Harriet said, pouring water into a pan. She knew that was untrue, because Harriet's friend Kelly didn't allow Catrin to wear makeup either, and Catrin was in the same class as Sara.

'Do you *want* me to be bullied?' Sara demanded.

'You won't be bullied for not wearing makeup. Anyway, it's against school rules.'

'I don't want to wear it to *school*,' Sara shot back, flicking her long hair over her shoulder. 'It's for Darlene's birthday party.'

'When is that?'

'November. The invite is in my bag, too. I've got to RSVP it. That's French for telling her I'm going.'

Blimey, Harriet thought, fishing it out and looking at the date. Darlene's mum was very organised. Harriet didn't usually begin thinking about her kids' birthdays until a couple of weeks before.

She was about to secure the invite to the fridge door, when she spotted the venue. Deri Castle? Surely that was a misprint?

'And I'll need something new to wear,' Sara declared.

'Will you now?' Harriet sighed.

'Please?' Sara was starting to whine.

'We'll see.'

Her daughter scowled at her. She knew, like all kids, that 'we'll see' usually meant no.

'I'll ask Dad.' Sara's expression was belligerent.

Good luck with that, Harriet thought. Declan paid the bare minimum towards his children's upkeep, and because he was self-employed and didn't declare half of what he earned, on paper he appeared to be living on the breadline.

'Good idea,' she said, with false cheerfulness. Maybe Declan would come through for his daughter, but Harriet doubted it.

Sara flounced out of the kitchen and Harriet called after her, 'Have you got any homework?' but the only response was the sound of a stroppy pre-teen stomping up the stairs.

Harriet let out another sigh. Being a single parent wasn't easy. Being a single parent with barely two pennies to rub together was flipping impossible. At least with the kids now back in school, she was able to pick up some extra shifts in the cafe, but she had a depressing feeling that most of any additional income would go on funding school activities and her daughter's burgeoning social life.

One step forward, two steps back... it was the story of her life.

–

'It's time to take Etta for a walk,' Harriet said after tea, and she waited for the grizzle of protest from her daughter. Bobby was happy enough to scamper along the riverbank with the dog, but of late Sara had become more reluctant, although she seemed to enjoy herself once she was there.

'Do I have to go?'

Yep, there it was – the whiny moan. 'Yes, Sara, you do. You can't stay in the house on your own.'

'Why not? Darlene does.'

'I'm not interested in what Darlene does or doesn't do. You're too young to be unsupervised.' Harriet was already sick of hearing Darlene's name. The child was swiftly becoming Sara's best friend, despite the two of them having only known each other a matter of weeks, as they'd gone to different primary schools.

'Scared I might nick your makeup?' Sara sneered.

Harriet blinked. This answering back and sassy attitude were new, and Harriet didn't appreciate it. 'If you want to pinch my makeup, feel free,' she said, hoping to take the wind out of her daughter's sails.

Most of it was old and dried up – a bit like Harriet herself. She'd never worn much anyway, just some concealer for the permanent dark circles under her eyes, mascara and lipstick when she remembered. However, the concealer had dried out, the mascara had gone gloopy and the lipstick wasn't the most flattering of colours. If Sara wanted it that badly, she was welcome to it.

'It's not fair,' Sara protested. 'Everyone else has makeup.'

'That's life,' Harriet said, biting back a smile when her daughter thrust out her chin, a mutinous expression on her face. When she did that, she appeared five, not eleven, and Harriet thought she looked adorable. Not that she'd say that to Sara's face, of course: there was only so much stropping Harriet could take. 'Put your shoes on.'

Sara narrowed her eyes and for a moment Harriet thought she might refuse, but with a loud huff, her daughter stomped into the hall to retrieve her trainers from under the stairs.

Bobby, bless him, was already wearing his and was hopping from foot to foot impatiently. Etta, sensing a walk was imminent, jumped up at him before dashing around in excited circles.

Harriet threw the dog's lead to her son and Bobby deftly caught it, clipping it onto the dog's collar while Harriet made sure she had poo bags and a ball in her pocket.

'I hate taking Etta for a walk,' Sara grumbled, as Harriet locked the front door behind them and they set off down the road. 'It's boring.'

'You wanted a dog,' Harriet reminded her. 'What happened to all those promises of "I'll feed her, I'll groom her, I'll walk her and I'll pick up her poop"?'

'*Mam!* Stop it,' Sara hissed, glancing over her shoulder to make sure no one had heard her mother mention the embarrassing subject of poo-picking.

6

There was no one else on the street, but even if there had been, it was unlikely to be Darlene, or any of Sara's other friends.

'Why? If you've got a dog, you need to pick up after it,' Harriet pointed out.

'Gross.' Sara gave a theatrical shudder and pulled a face.

'You used to do it—'

'Stop talking about it.'

'I pick up poo, don't I, Mammy?' Bobby tugged her sleeve.

'That's because you're a snot,' Sara said.

'Don't call your brother names. He's being a responsible dog owner.'

'Snotty, snotty,' Sara chanted.

'Mam, tell her!' Bobby shoved his sister, who promptly shoved him back. 'Mam, she pushed me.'

'He pushed me first.'

'Stop arguing, else you'll both be poo-picking for the rest of the week,' Harriet warned.

Sara opened her mouth. 'That's not fai—'

'Shh.' Harriet glared at her, then glared at Bobby for good measure.

They walked without speaking for a while. The children might be sulking, but Harriet didn't care – she relished the silence. However, Bobby soon perked up when they turned off the road and onto the path leading to the river, and he let Etta off her lead.

The dog scampered a few paces ahead, her nose down, tail up. This was probably her favourite place in the whole world, and Harriet smiled as she watched the dachshund sniff and snuffle her way along the path. No doubt she could smell the numerous other dogs who were also taken for walks along this stretch of the river, as well as the mice, shrews, voles and rabbits that lived in the undergrowth. Birds were plentiful, even though the swallows and swifts that were often seen swooping and diving over the meadows and fields to either side of the river had now flown south for the winter. There was a chill in the air, and the leaves of the trees lining the banks were turning the most glorious shades of burnt umber, nutmeg and cerise.

Harriet loved autumn. The run-up to Christmas with its fireworks and bonfires, the smell of woodsmoke in the air, the crispness of frost and dried leaves underfoot, the mists that hung over the river…

But although she might enjoy the outdoors, she wasn't looking forward to what went on indoors over the next couple of months, and her thoughts returned to the thorny problem of being able to afford all those Christmas presents that her children would ask for.

She hated disappointing them, but with Declan giving her only the bare minimum in child support, she had no choice. Sara still believed in Santa Clause, but even if she didn't Harriet had no intention of burdening her daughter's young shoulders with the knowledge that the family was only just holding its financial head above water.

As she watched Sara forget the sulk she was in at being forced out of the house for such a dreadful reason as taking the dog for a walk on a lovely September evening, and play hide-and-seek with her brother in the bushes, Etta joining in with gleeful abandon, Harriet shoved her worries to the back of her mind and concentrated on her blessings. She had two lovely healthy children, they had a roof over their heads and they lived in a beautiful part of the world. Not only that, she had an adorable pup and a part-time job that fitted in with school holidays. Aside from wishing she had enough money so she didn't have to struggle, what more could Harriet ask for?

Love? Romance? She heard Pen's voice in her head and scowled.

Pen owned Pen's Pantry where Harriet worked, and the annoying woman had been trying to set her up for some time now.

Harriet loved Pen to bits, but she didn't need a man in her life. She'd had enough trouble with Declan, and even if she hadn't, she couldn't face all that dating nonsense again. She wasn't in her twenties any more, and she had young children to boot. Maybe when they were older and had flown the nest, she might open herself to romance again. But not right now. Besides, there weren't many eligible bachelors in Foxmore, and none she fancied – so it was a moot point and Pen was barking up the wrong tree.

Speaking of trees and barking, Etta had managed to chase a squirrel up an ancient oak and was dancing around the base of the trunk, yelping hysterically. The little creature was high up on one of the spreading branches, chattering crossly.

With a smile, Harriet went to rescue the dog.

Chapter 2

What was it that old fella had called him just now? A tree hugger?

Owen Loxton chuckled quietly to himself. He'd been called worse, and the old guy had a point. Owen had never tied himself to a tree as such, but he had been known to protest vigorously about one being felled. These days, though, he did most of his protesting via a keyboard. He supposed he could be called a keyboard warrior, although he wasn't too keen on the term's negative connotations. He had paid his dues in the past and had earned his stripes, so to speak, when it came to protesting, and he had nothing to prove and everything to gain by using the powers of the internet to try to achieve effective environmental change.

Today he was in a little village at the southern end of the Snowdonia mountain range, his van parked on the edge of a small green. He had taken the opportunity to hand out a couple of leaflets to passers-by before diving into a cafe for a very late lunch, in the hope that if he had something substantial now, he would only need a bowl of porridge for supper later.

Owen wasn't entirely sure what he was doing here, but he had seen the sign for Foxmore and had decided to take a look. Besides, he was hungry, and he'd also fancied stretching his legs.

So far, he liked what he saw. The village was nestled in a wide glacial valley, with woodland cloaking its slopes and a river cutting through it. The tops of the hills were hidden by lowering autumn mists and he wondered whether there was any decent hiking in the area.

The village itself was pretty, consisting of a green with a Celtic cross in the centre, an old Norman church, a picturesque pub, and narrow streets leading off it which were lined with stone and slate terraced cottages.

There seemed to be a nice selection of independent shops, too. As he had driven slowly along the main street, he had spotted a butcher, a baker, a shop selling knick-knacks, an antique shop and – his heart had lifted when he'd seen it – an eco-refill shop. Ideally, he would love to see one of those on every high street, but there was some way to go before that happened. He was also pleased to see a cafe, as he had been driving since early morning and his stomach was starting to think that his throat had been cut.

The cafe was busy but there was a free table in the corner and Owen slipped into a chair with a contented sigh. He much preferred independent eateries like this to the national chains which tended to dominate most high streets, and picking up a menu, he scanned it hungrily.

The air was redolent with the aroma of coffee, and he was embarrassed when his stomach rumbled rather loudly.

A giggle made him look up to find a waitress standing next to his table, pad and pencil poised.

'I take it you're hungry?' she asked, smiling.

'Very. What do you recommend?'

'The specials are always good.' She pointed at a chalkboard on the wall behind the counter.

Owen peered past her to read it, but before he got to the end of the list of dishes, his eyes returned to her face.

He wouldn't describe her as beautiful, but she was arresting. There was something about her that made every other person in the cafe fade into the background.

Or was it just that he'd been without female company for too long?

No, that wasn't it. There was definitely something about her: navy eyes, sun-kissed skin and a smile so bright that it put the sun to shame. Reflexively, he checked out her left hand and saw she wasn't wearing a ring on her third finger – although that didn't necessarily mean she wasn't in a relationship.

He glanced at her face again, and her smile dimmed, a wary expression creeping into her eyes.

Damn! He was staring, wasn't he? And it was incredibly rude of him.

To cover his faux pas, he said, 'Have we met before?' Not exactly original, but he was relieved when her smile returned.

'I don't think so. I'd have remembered you.' Her eyes widened and she winced. 'I mean, I'm good with faces,' she explained hastily.

'I'm hopeless,' he said, trying to put her at her ease. He guessed she must have meant what she said – he was no oil painting and he knew it, so he didn't for one minute think his face was memorable because of his looks.

She smiled politely, and he realised she was waiting to take his order.

'Sorry.' He looked at the chalkboard again and picked the first vegan dish his gaze came to rest on. 'I'll have the chickpea stew, please, and a tea. Do you have herbal?'

'Of course.' She reeled off a selection and he chose camomile.

'Oh, and could I have some water?' he asked. 'Tap, preferably.'

She raised her eyebrows. 'Certainly.'

'I just don't believe in all that plastic-bottled stuff,' he said, wondering why he felt the need to explain. He didn't usually bother.

'Good for you.' She was about to retreat to the counter when she said, 'I saw you handing leaflets out earlier.'

'Er, yeah.' He cleared his throat as he prepared to explain. He would have given her one of them but he had handed them all out: although, no doubt he would find most of them stuffed in the nearest bin. 'We're trying to lobby the Welsh Assembly

Government to close all open-cast coal mines in the country. If enough pressure is exerted then maybe, just maybe, we'll be heard.'

'We?'

'Everyone who cares enough about the environmental impact that burning fossil fuels causes, and don't get me started on the destruction of huge swathes of land.' He stopped, realising that her eyes were starting to glaze over. He wondered why he bothered. No matter how hard he campaigned, no matter how passionate he was, it didn't seem to make any difference. It was like whistling into the wind.

'Right, I'd better sort your order out.' She tapped her pad with the pencil and he guessed he'd been a little too intense. He had a habit of doing that: unless the person he was talking to was as passionate about the environment as him, he often came across as a bit of a weirdo.

He watched the gentle sway of her hips out of the corner of his eye as she walked away, admiring her figure and how well she filled out her jeans.

Tearing his gaze away, his thoughts turned to work, so while he waited for his food to arrive, he put his tablet on the table, then shrugged his jacket off and hung it on the back of the chair. He might as well make use of the time to check his emails. He also had an article to submit, so he'd send that out while he was here.

When the waitress returned with his water, he asked if the cafe had Wi-Fi and was relieved when she said they did and gave him the password. Living in the van, he always had one eye on his data usage, keen not to go over his limit. He lived frugally and didn't want to spend money if he didn't have to.

He opened up the app and was engrossed in checking the article for a final time when he sensed someone at his elbow and realised his meal was ready.

Moving the tablet out of the way so the waitress could put the plate on the table, he smiled up at her.

'This looks delicious,' he said, eyeing the stew and accompanying sourdough bread with pleasure.

'It is. Enjoy. If you need anything else, give me a shout.'

'Who should I shout for?'

She narrowed her eyes. 'Harriet.'

He unwrapped some cutlery from a serviette. 'I'm Owen.'

She cocked her head in an acknowledgement of sorts but didn't offer anything further. He wasn't surprised. No doubt she got chatted up all the time. And why should she want anything to do with the likes of him? He was only passing through, and was a bit odd to boot.

Saying that, though, he had nowhere to go and nowhere to be, so he *could* stay for a few days and explore the local area if he had a mind to.

He had been heading towards the Llŷn Peninsula in the topmost northwest corner of Wales, purely because he had never been there before, but he quite liked the look of Foxmore so maybe he would hang around for a while.

Harriet left him to eat in peace, and as Owen tucked into his food, he checked out the local campsites. He much preferred to just pull off the road and find somewhere to park up, but that wasn't strictly legal, so he'd best use a campsite.

The cafe had quietened considerably by the time he had finished eating, and when he put his spoon down, he saw Harriet sitting at a nearby table, chatting to another woman, one he had seen serving behind the counter. They were taking a break, and he noticed that Harriet's sunny smile had disappeared and in its place she wore a sombre expression.

Owen didn't mean to eavesdrop, but with fewer customers in the cafe he couldn't help overhearing.

'She's growing up so fast,' he heard Harriet say. 'She's only been at secondary school a few weeks and it's already costing me a fortune. I thought it was bad enough when she was in primary.'

'In what way?' the other woman asked.

'Uniform and all the kit aside, they're asking for money for school trips, and she's already been invited to a birthday party. Goodness knows what I'm going to buy the girl for a present. Kids Sara's age aren't happy with a colouring book and a pack of crayons.'

The other woman patted Harriet on the hand. 'Have they ever been? I remember when mine were little; there was always one-upmanship when it came to birthday presents, and don't get me started on the party bags. It feels like you have to give the kids a present just for turning up. In my day we used to be happy with a balloon and a piece of cake.'

'Your day?' Harriet scoffed. 'Pen, you're not that old!'

'No, I just look it and feel it,' the woman laughed.

'You do not!'

'I'll be fifty-five next birthday. You're what, thirty-three, thirty-four?'

'Thirty-seven,' Harriet said, and Owen was surprised to discover that she was closer to his own age of forty-one, because he had assumed she was younger.

Abruptly, he pulled himself up.

Why should her age matter? Why should *anything* about her matter? He wasn't the kind of guy to leap into bed with a woman he'd only just met (even if she was up for it) and he didn't intend to be around long enough to get to know Harriet properly.

He would spend a couple of days in Foxmore, then he'd be off to Pwllheli or Abersoch in the hope of finding something worth writing about. Not only did he write articles for various publications, he also had a blog, *Planet B*, which provided the majority of funding for his lifestyle. The problem was, its success and popularity depended on him delivering fresh content every few days, which sometimes kept him awake at night.

When he tuned back into the conversation between Harriet and the woman called Pen (who, he suddenly twigged, was the cafe's owner – Pen, aka *Pen's Pantry*), the conversation had moved on.

'And now Sara is telling me that she needs a new outfit for this party,' Harriet was saying. 'She's already got a wardrobe full of clothes she doesn't wear. I'm getting sick of it – they don't appreciate what they've got, yet they want more. I'm fed up with buying stuff.'

'Then don't,' Owen heard himself say.

There was silence for a second as the two women stared at him.

If he'd had any sense, he would have left it there, but this was a subject close to his heart. He had spent the biggest part of his adult life trying to persuade people that there was already enough stuff in the world; that society's wanton desire to have the latest, the newest, the biggest, or the best, might be driving the economy forward but it was also driving the planet to destruction.

'Excuse me?' Harriet's expression reflected her icy tone.

Oh well, he had nothing to lose... 'I said, don't do it. Don't keep buying things.'

Harriet was looking at him as though he had two heads. It didn't faze him – he often evoked that very same expression in people.

'What am I supposed to do when my casserole dish breaks?' she demanded. Glancing at Pen, she said, 'Bobby knocked it off the counter and it smashed to smithereens!' She turned to Owen again and raised her eyebrows.

'Buy a second-hand one,' he suggested.

Harriet wrinkled her nose. 'I don't think so. I wouldn't know where it's been.'

'I would assume you'd give it a good wash before you used it,' Owen replied mildly.

'OK, say I do that—' she didn't sound as though she would '—it wouldn't stop my daughter from demanding something new to wear to this party. And what are you playing at, listening to other people's conversations?'

'I didn't mean to. You weren't exactly quiet.'

'I wasn't shouting from the other side of the room, either.'

'You've got to lead by example,' Owen ploughed on.

'Pardon?'

'When you buy things. Don't buy anything you don't need, don't buy something new just because you're fed up with what you've got, and when you do have to buy something, try to buy it second-hand.'

'Yeah, right. My children are *so* not going to go for that!' She rolled her eyes at the other woman.

To Owen's surprise, Pen said, 'It's a good idea.'

Harriet frowned. It made her look like a cross kitten. 'Whose side are you on?'

'Yours. If you can't persuade Sara to wear something she's already got, then buy second-hand. She gets something new without the "new" price tag.'

Owen could see Harriet thinking. The price-tag comment seemed to have hit home.

'I suppose I could check out eBay or Vinted.'

'Or Aled Harris holds a boot sale on his field every Saturday,' Pen said. 'I haven't been, but I hear it's well attended.'

'Boot sales are brilliant,' Owen said enthusiastically. 'Better than online second-hand shops because you don't have to pay postage... You might also pick up a casserole dish,' he added.

Harriet's expression gave nothing away. 'I might.'

He was losing her. She really wasn't keen on second-hand cooking utensils, was she? Typical. Never mind saving the planet – which should be everyone's main concern – she wasn't even prepared to consider the savings to her own pocket.

'Do you ever buy anything new?' she asked.

'Not if I can help it.'

'So that's a yes, then?' Her tone was triumphant, as though she had caught him out in a lie.

'I haven't bought anything new for over a year,' he replied mildly. 'I bet you couldn't manage a week.'

'I bet I could.' Her expression was challenging.

'If you're just planning on delaying your purchase of a casserole dish for a week, that doesn't count. And neither does not taking your daughter shopping for seven days,' he added hastily.

She pursed her lips and his gaze settled on her mouth for a moment, before returning to her eyes.

'I'll go one better,' she declared. 'I won't buy anything new for a month.'

He pulled a face. As soon as the month was up, she'd shop like crazy – *if* she kept to her promise at all.

'Whatever. Can I have the bill, please?' He was tired of trying to change the world one person at a time. It was like trying to push a ten-tonne boulder uphill with his bare hands. The phrase *fighting a losing battle* came to mind.

'You don't believe me, do you?' Harriet got up and walked over to the counter.

Owen sighed. 'No.' He followed her to the till point and took out his wallet.

'OK,' she said, her hands on her hips and a defiant look in her eye. 'I won't buy anything new between now and Christmas.'

His smile was sad. He'd heard it all before.

'You will,' he replied. 'How much do I owe you?'

She handed him a slip of paper. He squinted at it, then pulled out a ten-pound note. 'Keep the change.'

'I don't want a tip.' The till popped open and her fingers scrabbled for some coins. There was a spot of colour on both her cheeks and he guessed he'd made her cross.

She slapped his change down on the counter.

Pointedly, Owen picked up the coins and dropped them into a charity collection box which was sitting on the counter. Ironically, it was a Friends of the Earth one.

'I mean it,' she said. 'About not buying anything new until Christmas.'

'You won't stick to it. As soon as I leave Foxmore, you'll be back to your wasteful ways.'

Harriet straightened and her nostrils flared.

Ooh, he'd hit a nerve and had made her angry. Good. Angry people were what this planet needed. Complacent, contented people did nothing to change the status quo.

'I'll prove it to you,' she snapped. 'Don't leave. You could always stay here and keep tabs on me.'

Owen barked out a laugh. She thought she was winning the argument and that he had somewhere else he needed to be, so he'd have no choice other than to leave.

He decided to call her bluff. 'OK.'

'OK, what?'

'I'll stay in Foxmore. Where's the best place to park my van?'

'Oh, I… er, um. I'm not sure.'

There, that had her! Owen felt quite smug and wondered how soon she would back down.

'There's a campsite about one mile up the road, you could give them a try,' she said, and his smugness faded. She was serious.

Or was she calling *his* bluff, seeing how far he'd take it? 'I'll go straight there,' he said, his gaze not leaving hers.

'Good.' She nodded.

'Good,' he repeated.

They were at a standoff. He supposed he could spare a few weeks. After all, he didn't have anywhere he needed to be, although he did have to find something to write about on his blog if he was to—

Owen mentally slapped a hand to his forehead. Harriet and her buy-nothing-new-for-three-months challenge was the *perfect* subject matter. He could follow her progress, and make a note of what she found easy and what she found difficult about the challenge. Having children and the pressures they brought would add further depth and interest to the story.

But how would she feel about being in the spotlight? He had hundreds of thousands of followers who would be charting her progress with interest.

If he asked her for permission to write about it and she refused, could he, in all conscience, still write it? Probably not.

However, if he didn't ask and wrote it anyway, Harriet would never know. So where was the harm in it?

Owen, my man, he said to himself, *you're a genius!*

Chapter 3

'What?' Harriet demanded after Owen left the cafe, conscious that Pen was giving her a look. She watched him climb into a brightly coloured camper van. 'It's a good idea. Both for the environment and for my bank balance.'

'You keep telling yourself that,' Pen said. She was smirking.

Harriet knew exactly what she meant. 'He's not my type. He's too...' She couldn't think of the right word.

'Passionate?'

'Intense.' Harriet glared at her boss.

'Not bad-looking either,' Pen added.

'I didn't notice.'

'I don't believe that. He's tall, too.'

'His height is of no concern. I'm not height-ist.'

'How tall are you?'

'Five-foot-eight, as you well know.' Harriet glared down at Pen's five-foot-three frame.

'I like a man to be taller than me.'

'I'm not surprised,' Harriet shot back. 'Most men *are* taller than you.'

'A tall man makes you feel safe and protected, don't you think?'

'No.'

'No?'

'I'm not thinking about it.'

Pen carried on, 'What about his eyes? He had nice eyes. What colour would you say they were?'

'Amber,' Harriet replied, without thinking.

'Woo-hoo! *Amber?* And you're trying to tell me you didn't take any notice of him?'

Harriet lifted her chin and stuck her nose in the air. 'I'm not speaking to you any more.'

'Not even to tell me you'd like to work tomorrow?'

'Not even then.'

Pen chuckled. 'I'll see you at nine thirty. You'd better get off home: Bobby will be out of school soon.'

Harriet checked the time. 'He's got football practice so he won't be home for another hour.' Sara finished at three, but with the secondary school being some distance away and her daughter having to catch the bus, Harriet had a few minutes to herself until madness descended on the house.

She undid her apron, folded it neatly and popped it on a shelf under the counter, then went out the back to fetch her bag. When she came back into the cafe, she saw Pen standing by the window, gazing out of it.

'His van is still there,' Pen observed.

'So it is.' Harriet stared at it – it wasn't exactly subtle, was it? Not with what looked like a jungle painted on it. And was that a parrot? She squinted: yep, a parrot, and there was a monkey peeping out from behind a tree, too, and… a leopard? Goodness, he certainly didn't mind being noticed.

'Is he in it, do you think?' Pen wondered.

'I don't know and I don't care.'

'You cared enough to let him talk you into not buying anything new for the next couple of months,' Pen quipped.

'With the state my finances are in at the moment, it's hardly going to be difficult,' Harriet shot back.

Although, saying that, maybe she had been a little hasty. Christmas was coming and she didn't think her kids would thank Santa if he brought them someone else's discarded and unwanted items. And she still had the thorny problem of Sara's birthday invitation to deal with. Her daughter wouldn't take kindly to being told that Darlene wasn't going to be given an expensive gift. The way things were going, Darlene would be lucky to receive a gift from Sara at all.

Harriet said goodbye to Pen and made her way home, trying not to appear too interested in Owen's van as she sauntered past.

Was he inside? she wondered. And had he meant it when he'd said he intended to stay around to make sure she kept her word?

To be honest, she would be very surprised if he hung around longer than a week. Two, at the most. Foxmore was lovely and Harriet wouldn't want to live anywhere else, but she couldn't picture a man like Owen making the village his home for any length of time.

How long would he be able to live in that van for anyway? Not permanently, surely?

Then again, such a thing wasn't unheard of, although she couldn't imagine it. She liked her creature comforts too much – such as heating and the TV, for example. And showering.

She hoped he had a loo in there, because the thought of having to tramp across a wet, muddy field every time she needed to spend a penny made her shudder.

And there was something else that was bothering her. Didn't he have a job? Although, saying that, many people did work from home these days, so it was entirely plausible that he was gainfully employed and still able to travel around the country in a camper van: if, in fact, that was what he was doing. He might just have rented it for a holiday, for all she knew.

But then again, he *had* implied that he could stay in Foxmore for a while…

Wishing she knew more about him, yet at the same time irritated that he was taking up valuable headspace, Harriet had just returned to the problem of Sara and the forthcoming birthday party, when something made her pause.

Did buying birthday cards count as buying something new? She supposed it must.

Did that mean she'd have to try to find a second-hand one?

The idea made her giggle. Who'd ever heard of second-hand birthday cards? How ridiculous!

Yet another thought popped into her head — maybe Sara could make one? There were lots of bits and pieces in the house which Harriet had put to one side in case they came in handy for arts and crafts sessions with the kids on rainy days — old Christmas cards, ribbon, those shiny wrappers found on Christmas chocolates, scraps of fabric — plus the glitter, bits of coloured card, marker pens and glue that everyone with young kids had hanging around the house.

Surely Darlene would appreciate a card that had some thought put into it, rather than one grabbed off a rack in the supermarket while doing the weekly grocery shop?

Or maybe not.

Kids could be funny about things like that. Sara might even be bullied for daring to be different.

What about a digital card instead?

Harriet wrinkled her nose. That didn't sound right, either. She didn't think digital or e-cards were suitable for children of Darlene's age.

Maybe a TikTok video?

Ha! Harriet wouldn't know where to start, but Sara probably would. However, Harriet didn't feel like suggesting it, although it might be worth it just to see her daughter's face — Sara would be horrified.

As Harriet walked home, she debated the wisdom of accepting the challenge she'd been set. She hated backing down, but she couldn't see how it was doable. She had so much going on in her life, where would she find the time to scour second-hand shops for the things she needed?

If she saw Owen again (and let's face it, it was unlikely), she'd tell him that the challenge was off.

With the decision made, she thought she would feel lighter, but to her surprise, she didn't.

She felt guilty — because Owen was right. If she was serious about wanting her children to be less wasteful, she had to lead from the front. If *she* wasn't prepared to buy less stuff, why should *they*?

Sara would be a hard nut to crack, and Harriet recognised that she might never make any headway with her daughter, but Bobby, being that bit younger, might be more amenable, especially if she turned it into a game.

Harriet opened her front door and stepped into the hall, realising that she had talked herself into a complete about-face and was once again considering giving Owen's challenge a go.

The deciding factor, however, came when she spotted the brown envelope on the hall floor.

It was a bill, and as usual, it was for far more than she had anticipated.

–

A knock on the van's side window nearly gave Owen a heart attack, and he leapt to his feet, his pulse racing.

'Excuse me – are you in there?' It was a woman's voice and it sounded vaguely familiar.

With a sudden surge of excitement, Owen strode to the door and yanked it open, but was disappointed to see Pen from Pen's Pantry gazing expectantly up at him, and not Harriet.

'Er… hi,' he said, wondering what she could possibly want.

'Sorry to bother you, but I noticed that your van hasn't moved and I thought you might be having difficulty trying to find somewhere to pitch up. You can't stay here overnight, obviously.'

'Obviously,' he agreed. The road encircling the green wouldn't be the best place to park, especially since someone would invariably tell him that he had to move on. He wondered what she was going to suggest: he'd yet to give the campsite that Harriet had mentioned a call because he had been too busy drafting a blog post – although he didn't intend to publish it yet. First, he wanted to make sure Harriet was going to at least give it a try. But he had wanted to write it up while the idea was fresh in his mind.

Owen had a feeling she was going to chicken out, though. But even if she did, he had it covered: he would open the challenge up to his followers and ask for volunteers. Then he would pick one and pay them a visit. All would not be lost and he knew his readers would relish the challenge, and a great many of them would go along with it.

Owen wondered why he hadn't thought of this before; after all, not buying new was second nature to him. Then again, he mused, where was the challenge in that? The selling point of this idea was that it would be a completely new concept for Harriet. He didn't want someone who was already half doing this. He wanted to write about someone for whom buying second-hand, or resisting the urge to buy in the first place, was a totally alien concept.

Pen was still staring at him, and Owen realised she must have said something and he'd missed it.

'Sorry, could you repeat that?' He gave her an apologetic smile.

Pen grinned back. 'I said, I've spoken to the farmer who owns the land up the road. He's got a field that he doesn't know what to do with—' she lowered her voice '—he tried to get one of the big supermarket chains to build a store on it, but the villagers were having none of it.' She took a breath. 'Anyway, I asked if you could park your van there. There's no toilet or shower block, but I think it has a cold-water standpipe. For the sheep,' she added. 'Although, I believe the water might come directly from a stream on the mountain, so it's probably Baltic.'

'I don't mind,' Owen said, touched by the woman's thoughtfulness. 'If you give me directions, I'll move this eyesore.'

'Oh, and I've brought you this.' Pen handed him a paper package. 'It's a vegan pasty. I didn't know if you ate meat or dairy, and I didn't want to take the chance, so vegan it is! I don't get much leftover food, but when I do, I hate seeing it go to waste.'

'That's so kind, thank you. How much do I owe you?'

'Nothing.'

'Please let me pay you for it,' he pleaded, turning away to find his wallet. As he did so, he was conscious of Pen's curious gaze as she peered around him into the van.

'I wouldn't dream of taking your money,' she argued, her eyes scanning the interior. 'You've got it nice.'

'I like to think so. It suits my needs.'

'Here on your own?'

Owen bit back a smile. 'I am.' Pen was fishing, and he wondered whether it was Pen herself who was curious or whether her nosiness was on Harriet's behalf. For some reason that he didn't want to go into too closely, he hoped it was the latter.

'On holiday?' she asked.

'Not really.'

'Where are you from?'

Pen wasn't backward in coming forward, was she? But he answered her readily enough. 'Narberth, near Tenby, originally, but I lived in the south-east for a while.'

'Down Merthyr Tydfil way?'

He laughed. 'Not South-East Wales, the south-east of England.'

'I see. What brings you to this neck of the woods?'

'Nothing in particular.'

'What do you do for a living?'

Owen was beginning to think that the price of the pasty which he was still holding in his hand was more than he wanted to pay.

'A bit of this and a bit of that,' he replied warily. If he did intend to go ahead with featuring Harriet on his blog, he didn't want to let on that he was a writer, because he had the feeling Pen was part terrier, and she wouldn't stop gnawing until she'd winkled out of him what it was that he wrote.

'Ah, I see,' she said. 'I'll ask around, see if anyone needs a hand. Sometimes one of the farms hereabouts can do with an extra body. Any speciality, like carpentry or dry-stone walling?'

'Um, no.'

'General labouring, then. I'll put some feelers out. If you call in tomorrow around lunchtime, I can let you know if I hear anything. Bye.'

'Er, Pen? Those directions?'

'Yes, of course. Silly me!' She gave them to him, then scuttled back into her cafe, leaving Owen feeling as though he'd just done a round with MI5.

Bemused and hoping he hadn't given too much away, he returned to his laptop and the post he was writing. He had given Harriet a pseudonym to protect her identity, and had chosen the name *Dawn* for no other reason than he hoped this series of blog posts would encourage people to see the light. But then again, he supposed he was preaching to the choir, because those people who read his blog on a regular basis were mostly already converted.

Maybe it would be an idea to cast his net wider? He often got a bump of interest if he posted something that caught the eye of an organisation or a publication. How about if he directly approached one or two who might be interested, and see if they would give him a bit of free advertising by tweeting about it or mentioning it on any of their other social media accounts?

It was a thought.

While he was on a roll, he had better consider the issue of images. It was a known fact that photos caught the eye and encouraged people to click on a link or to read on, and while he wouldn't be able to take photos of Harriet (and certainly not of her children), there was nothing stopping him from taking the odd snap of any pre-owned items she might buy, and he could always pad those out with 'finds' that he'd hopefully spot in charity shops or the boot sale Pen had mentioned in the cafe earlier.

However, all this was pie in the sky at the moment, until he knew for sure that Harriet was definitely on board. Although he would dearly like her to keep her end of the bargain until

Christmas, the most important thing was that she started it in the first place. Even if she packed it in after a couple of weeks, at least he would have been able to write about the difficulties she had faced and the issues preventing her from continuing with the challenge. Valuable lessons would be learnt, which he could pass on to his followers.

Owen realised that he was unaccountably excited about this.

But whether it was the prospect of seeing rather more of Harriet or writing about the challenge he had hopefully goaded her into accepting, he had yet to determine.

Chapter 4

Harriet hadn't intended to go into the charity shop that morning. Or any other morning, for that matter.

It was simply a habit of hers to glance into shop windows as she walked along the high street on her way to work. It didn't matter if the shop was the hairdresser's or whether it was the convenience store with its 'for sale' board, she always had a gander. Her favourites were the antique shop (though the prices made her eyes water) and the soap and candle shop, ingeniously called Wash N Glow. She'd loved both of their Christmas windows last year, and she was looking forward to seeing what the owners would come up with this year.

It was only natural, then, for her gaze to sweep over the window displays of the double-fronted charity shop. The first window had two mannequins on stands, sporting clothes in autumnal colours, and her attention was drawn to a knitted hat in a nut-brown shade with a faux-fur trim. It looked cosy and warm, but she had a perfectly good bobble hat at home and didn't need another.

However, she did need a casserole dish, and there was one sitting on a table in the second window. Harriet came to a halt and gazed at it. She had been anticipating buying the exact same glass dish with a lid as the one that had been broken, but this one looked as though it would do the trick. And the price wasn't to be sneezed at.

Without giving herself a chance to change her mind, Harriet pushed the door open and stepped inside.

'Hello, Mrs Moxley, can I have a look at that casserole dish in the window, please?'

'The cream enamel pot with a lid?'

'That's the one. Is it really only one pound fifty?'

'Let's have a look, shall we?'

Harriet followed Mrs Moxley's purple-haired progress over to the window and watched as the pensioner carefully lifted it off the table.

'I didn't know you worked here,' Harriet said, as the woman made her way back to the counter. 'I thought you helped out in Sero?' Sero was the recently opened zero-waste shop that was run as a co-operative by many of the villagers. Harriet wished she could afford to buy a share, but as well as not having the money, she didn't have the time to help run it.

'Here you go, luvvie.' Mrs Moxley put the casserole dish down in front of Harriet. 'I've been volunteering for a while now. We don't see you in here much.'

Harriet heard the subtext: if she came into the charity shop more often then she would know who worked there and who didn't.

'Your dad is a regular,' Mrs Moxley added.

'He is?' How come Harriet didn't know that?

'Oh aye, whenever he's in Foxmore to pick up your kiddies, he pops in.'

'Sara and Bobby, too?' Harriet couldn't imagine Sara being happy with mooching around a charity shop.

'No, he doesn't bring them with him. He comes in before he picks them up.'

'What does he buy?' Harriet asked curiously, the enamel pot lying forgotten on the counter.

'Records. Old 78s mostly. He's always on the lookout. If we get any in, and that's not often, mind you, I put them to one side for him. What do you think?'

'That's very kind of you.'

'Not about that – about the pot. You can use it on the hob or put it in the oven. When I was a girl, my mam used to have loads of this stuff, from a bread bin to a roasting tin.'

Harriet picked up the pot and turned it over in her hands. 'It's in good condition.'

'We don't sell rubbish in here. Mind you, in my day people didn't get rid of stuff the way they do now. These days they throw it out as soon as look at it. My mam would turn in her grave at the things people get rid of. She lived through the war, you know.'

Harriet smiled absently. She was still checking out the pot, wondering how many casseroles had been prepared in it and whether it had been washed thoroughly each time.

Of course it must have, she told herself. It certainly looked clean enough.

She checked the sticker again: one pound fifty. A bargain.

'I'll take it,' she said, reaching into her bag for her purse and a tote to put her new purchase in.

'Take my advice and don't scrub it with a scouring pad if you get burnt food on it. Leave it to soak overnight in warm water and add a denture tablet. It'll be as good as new in the morning.'

'Thanks for the tip,' Harriet said, handing over some coins.

Pleased with her purchase and thinking how retro the pot was, she began to walk out of the shop when the knitted hat caught her eye again and temptation tugged at her.

This hat was much nicer than the one she had, which was starting to look a bit shabby and had lost some of its stretchiness. Maybe she could treat herself to a new one, considering she had saved a few pounds by buying a second-hand casserole dish?

She was about to ask if she could try it on, when common sense kicked in: she had a bill to pay. Besides, remembering what Owen had said about not buying anything you don't need, she realised that she had been trying to justify the purchase of a new hat (new to her, anyway) simply because she wanted it.

Only a few minutes ago she had been telling herself she had a perfectly good hat at home.

Feeling inordinately pleased, both with finding a bargain and for resisting temptation, Harriet hurried off to work.

Owen would be proud of me, she thought, as she rounded the corner into the green. Then she felt a flash of disappointment when she didn't see his van, and she hoped he'd gone to the campsite she had told him about and hadn't left Foxmore for good.

Still, even if he had left the area, he had given her something to think about when it came to her future buying habits. And if he had gone, she wouldn't need to worry about making a card for Darlene's birthday, because he wouldn't be here to know if she bought a new one. They did some lovely cards in the shop on the high street, even if they were rather expensive.

'He's single,' Pen announced as soon as Harriet entered the cafe.

Harriet stowed her bags and coat in the room at the back, and tied her apron around her waist before she asked, 'Who is?'

Harriet knew who Pen meant, but she didn't intend to give her boss the satisfaction. Pen was far too smug already.

Pen gave her a look. If she wore glasses, the woman would have been peering over the top of them.

Harriet gave in. 'How do you know?' She had to admit, she was curious.

'I asked him.'

'When? Has he been in already?' Disappointment at having missed him teased her mind, but at the same time she was relieved that he was still in the area. However, she didn't want to examine why she felt relieved, so she shrugged and got on with her job.

'Not yet.' Pen was grinning at her. 'Are you hoping he will?'

'Certainly not!' Harriet cleared a table and wiped it down before pushing the chairs back into position. Then she returned to the counter where Pen was cutting a large cake into suitably sized servings.

36

Curiosity got the better of her again, and she asked, 'When did you speak to him?'

'Yesterday, after I closed up. He was still parked on the green, so I took him a pasty.'

'And demanded payment in the form of information?' Harriet guessed.

'He didn't *have* to talk to me.'

'It would have been rude if he hadn't,' Harriet pointed out.

'He's from West Wales originally, near Tenby, but he's been living in England. Do you want to know where he is now?'

'Not really. Excuse me.' Harriet took a customer's order and set about fulfilling it.

Pen wasn't to be deterred. 'I spoke to Aled Harris and he agreed to let Owen park his van on his bottom field. Not the one the boot sale is held on – that's Holly Field – the one next to it.'

'My, my, you have been busy.'

Pen grinned. 'How did Sara take the news that she won't be getting a new outfit for her friend's birthday party?'

'I haven't told her yet.'

'Chicken.'

Harriet clucked her acknowledgement. 'Anything for a quiet life for one more day. When I do tell her, they'll probably hear the shouting in Dolgellau.'

'That far, eh?'

'Ten miles is nothing,' Harriet warned grimly. 'Sara's got a bell on every tooth when she gets going.' She brightened. 'I bought a casserole dish this morning.'

'Aw, Harriet, you promised!' Pen's face was a picture of disappointment and Harriet took great delight in explaining.

'I popped into the charity shop next door to A Cut Above on the way into work, and they had an enamel pot with a lid. It's quite retro.'

'Let's see?'

Harriet finished serving a customer, then nipped out the back to fetch her purchase.

'It's in good condition,' Pen observed, tipping it this way and that. 'Not a chip in sight.'

'I don't think you're meant to cook chips in it,' Harriet said, deadpan.

'Very funny.' Pen gave it back to her. 'See, that wasn't so bad, was it? How much did you pay for it?'

'One-fifty.'

'You've got a bargain.'

'I thought so, too.'

'Don't forget to give it a wash before you use it,' Pen teased, and Harriet rolled her eyes.

Still, if Pen thought she had made a decent purchase, then she must have done. Maybe there was something in this not-buying-new challenge after all…

–

Not wanting to fire up the wood burner just to heat some water, Owen decided to make do with a cold shower, so he filled his portable water bag from the standpipe near the gate and hung it up in the tiny shower cubicle. On sunny days, and if he had enough time, he would hang the bag up outside to allow the heat of the sun to warm the water naturally, but that took a good few hours and he wanted a wash now.

Owen stripped off, gasping as the icy water cascaded over his skin, and he hastily reached for the soap. Weren't cold showers supposed to be good for you? Something to do with boosting the immune system? After the number of freezing showers he had taken over the years, he should be as healthy as a horse. To be fair, he was rarely ill, and he put it down to living a simple and mostly outdoor life. However, since he'd turned forty, he had noticed the odd twinge in his back, and his right knee sometimes played up first thing in the morning, and it could take as long as an hour for the aches and pains to settle down.

His dad maintained that those kinds of things were an inevitable result of ageing, but Owen refused to believe it, despite having a sneaking suspicion that his father might be right.

Maybe he just needed to replace his mattress? In this instance, he would buy new, but only because a used mattress usually tended to be nearing the end of its life and he would only end up having to buy another one in a couple of years. Owen had certainly had his money's worth out of this one, though, having had it for eighteen years, so he couldn't complain. The current advice was to change a mattress every seven years, but Owen was convinced that the 'advice' was a marketing ploy on behalf of mattress manufacturers everywhere.

Shower over, Owen hastily towelled himself dry, then rooted around for some clean jeans and a T-shirt. He'd throw a hoodie over the top because the morning was a little fresh, which was only to be expected considering it was nearly October, although it was forecast to be a nice day, and perfect for getting out and about exploring the local area.

Hungry again (he had already eaten rolled oats with syrup and sliced banana at six a.m.), he decided he'd have a second breakfast at the cafe. If he ate something substantial now, it would set him up for the rest of the day until supper.

Feeling content with his lot, he locked the van, then sauntered down the lane towards the village, in no hurry. He had nothing in particular to do and nowhere in particular to go, and he relished the freedom. Who wanted to be tied down to a nine-to-five job and a house that was mortgaged to the hilt, when you could work when the mood took you, pitch up where you fancied and be answerable to no one? Not him!

The hillsides and mountains around Foxmore were inviting, but Owen decided he would check those out another day. Right now, he wanted to explore the village itself, then take a walk by the river.

He loved running water, the sound of it, the smell, the way it trickled along the shallows and ran darkly in deeper parts. And he loved wild swimming, although he would probably give that a miss for now. He'd had his fill of icy water today.

He would do some foraging, though, because there was nothing nicer than eating what you grew or found, and considering he didn't have a garden to grow veggies and fruit in, he would have to make do with what he could forage. There should still be some blackberries around, and the hawthorn berries and rosehips were usually abundant in the hedgerows at this time of the year. If he was lucky, he might find a few late-fruiting wild strawberries, and when he ventured to the hills above the village, he would make sure to take a basket with him to collect the last of this season's blueberries. He would keep an eye out for hazelnuts and sweet chestnuts along the riverbank, too.

In a very short time Owen had left the houses behind and was walking along a dirt track towards the river.

He smelt it and heard it before he saw it, and he stopped to listen to the burble of running water as he breathed deeply, enjoying the clean, fresh air.

The trees were getting ready for winter. They were turning colour and a steady patter of dry leaves drifted down from the branches overhead like oversized confetti. They crunched under his feet as he walked, and he scuffed his way through them, kicking them into the air, feeling like a big kid.

He had his rucksack with him, and when he found a patch of brambles resplendent with juicy black fruit, he picked enough to fill a Tupperware box, but made sure he left plenty for the birds and other animals to feast on. His mouth watered when he thought about mixing them with yoghurt for a healthy dessert. He might even have enough to make a small pot of jam.

Owen picked a handful to eat now, and perched on a fallen log to devour his snack, letting the sights and sounds of nature fill his heart and soul.

The residents of Foxmore were lucky to have such a beautiful unspoilt river on their doorsteps and, combined with the hills and moorlands above, he had to admit this was a darned nice spot to live in. If ever he thought about settling down, Foxmore would be the sort of place he'd consider.

He didn't know how long he sat there, but when his stomach growled, he decided to head back to the village and pop into Pen's Pantry – ostensibly to have a bite to eat, but in reality to see if Harriet was there and, if she was, whether she was serious about taking him up on his challenge.

He had a feeling she would back out. He'd heard her say that her daughter wanted a new dress for a party, and he guessed she would probably give in to the girl's demands.

He could feel a grin spreading across his face when he spied Harriet through the window as he approached the cafe. She had her back to the door, but she soon turned around when Pen nudged her as he stepped inside.

'Owen!' Pen called. 'How was the field?'

'Good, thanks.'

'Take a seat. Harriet will be over to take your order in a minute.'

Owen did as he was told, choosing a table on the opposite side to the counter and sitting with his back to the wall so he had an uninterrupted view of the room. And Harriet.

She was looking particularly pretty this morning, with her hair piled on the top of her head and a few wisps curling around her cheeks. She looked as though she had been in the sun, her face glowing, although that might equally be from the warmth inside the cafe, he guessed.

'She's bought a casserole dish,' Pen called over to him. 'Harriet, show him.'

Harriet's glow intensified. 'Not now,' he heard her hiss.

'You'd like to see it, wouldn't you, Owen?' Pen persisted.

He shrugged, thinking *not really*, but was too polite to say. He'd known that Harriet wouldn't be able to stick to her pledge of not buying anything new from now until Christmas, but he honestly hadn't expected her to cave in quite so fast; it had been less than twenty-four hours, for goodness' sake!

Maybe his thoughts had shown on his face, because Pen made her way over to him and lowered her voice. 'She bought it second-hand.'

Owen perked up and sat up straighter. That was more like it! 'She did?'

'Uh-huh.' She turned to Harriet. 'You might as well show him – after all, you would never have bought it if it wasn't for Owen and his challenge.'

Harriet looked positively thunderous. With swift, jerky movements, she wiped her hands on a towel, threw it onto the counter, then stalked out the back.

Owen was conscious of the curious gazes of a number of the cafe's clientele, and he wondered whether Harriet was embarrassed at having bought something second-hand. They were clearly speculating as to what the challenge could be, and he debated whether she'd enlighten them.

He thought not, considering she hadn't been too keen on the idea in the first place, and he had to admit to being taken aback that she had actually bought a pre-owned casserole dish.

Harriet, carrying a tote bag, stomped up to his table. The look she gave Pen made him wince, but all Pen did was beam at her.

Crossly, Harriet took her dish out of the bag and plonked it on the table. 'There. Satisfied?'

Owen wasn't entirely sure she'd been talking to him, so he kept his head down and examined the casserole dish instead. He had been expecting to see a glass one, but this was an enamel pot and it was in excellent condition. A sticker on the side of it declared it to be one pound fifty.

'You've got yourself a bargain,' he declared.

Harriet glared at him for a moment, then her expression softened and a smile hovered on her lips. She had nice lips – full and pink – and he imagined how it would feel to kiss them. Then he pulled himself together. There was no way he should be imagining kissing Harriet.

'I have, haven't I?' she said, and a grin broke out. She had the most gorgeous smile, and he smiled back at her.

'When you two have finished making eyes at each other,' Pen said, 'can you let me know if you intend to order anything, Owen?'

Harriet huffed. 'We weren't making eyes at each other. Pen, I honestly don't know what's got into you lately.'

'Er, sorry Pen, no eye-making,' Owen said, feeling self-conscious. Had he been that obvious? But even if he had, Harriet hadn't been looking at him like that. Pen, he decided, had an active imagination. 'I'll have the rainbow salad falafel wrap with houmous, please, and a mint tea.'

'Coming right up.' Pen took a step towards the counter, then paused, giving Harriet a pointed look. 'Does this mean you're going to stick to your vow of not buying anything new from now until Christmas?'

'I suppose it does,' Harriet said. She didn't look happy about it, though, and Owen sympathised.

It wasn't easy transitioning from buying what you wanted, when you wanted it (within reason, of course), to having to seriously think about everything you purchased. Still, it was better for the planet, and that was all that mattered.

He was still holding the enamel pot in his hands when he realised Harriet was waiting for him to hand it back.

It was then that a major flaw in his plan occurred to him – *how on earth was he going to take a photo of this to put on the blog?*

Chapter 5

'Poor baby, have you missed your mam?' Harriet crooned as Etta scrambled to climb into her lap. She hated leaving the dog alone when she was at work, but she didn't have a great deal of choice. Sometimes, if she was able, she would dash home on her break and let her out for a wee, but when she did that, it seemed to unsettle the pooch more.

Laughing, Harriet tilted her head back, fending off sloppy, enthusiastic licks, and cuddled Etta to her, holding the wriggling body close.

'I expect you want to go out,' she said, getting to her feet and opening the kitchen door to allow the dog into the garden. She left it open, and reminded herself what she was making for tea. There was a menu on the fridge, which she set weekly and stuck to religiously to ensure that she had the ingredients to make their evening meal each day, and that she didn't waste any food.

Today it was fish fingers and chips, luckily, because what Harriet was going to tell her eldest child over tea wouldn't go down well, and she was vainly hoping to distract Sara while she was tucking into one of her favourite meals.

Meh, who was she kidding? It was never going to work. Sara wouldn't be keen on making a card for Darlene's birthday at the best of times, and after finding out she'd either have to wear what was in her wardrobe or trawl around the boot sale on Saturday, she would probably have a meltdown.

If Harriet blamed herself for her daughter's attitude, she blamed Declan more. While she had been busy trying to set boundaries, Declan had indulged the children to the point that it had become a rather large bone of contention between them. Then he'd buggered off, and now not only had all the spoiling and the treats stopped, but the kids were lucky if they saw him from one month to the next. In fact, she couldn't remember the last time they had spoken to him, let alone had a visit from him. Bobby had stopped talking about his father, and Sara only mentioned him infrequently – like when she was trying to play Harriet off against him. Harriet recalled the conversation she'd had with Sara when she had threatened to ask her dad if he would buy her something new to wear to Darlene's party. Harriet assumed the answer had been no, if the child had actually managed to speak to her father, because more often than not, he didn't answer his phone.

Her heart bled for her children, but there was nothing she could do about their father's lack of regard.

Bobby barrelled in through the door first, quickly followed by Sara, and the pair of them headed for the fridge, casting aside bags and coats as they did so.

Harriet had a feeling of déjà vu. It was the same scenario every school day, and she mentally counted the seconds off in her head before one of the children asked what was for tea.

'Fish fingers,' she informed them.

'Yay! My favourite.'

Harriet smiled stiffly, wondering how long her daughter's good mood would last once she knew about the card and new outfit situation. 'Have you got any homework? No, Bobby, you can't have another yoghurt – you haven't finished the one you've got in your hand yet. If you're hungry, have some fruit. Or there's a nut-and-seed bar in the cupboard. And please can you put your PE kit in the laundry basket? Sara, homework.'

Harriet might as well have been talking to the wall, for all the good it did.

Bobby left his bags on the floor and made a dash for the stairs, and Sara headed for the living room and the TV.

'Kids, get back here and sort out your school bag: Sara, no TV until you've done your homework.'

A chorus of groans, 'it's not fair', and elaborate sighing followed, but at least the children dragged themselves back into the kitchen and did as they were told.

'Did you have a good day?' she asked, directing the question to both of them.

'It was all right,' Sara mumbled, scooping her bag up off the floor and slinging it over her shoulder.

'Have you got any homework?'

'Loads.'

'What subjects?'

'History. We've got to do some research on where we live.'

'That sounds interesting.'

'It's dumb.'

'Riiight. How about you, Bobby? Did you have a good day?' Harriet turned her attention to her youngest, who had his head in the fridge again. 'What did I say about eating another yoghurt?'

'But I'm hungry.'

'Fruit,' she reminded him. 'Or a nut-and-seed bar.' She made them herself and she knew exactly how much goodness was in them.

Bobby pulled a face, but took a banana from the bowl, peeling it reluctantly.

Why did everything have to be a battle? she wondered, wishing Declan were there to take some of the weight off her shoulders, even if he hadn't been much use on the discipline side of things.

Harriet shook her head to clear it. What on earth was she thinking, wishing that Declan still lived with them? He had made his feelings pretty clear, so why she would want him back was beyond her.

If she was honest, she didn't. It would just be nice to have another adult in the house, that was all – someone she could sound off to when things got a bit much, someone she could share her worries with, share her hopes with… Share *anything* with, really.

Tea didn't take long to prepare, and within half an hour it was on the table and she was shouting for the children to wash their hands and come eat.

Bobby was first to sit down, his hands still suspiciously grubby, so Harriet sent him away to wash them again.

'We'll eat this then take Etta for a walk, yeah?' Harriet said. Déjà vu again…

'Can I have a mobile phone?' Sara crammed a chip into her mouth.

Harriet's spirits sank. 'No, cariad, you can't.'

'But, Mam, everyone in school has got one. I'm the only one who hasn't.'

'We can't afford it. Sorry.' She suspected Sara was exaggerating again, but even if she wasn't, Harriet thought her too young to have a mobile, even if money wasn't an issue.

Sara's expression turned mutinous, and she narrowed her eyes and jutted out her chin.

'Maybe next year,' Harriet said.

'Can I have a mobile, too?' Bobby knew he was pushing his luck, Harriet could tell, but she didn't blame him for trying.

'Definitely not. How about we get the craft box out after we've taken the dog for a walk? That would be fun, wouldn't it?'

Bobby perked up, but Sara didn't look convinced. Uncannily, Harriet had the feeling that her daughter knew she was up to something, and considering that the craft box was usually reserved for rainy days, Sara was right.

'I thought it would be a nice touch if we made Darlene a birthday card,' Harriet added casually.

Sara stared at her in disbelief.

'It'll be more personal than if we bought one,' Harriet persevered, knowing from the expression on her daughter's face that she'd already lost the battle.

'I'm not giving Darlene a handmade card,' Sara said in a flat voice.

'It's no different to buying a handmade card off Etsy,' Harriet pointed out, ignoring Sara's 'yeah, right' look, and wondering whether she should go ahead and just buy one anyway. Owen would never know.

'It'll look awful,' Sara snapped.

'It mightn't.' Harriet tried to be chirpy. 'If we're any good at this, we could start our own Etsy shop. What do you say?'

'We'll be millionaires!' Bobby cried, ignoring Sara's sneer. 'I bet I can make the best one.'

'Bet you can't.' Sara's retort was automatic and Harriet knew that her heart wasn't in it. Sara's default setting was to contradict everything Bobby said.

'I think both your cards will be fantastic,' Harriet enthused.

'Huh.' Sara finished her meal and pushed her plate away.

'I'll quickly wash up, then we'll get going.' Harriet got to her feet and collected the dirty dishes. 'Sara, it's your turn to dry; Bobby, can you find Etta's lead?'

Sara rolled her eyes but did as she was asked. Harriet made sure the children did some chores – although she had to remind them constantly.

'Mam, can I go shopping with Catrin on Saturday? She's going to Dolgellau and her mam said I can go with them.'

'If you want,' Harriet said. It was kind of Kelly to let Sara go with them; Catrin and Sara had been friends since primary school, and Harriet was relieved that Sara wanted to spend time with her, as she hadn't heard Catrin's name mentioned for a while. It had been Darlene this, and Darlene that, lately.

'I thought I could buy something to wear to Darlene's birthday party,' Sara added.

'I don't think that's a good idea.' *Drat, I should have anticipated that*, Harriet thought.

'Kelly can help me choose. She's sensible.'

'I know she is, my lovely, but it's not fair on her. I wouldn't like it if the shoe was on the other foot. I'd be worrying whether

Kelly would approve. Anyway, I'm sure you've got something in your wardrobe that you can wear.'

'I haven't.' Sara was adamant.

'What about that dress you wore for Granny's birthday?'

'It's too babyish. And it doesn't fit me. I've grown,' Sara announced. 'See? I used to be up here—' she put a finger on Harriet's arm '—and now I'm this tall.' She placed her hand on the top of her head, then transferred it to a spot just below Harriet's shoulder.

Sara might be overly optimistic when it came to her height, but Harriet realised the child was right – her daughter had indeed grown. She seemed to have shot up since last week. And so had Bobby, she thought. The joggers he had on today were at half-mast. Both children were in urgent need of new clothes, and Sara might have a wardrobe full, but how many of them still fitted her properly?

Harriet groaned – if she had to buy new clothes for both of them, it was even more imperative that she bought second-hand.

'Let's have a look through your clothes first, eh? See what fits and what doesn't, then we'll go from there, shall we?' Harriet suggested.

'When? Today?'

'Not today. How about Friday?'

'Then I can go shopping for new clothes on Sunday!'

'Sorry, no, we're going to Granny and Grandad's on Sunday.'

'The Saturday after?'

Harriet said, 'Possibly.' She wanted to see whether any of the clothes already in her daughter's wardrobe were suitable first.

Typically, Sara heard only what she wanted to hear. 'Yay!' she cried, twirling the tea towel that she was clutching around her head and dancing out of the kitchen. Then she dashed back in, thrusting the tea towel at Harriet. 'You're the best mam in the world,' she declared, before skipping out again, leaving Harriet feeling a total failure, because she had no intention of taking her daughter on a mammoth shopping trip to the nearest town any time soon.

Harriet dreaded breaking the news to Sara that her clothes shopping was going to be done here in Foxmore – in the charity shop. Or, failing that, the car boot sale.

Harriet felt like crying. It was one thing being noble about not buying anything new for the rest of the year, but it was another thing entirely being forced into it by circumstances, and she was not looking forward to telling Sara. And not just because her daughter would be upset. Didn't every parent want their children to have the best?

Looking back, Harriet certainly hadn't wanted for much when she was growing up. She knew her parents had sacrificed a lot to ensure that she and her brother had a wonderful childhood. Never once had she considered how her mam and dad had been able to afford her ballet lessons or her brother's rugby tournaments, her passion for horse riding or Simon's for playing the guitar. Of course, neither she nor her brother had got *everything* they had wanted – there had been limits – but she had never felt a lack of anything. And it broke her heart to think that her two children would be forced to stop and think about the price of everything from now on.

Sara and Bobby, bless them, were oblivious to her mood as they stepped outside, Etta pulling excitedly on the lead, and for once Sara hadn't moaned about walking the dog.

'This is the wrong way for the river, Mam.'

Bobby's voice brought her out of her dismal thoughts, and Harriet realised that they were heading out of the village and towards Aled Harris's farm. Her feet must have subconsciously brought her this way because this was where the boot sale was held, and she had been so wrapped up in thoughts of second-hand stuff that she hadn't paid attention to where they were going.

She hadn't been down this way for ages, so it made for a change, and Etta would love all the new smells in the open fields. Before they'd had the children, she and Declan used to go for long walks on the hillsides surrounding Foxmore, but after the kids had arrived, those long walks in the mountains had dwindled to nothing. Harriet had hoped that having Etta would encourage the family to get out and about more, but then Declan had left and the most Harriet could manage was a stroll along the riverbank once a day. And even that went by the wayside when the nights drew in and the weather was foul.

'Mam, this is the wrong way for the river,' Bobby repeated.

'I thought we'd have a change of scenery,' Harriet said. 'We always go down to the river.'

'We're not going up there, are we?' Sara grimaced, pointing to Aled's farm and the hillside above it.

It was quite a trek to get to the top, and although Harriet would have been up for it once upon a time, she didn't think she could manage it now. Besides, it would be dark soon, and there was no way she was trekking up any mountain in the dark.

'We'll just go as far as Aled's bottom field and if there aren't any sheep in there, Etta can have a good run around, then we'll go home,' she told Bobby, as they reached the edge of the village and began walking along the path next to the lane.

It was only when the path veered off towards the field and the public right of way – and she spotted his van parked against the hedge – that Harriet remembered Owen was camping there.

Oh, really? She had only *just* remembered? Pull the other one!

She ignored the sarcastic voice in her head and carried on walking. Anyway, it was too late to turn back now without the kids asking questions. Besides, Etta still needed a walk. And Owen had seen her...

'Who's that man?' Bobby asked as Owen waved to her. He was sitting outside the van, tending to an open fire. 'What's he doing?'

'His name is Owen and he's camping here.'

'He's got a fire. Wicked!' Bobby scampered off, Etta in tow, heading for the van and the fire pit in front of it.

'Don't get too close,' Harriet shouted after her son. 'And don't let Etta off the lead!' The last thing Harriet needed was a dog with a burnt nose because she'd stuck it into the flames. Etta might be a sweetie, but she wasn't the brightest mutt in the kennel.

By the time she and Sara caught up with Bobby, Etta was being fussed by Owen and was lapping up the attention. Bobby was staring at the van with his mouth hanging open.

'Are you on holiday?' she heard her son ask.

'No, I live in this all year round.'

Bobby turned to look at her. 'Can he do that, Mam?'

'He can, although I'm not sure I'd want to. Not with you lot – we'd get on each other's nerves.'

'I take it these are yours?' Owen said.

'They are,' Harriet replied proudly. 'Sara and Bobby, and the dog is called Etta.'

'I'm Owen,' Owen said.

'We know. Mam told us. What's that?' Bobby was staring at a large cylindrical black bag hanging from a hook at the rear of the van. It looked a little like a punchbag, except it had a hose coming from it.

'It's a solar shower,' Owen replied. Harriet was about to ask what that was, when he must have seen the confusion on her face. 'I fill it with water from the standpipe over there and leave it in the sun for the day. The sun heats the water, then I take a shower with it.'

'In the field? Like, with no clothes on?' Bobby's eyes were out on stalks.

Owen chuckled. 'No, I have a proper shower room in my van, but I prefer using solar power to heat water when I can, rather than the van's battery.'

'You've got a shower? In there?'

Owen nodded. 'And a kitchen with a fridge and an oven, as well as a bed and living room.'

'How does it all fit in?'

'It's quite cosy,' Owen said. 'Would you like to see inside? You, too, Harriet, if you want.'

Oh, Harriet wanted: she was practically dying of curiosity. 'If you don't mind?'

'I wouldn't ask if I did,' he said, smiling. 'Thank goodness I cleaned up today. Just kidding,' he added, when she raised her eyebrows. 'You can't live in such a confined space without being tidy.' He gestured for her and the children to step inside.

It was one of those vans with a sleeping compartment over the cab and a side door to reach the living quarters, and Harriet felt rather strange as she followed Bobby, who had shot inside and could now be heard exclaiming loudly.

'Wow! This is so cool. Can we have one, Mammy?'

Harriet stuck her head through the doorway and gasped. She'd never seen inside a camper van before, not in real life, and she was struck by how well-appointed and homely it was.

'Go in,' Owen urged, and she reluctantly climbed into it and made her way to the living room at the end. It was U-shaped, with a table in the middle. On it sat a laptop and a ceramic mug.

Harriet gazed around, amazed by how nice it was. Owen was right – it was cosy and very tidy. And was that a wood-burning stove in the corner? It was tiny and sat on a raised platform with a cupboard underneath. There was a door next to it, which Sara opened before Harriet could tell her not to.

'It's got a toilet!' Sara exclaimed. 'And a shower. He wasn't telling fibs.'

'I didn't for one second think he was,' Harriet said, mortified. She sent Owen an apologetic look over her shoulder. 'Is that a wood burner?'

'It is. Originally, that space was a wardrobe, but I had it taken out and installed a stove instead. It's surprising how much heat it kicks out.'

'Cool,' Bobby said.

'Hot, actually,' Owen replied, and it took Bobby a second to get the joke.

'He's funny, Mam. I like his house.'

'I like it, too,' Sara said. 'But you haven't got a bath. I like a bath with lots of bubbles and bombs in.'

'Bombs?' Owen frowned.

'Bath bombs. They are round things that you put in the bath, and they go all fizzy and smell nice.'

'She had some for Christmas last year.' Harriet felt the need to explain that she hadn't bought them, that they'd been a gift.

'Fizzy, eh? Sort of like lying in a bath of lemonade?'

Sara gave him a 'you're being silly' look. 'Do you ever have a bath?'

'No. I can't remember the last time I had one.'

'Do you miss it?'

'Not really. Although it might be nice to lie in fizzy water,' he said, chuckling.

'He could come to our house for a bath, couldn't he, Mam?' Bobby had been following the conversation and he sounded very pleased with himself to have thought of a solution to Owen's lack of recent bath experiences.

Harriet was horrified, and even Sara looked shocked. 'You can't just invite people for a bath,' she said, amazed that her son would even suggest such a thing.

'Why not?'

'Because, because...' Harriet floundered, not knowing where to start.

'He could come for tea, then have a bath afterwards,' Bobby said.

'Shut up, you div,' Sara hissed, elbowing him.

'What?' Bobby demanded, and Harriet could see that he was genuinely bewildered.

'Er, I don't think that's a good idea, sprout,' Owen said. 'But thanks for the offer.' He caught Harriet's eye and she realised he was trying hard to hold back his mirth.

She bit her lip, her own laughter not far from the surface. God, she loved that boy!

'Come on, let's leave Owen in peace,' she said, ushering her children outside. 'Etta hasn't finished her walk yet and it'll be dark soon.'

After saying their goodbyes (Bobby with a great deal of reluctance), Harriet shooed her children towards the kissing gate at the opposite end of the field. Hopefully, by the time they had circumnavigated the next pasture and retraced their steps to the lane, Owen would be safely tucked up in his van. Not that she didn't want to see or speak to him – she did. But that was the problem: Harriet didn't need to make her life any more complicated than it already was. And she had a feeling that if she gave in to her rapidly growing attraction to Owen, her life would become very complicated indeed.

–

After overhearing Harriet talk about her children in the cafe, Owen had felt as though he'd already met them. But now that he'd met them for real, they were nothing like he'd imagined, he mused, as he watched them wander across the field, the dog scampering ahead.

His eyes were drawn to Harriet's tall, upright figure, the jacket she was wearing doing little to hide her curves. He studied her small waist and full hips, her long, slim legs encased in a pair of faded jeans. She was wearing her hair down, cascading over her shoulders, and from the back he thought she could be mistaken for a teenager herself.

Her daughter was the image of her, and Owen imagined Harriet would have looked very similar at the same age. He had expected Sara to be a bit of a madam, but she'd seemed like a normal kid – although he wasn't quite sure what a normal kid was like, as he'd not had much to do with children. The boy was a poppet, though, and Owen grinned as he remembered the horrified expression on Harriet's face when Bobby invited him to their house for a bath. It had been priceless.

Owen smiled ruefully as he doused the flames, thinking that it might be quite nice to have a bath for once. It had been such a long time since he'd had a soak, although he wasn't sure about a bath bomb. He briefly thought of heating some water and using the small tin bath he used for washing his clothes. But when he tried to imagine folding his six-foot-one frame into it, he chortled at the vision of getting stuck and having to carry a tin bath on his back like a snail's shell as he tried to extricate himself from it. It wouldn't be a good look.

After ensuring the fire was out, Owen went back inside the van for the night. He had some work to do, and meeting Harriet again had reminded him that he needed to write up her enamel-pot purchase. That she had bought it second-hand had surprised him; he'd never thought she would take him up on his challenge, despite her saying she would. He began to think that the *Don't Buy New* series of blog posts that he had planned might grow wings and fly after all, without the need to ask for volunteers.

He did feel slightly uneasy that Harriet didn't know she was centre stage, but he justified not telling her by trying to convince himself that it was more authentic this way; if she knew other people would be following her progress, it might influence what she did or didn't buy. But no matter how much he kept telling himself that was the reason, the truth was that he was worried she might refuse. And if she refused and he wasn't able to share it with readers of *Planet B*, then it might make staying in Foxmore pointless and uncomfortable. And he really wanted to stay here.

Before he could address the issue of whether it was Foxmore that had captured his attention or Harriet herself, he heard a vehicle pull up alongside the gate and a door slam as an elderly gent got out.

Aled Harris owned the farm that the field was part of, and he'd been pleased with the prospect of earning a bit of cash from Owen's stay. Owen knew that many farmers were short of money, and he didn't begrudge the bargain he'd struck with the old chap. He guessed Aled to be in his late sixties, still going strong when other men his age would have retired; farming wasn't an easy way of life.

'Awright, butt?' Aled asked. 'Thought I'd see how you are settling in.'

Owen smiled. He hadn't been called butt or buttie, as it was short for, in a long time. 'Fine, thanks,' he said.

There hadn't been any settling in to be done. He had picked a spot not too far from the water tap, and the trough underneath it, and had parked up. It had been as simple as that. It wasn't like camping with a tent – he was like a snail, carrying his house with him wherever he went.

Aled was studying the van, his eyes crawling all over it, curiosity coming off him in waves. But, unlike with Harriet, Owen didn't feel like inviting the man to take a look inside.

'Good, good…' Aled nodded. 'I hear you're after a job?'

Owen blinked. 'Not exactly.'

'Oh?' Aled looked taken aback. 'The word is that you're a jack of all trades. I heard that you do a bit of this, and a bit of that.'

'I have been known to,' Owen replied warily, wondering where the conversation was heading.

'I could do with a bit of help, see,' Aled continued. 'Nothing much, mind, and it'll only be a few bob because I can't afford that minimum-wage nonsense, and I thought you could do with the work, like. What do you say?'

Owen was inclined to say no, but curiosity got the better of him. 'What sort of work?'

'As I said, it's nothing much, but it'll be enough to buy a pie and a pint in The Jolly Fox. Are you interested?'

Although writing articles and his blog provided Owen with more than enough funds for his needs, he wasn't averse to doing a bit of something else from time to time to supplement his income. He had been known to do anything from fruit picking to casual labour on a building site over the years, although he didn't make a habit of it these days.

'It depends,' he replied, and Aled frowned. Owen could tell that the man had assumed that just because he lived in a van, Owen would have jumped at the chance to earn a bit of money. 'What would you want me to do?'

'I hold a boot sale in the field next to this every Saturday morning. Now, seeing as you're already on site, so to speak, I thought you could help with the marshalling of the pitches. As I said, the pay won't be much but I expect every bit helps, don't it? How about twenty quid?'

Owen didn't answer; he was too busy hoping that the boot sale wouldn't spill over into the field his van was parked in.

Aled mistook his hesitation. 'Thirty, then,' he said, 'but that's my final offer. Take it or leave it.'

Owen took it. What did he have to lose?

—

'Owen is cool,' Bobby said. 'I want to live in a van when I grow up. He can go anywhere he wants.'

'I thought you wanted to be a tractor driver?' Harriet said.

'I can do that, too.'

'No, you can't,' Sara piped up. 'Mam, tell him – he can't drive a tractor and a van at the same time.'

'I can if I tow it,' Bobby argued. 'Can't I, Mam?'

'I suppose.' She unlocked the front door. 'Take your trainers off, please; I don't want mud trampled through the house.' Grabbing an old towel, she picked Etta up, patting her paws and tummy dry. The dog squirmed and wriggled until Harriet put her down, then she dashed to her water bowl and had a long drink, before jumping on the sofa and curling up in a ball.

'Right, then.' Harriet clapped her hands. 'How about a mug of cocoa, and we get the craft box out?'

'I don't want to make a card. It's lame.' Sara pouted.

'I do,' Bobby said. 'Can I still make a card even if Sara doesn't want to?' He looked anxious.

'Of course you can,' Harriet assured him. 'Why don't you fetch the box? Sara, get the mugs out, please.'

Sara made a show of not wanting to have anything to do with card-making, and huffed and puffed for the first few minutes as the three of them sat around the table, mugs of steaming cocoa in front of them and a variety of coloured card, string, ribbon, glitter, beads and scraps of fabric spread across the wooden surface.

But once Sara had started cutting and sticking, Harriet could tell that her daughter was enjoying herself, especially when Harriet allowed her to use the ancient laptop to research card ideas online.

'That's brilliant!' Harriet exclaimed, when she saw Sara's finished result. She had drawn the figure of a girl, and had added fabric, beads and glitter to make a dress, and had used coloured thread to write out the words 'Happy Birthday Darlene'.

'Is mine good, Mammy?' Bobby asked. 'I made a card for Tristan, and I made one for Owen.'

'For Owen?'

'It's his van. See?'

'So it is! Well done, you two. Sara, do you think you can make an envelope?' Sara had done a brilliant job – Darlene would be thrilled to receive such a lovely, thoughtful card.

'What's the point?' Sara muttered.

'Can I make an envelope, Mam?' Bobby was brandishing the card he had made for Owen.

'Of course you can.' Harriet would have to have a fiddle around using a spare piece of paper to get the dimensions right before she showed the children how to make envelopes, but she was certain it could be done. 'And the point, my lovely girl, is that you can't give a card without putting it in an envelope.'

'That's OK, I don't need to make an envelope because I'm not giving this card to Darlene. I'm going to buy a proper one when we buy her present. She wants a Pandora bracelet.'

Flipping heck! I bet she does, Harriet thought, wondering if the cheeky little madam had told everyone what present she wanted them to buy.

'No chance,' Harriet said.

'But that's what she's asked for,' Sara protested.

'Then she'll have to ask for it from someone else, because she's not getting that from us!' Harriet was thunderstruck at the cheek of it.

'I'll buy it myself.'

'You will not!'

'I will, too! I've got money.'

'Do you know how much those cost? More than you've got in your piggy bank.'

'You're mean. Everyone else is buying Darlene what she wants.'

'I highly doubt that,' Harriet said.

'She'll hate me.'

Good, Harriet wanted to say. Darlene sounded like a thoroughly spoilt little girl, and the less Sara had to do with her, the happier Harriet would be. If she could forbid Sara from being friends with the child, she would, but she couldn't stop Sara from bothering with her in school, unfortunately.

'I've got an idea,' Harriet said, a warning tone in her voice. 'How about if you don't go to her birthday party at all? Then you won't have to give a card or a present. Problem solved.'

Sara looked aghast. 'But I've *got* to go! *Everyone* will be there!'

'Not everyone, surely?' Her daughter was prone to exaggeration.

'Everyone,' Sara declared. 'Darlene is having her party at Deri Castle and she's invited the whole class.'

'I meant to ask you about that – I thought it was a misprint, that her mum must have written it down wrong.'

'It's deffo at Deri Castle.' Sara was adamant.

'Wow! That's not going to be cheap.' As far as Harriet knew, it was more renowned for hosting weddings than kids' parties.

It was also a country club and spa, and she'd never set foot in the place, despite it being only fifteen or so miles away.

'I *know*!' Sara looked starstruck. 'She's having a pamper party and I'm getting my nails painted purple. Or maybe orange, with glitter on the top.'

'I bet the boys will be thrilled about that,' Harriet said dryly.

'What boys?'

'I thought you said she's invited the whole class?'

'Not the *boys*. Duh!'

Did Sara just 'duh' me? Harriet raised her eyebrows and gave her daughter The Look. The one that meant she had gone too far.

'Sorry,' Sara mumbled, contrite for all of a split-second. 'And we're having high tea.' She paused. 'What's high tea?'

'It's a posh term for sandwiches and cakes,' Harriet said, wondering how she was going to top that when it came to Sara's birthday party. Annoyed, she told herself not to think about it yet: she had Christmas to survive first.

She also had another problem – how on earth was she going to tell her daughter that she wouldn't be having a new outfit to wear to this over-the-top kids' birthday party?

Chapter 6

'You're going to have to buy Sara something without her knowing where you got it from,' Pen advised the following morning, after Harriet told her about her dilemma. 'For Pete's sake, mun! Deri Castle for a blimmin' kiddies' party? The mother must have more money than sense. She could have done the same thing at home for a fraction of the cost.'

'I know,' Harriet groaned. 'Talk about raising the bar.' She had to smile at Pen, though: her boss was quite indignant on Harriet's behalf.

Pen carried on, 'Mark my words, you don't want to get into a competition with her. You'll never win. I don't know the woman, but she sounds like a right two-sheds to me.'

'Two-sheds?' She'd never heard that expression before.

'Aye, you know the sort – you say you've got a shed in your garden, and they'll tell you they've got two, both of 'em bigger and better than yours! Whatever you do, she'll go one better – with knobs on.'

'You're right,' Harriet agreed. But knowing Pen was right didn't change the situation or solve her immediate problem of what Sara was going to wear to the party. 'And to top it all off, parents are also invited to stay for the duration,' she added. 'Apparently, according to Sara, Darlene's mam doesn't think it fair for parents to drive all that way just to drop their kids off, only to have to go back again after a couple of hours. I'll have to take a flask of coffee and sit in my car – I doubt if I can afford as much as a glass of water in a place like that.'

She wiped down a table and checked that no one needed serving. The cafe was fairly quiet for once, although it would soon pick up again: it was never quiet for long.

Pen sniffed. 'I bet you there'll be refreshments laid on, even if it's only a cuppa. She sounds like the type who wants to show the rest of the world she can afford to be generous. It'll also give the chance for everyone to check out the prices. I've come across her sort before. Bloody two-sheds,' she repeated.

'I had a quick look in the charity shop before I came in,' Harriet said, returning to the problem of what her daughter was going to wear. 'But I didn't see anything I thought Sara might like.' She noticed that the cutlery basket needed replenishing, so she went out the back and emptied the dishwasher.

'You'll have to go to the boot sale. Failing that, try Vinted,' Pen called after her.

Harriet brought a handful of clean knives and forks with her, figuring that she may as well wrap them in serviettes while she had the time. No doubt she would be rushed off her feet in an hour.

'I'm thinking that I might just have to bite the bullet this time and buy her something new,' she was saying, as she used her behind to push the door open.

'You can't do that!' Owen's voice made her jump, and when she looked around, she saw him standing next to the counter, a disapproving expression on his face.

Harriet sighed. She'd been hoping Owen would never need to know. Although, saying that, she would probably have felt guilty about cheating, so she'd have had to come clean anyway. Wishing she hadn't accepted the stupid challenge in the first place, she tried her best to explain.

'So, you see, I haven't got a great deal of choice,' she added, after she had finished telling him about her problem.

'Of course you've got a choice. You can choose not to participate in such blatant consumerism,' he said.

'That's easy for you to say – you haven't got any kids.' Harriet stopped abruptly. 'Have you?'

'No...'

'Well then!' Basically, she was telling him to butt out, without saying the words.

Owen appeared to take the hint, as he didn't say anything more on the subject. He also appeared to be disappointed, although what difference it was to him whether she bought her daughter a new dress or not was beyond her. Apart from it not helping the planet, of course, so there was that. And he was clearly very passionate about the environment.

One little purchase wasn't going to make the slightest difference in the scheme of things, though, so he needn't look so sad about it.

Then again, she reasoned, if everyone thought the same way – that the one new pair of shoes, vase or coffee table they'd had their eye on wasn't going to make any difference – then everyone would carry on buying new, wouldn't they, and knickers to the planet.

Grrr, she was cross with him for making her feel so guilty.

There was one thing she *was* happy about, though, and the knowledge kept tugging at her like a five-year-old pulling on her sleeve for attention: she was as sure as she could be that Owen didn't have a significant other. There hadn't been the remotest hint of a woman's presence in his van. She knew because she'd looked.

Harriet pulled herself together. This wasn't the time or the place to be thinking about Owen's domestic arrangements, and neither was it any of her business. She never should have asked him whether he had children, and she certainly shouldn't have asked him in such a confrontational manner.

'Sorry, that was rude of me,' she said.

Owen was peering at the specials board. He still looked disappointed. 'That's OK.' He turned to face her. 'I didn't think buying second-hand was your cup of tea, to be honest.'

'Why not?'

'Er...'

'Tell me.' She put her hands on her hips.

'You don't look the type.'

'And what type is that, may I ask?'

'Never mind. I shouldn't have said anything.'

'I want to know.'

'The type to compromise,' he said, wincing.

'What do you mean?'

He let out a sigh and shrugged. 'Let me put it another way – you're not as passionate about saving the planet as I am.'

Harriet squinted at him. That's not what he had meant at all. He was trying to be diplomatic, but she wanted to know.

'I might not be as passionate, but I do care,' she said. 'What were you going to say before you decided to be tactful?'

He shot her a look, and she smirked. She had two children: she was used to spotting lies, even if this was only a little white one.

'OK, you asked for it.' He took a breath and she wondered just how bad this could be, as he said, 'You strike me as the sort of person who, if she wants something, she simply goes out and buys it.' His glance swept over her, from the top of her piled-up hair to the leather brogues on her feet, and everything in between. It felt less like the assessing look she knew it to be and more of a caress, and a tremor travelled down her spine. 'With little thought to the cost or the impact on the environment,' he added.

Harriet was aware of Pen's sharp intake of breath, and she sent her boss a quick look to reassure her she wasn't going to blow her top.

'Have you decided what you want?' she asked, mildly.

Owen blinked at the change of subject but rallied well enough. 'Er, yeah. Could I have the pumpkin soup, please? And a mint tea?'

'Take a seat. I'll bring it over.'

Harriet took her time ladling the soup into a bowl and putting it on a tray, along with several slices of seeded bread and a knob of vegan spread. She quickly popped a tea bag into a mug, then poured herself a coffee.

As she unloaded the tray, Owen gave her a tentative smile. He was clearly hoping she had forgiven him for being so blunt. She soon wiped it off his face when she pulled out a chair and sat down opposite.

'You eat, I'll talk,' she said, and waited for him to unfold his spoon from the serviette it was wrapped in and dip it into his soup.

'Mmm, this is delicious,' he said, taking a sip.

'I know. I made it myself.'

He cocked his head in acknowledgement and ate another spoonful, following it up with a morsel of bread.

As soon as his mouth was occupied, Harriet began to speak.

'You're wrong about me,' she said. 'I wish I did have the money to simply go out and buy whatever I want, whenever I want. But I don't.'

He swallowed hastily, and she could see he was about to say something, so she held up her hand.

When he subsided, she continued, 'I'm very careful with money – I have to be. I'm a single parent with two kids, a house to run and a greedy dog. I've got an ex-husband who only believes in paying the minimum amount of maintenance, and a part-time job that barely keeps my head above water. What you see—' she gestured to herself '—is the result of buying good-quality things and looking after them. Yes, a couple of years ago your assessment of me would probably have been right. But not any more. I've not bought any new clothes for myself for over two years; I've not been to the hairdresser for eighteen months.'

'She's right,' Pen chimed in from where she was lurking near the cake display. 'I cut her hair for her now.'

'Thanks, Pen.' Harriet shot her a grateful look. 'So, you see, you've got me all wrong. I bought that casserole dish not because of your stupid challenge, but because I wouldn't have been able to afford one otherwise. And don't you *ever* question

67

me about wanting the best for my kids. And if that includes buying my daughter a new dress for a party so she doesn't feel embarrassed, then so be it. So there!' she added, for emphasis. Then she wished she could take that last bit back, as she realised she sounded like Bobby when he was cross.

She also realised that Owen had stopped eating a while ago and had put his spoon down, the soup growing cold in the bowl.

'I'm sorry,' he said. 'I had no right to assume or to judge. I've been on the tail end of that kind of thing enough times, so I ought to know better.'

'Because you live in a van?'

He nodded.

'Here, let me warm that up for you.' Pen darted between them and whisked his meal away before either of them could say a word.

'Is she always like that?' he asked, jerking his head towards Pen.

'I'm afraid so. Her heart's in the right place, though.'

'I noticed. She brought me a leftover pasty the other night.'

'You do realise she only did it because she was being nosy, and that the pasty wasn't leftover at all. We always sell out, so she must have put it to one side especially.'

'I did have my suspicions,' he replied with a grin. 'I am sorry, though. I shouldn't have set you such a stupid challenge.'

Harriet winced as she heard her words echoed back at her. 'It's not silly,' she said. 'In fact, it's incredibly worthwhile. I just don't think I can stick to it when it comes to this blasted birthday party.'

'You don't have to stick to it at all,' he told her gently.

'I want to,' she said. 'But I may need some help.'

She noticed the way his eyes lit up as she said those words, and her heart melted a little. He really was incredibly passionate about the environment, wasn't he?

'I'll help in any way I can,' he said. 'What do you need?'

'Advice, mostly, I suppose.' Apart from the charity shop on the high street, Harriet wasn't sure where to start when it came to sourcing pre-loved purchases (she much preferred that term to second-hand); she had no experience of eBay or Vinted, or any of the other second-hand sites.

When she said as much to Owen, he explained roughly how they worked, but Harriet wasn't totally convinced.

'What if I buy something and it doesn't fit, or Sara doesn't like it, or…?'

'That's the chance you take.'

Harriet frowned. 'I honestly don't think it's a good idea. I like to see what I'm buying before I buy it, or at least I'd like to be able to return it and get my money back.'

The cafe was filling up around them, but Harriet was only vaguely aware of it – she was far too wrapped up in what Owen was saying.

'If that's the case, these sites aren't for you,' he told her. 'You'll be better off going to charity shops or boot sales.'

Harriet pulled a face. This was getting far too complicated and seemed an awful lot of effort when she could just pop into Dolgellau instead.

But – and this was the problem she kept returning to again and again – she simply didn't have the money to pop anywhere. Yet the children were in desperate need of new clothes. They were growing so fast, it was frightening, Bobby especially. He was shooting up at a rate of knots, so she didn't have any choice other than to buy second-hand if she didn't want him to walk around in half-mast trousers and too-small jumpers.

'I suppose I'll have to give the boot sale on Holly Field a try,' she said, sighing loudly. It wasn't something she was looking forward to in the slightest, but at least Sara wouldn't be with her on Saturday, so that was some consolation.

'I'm going to be there,' Owen said.

'Buying or selling?' Harriet wondered: he hadn't appeared to have a lot of excess stuff in the van.

'Neither. Aled Harris asked me to help.'

'I hope he's paying you.' Harriet was well aware of the farmer's reputation for meanness.

'He is,' Owen laughed. 'Once I've helped to set the boot sale up, I can have a look around with you, if you like?'

Harriet liked very much. Far too much. 'I'm sure Bobby will love to see you again,' she said. 'He couldn't stop talking about your van. He was quite taken with it.' She could feel heat steal into her cheeks. 'I'm sorry if he embarrassed you.'

'He didn't. He did make me laugh, though. You should have seen your face!'

She put a hand to her flaming cheek and giggled. Then she suddenly became aware that Pen was having to cope on her own because Harriet was too busy enjoying herself, and she immediately felt contrite. 'Oops, I'd better get back to work before I get the sack. See you on Saturday?'

'If not before. There are a few more things on the menu I'd like to try.'

Harriet cleared away the used dishes on a nearby table and, out of the corner of her eye, she watched him tuck into his reheated soup, feeling confused. She was pretty sure she'd been flirting, and she was surprised at herself. The last time she had flirted with anyone had been when she'd met Declan for the first time – and look how that had turned out!

She couldn't deny that she fancied Owen, though. He wasn't her usual type, being too intense; but then again, she had been away from the dating scene for such a long time that she wasn't sure she had a type any more.

Wait up... what was she doing, thinking about Owen and dating in the same sentence? Seeing him on Saturday at the boot sale was hardly a date. And even if he asked her out, she wouldn't go. She'd had enough of men to last her a lifetime. Or until the kids were grown and flown. The thought of having to go through all the palaver of meeting someone, getting to know them, introducing them to the children and hoping they got on... No thanks! She could do without the aggro.

'You like him, don't you?' Pen said, after he had paid and left. She was peering at her with a knowing expression.

'I do not.'

'You could have fooled me.'

'Looks like I did. Because I don't.'

'You were flirting with him.'

Oh, for goodness' sake! Trust Pen to have noticed. 'I was being friendly. Are you going to serve Lowri, or shall I?'

'You serve her,' Pen said. 'It's about time you did some work.'

Harriet threw her a dirty look, Pen's chortles following her as she walked over to Lowri's table. 'We don't see you in here very often,' Harriet said. 'What can I get you?'

'A chai latte, please, and a slice of whatever that is.' Lowri pointed to the cake in the top of the chiller.

'Red velvet cake.'

'It looks yummy.'

'It is. How is that gorgeous daughter of yours?' Harriet bent over to peer into the pram, and a pair of deep blue eyes gazed solemnly back at her. 'Aw, isn't she cute! I'm getting all broody.'

'You'd soon change your mind if she had you up three times in the night.'

'She's still so tiny – she needs her feeds.'

'She didn't want feeding at all. She wanted cuddles,' Lowri grumbled. 'She had better start sleeping through the night soon, because I'm going back to work shortly.'

Harriet remembered those sleepless nights well, but she was lucky that Declan had earned enough so Harriet could stay at home when the children were babies. But Lowri owned A Cut Above, and when it was your own business, Harriet supposed it was harder to take time off.

As she made Lowri's chai latte, she once again wondered what Owen did for a living. Pen had told her that he did a 'bit of this, and a bit of that', but what were the *this* and *that* exactly? Aside from handing out leaflets and doing a spot of work for

71

Aled Harris, she had no idea what he did. She was tempted to ask him the next time she saw him.

A shiver of excitement shot through her at the thought of seeing him on Saturday, and she stamped down hard on it. Even if she was amenable to some romance, she didn't think Owen was interested in her. Not in that way. All he seemed to be interested in was making another convert to the 'don't buy anything new' crusade.

Oh, well, it was for the best, because if he *had been* interested in her, Harriet had the unsettling suspicion that she might be unable to prevent herself from acting on the attraction she felt for him.

Chapter 7

Owen loved early mornings, when there were few people around, and he could sit outside the van with a brew in his hand and listen to the sounds of the world waking up.

Not this morning, though, because today was Saturday and he had work to do. He could already hear the rumble of a diesel engine trundling down the lane and he guessed Aled wanted to get started.

Owen had been to many a car boot sale in his time, so he had a fair idea of what was expected of him. No doubt the sellers would be on one side of the field and the punters would park on the other.

He was proved right, as the field next to the one he was camping in was already mapped out with stakes and tape to indicate the rows for the sellers' vehicles. It was his job to ensure that they stayed within the lines and left enough room between them. Plus, a car would only be entitled to one bay, whereas a long-based van would qualify for two.

'Have you been doing this long?' Owen asked, after Aled explained that he'd be collecting the money at the gate, and that Owen was to perform the role of parking attendant.

'Since the summer.' Aled scowled. 'I gotta do something to make the farm pay. There ain't any money in sheep these days.' He stuffed his hands into the pockets of his worn waxed jacket and snorted. 'I was supposed to be selling this field and the one you're in to Cornerstone – the supermarket.' Owen nodded to show he'd heard of them, as the man continued, 'But those damned villagers were having none of it. Selfish buggers.

They prefer to drive to Dolgellau for a loaf of bread than have a supermarket right on their doorstep. So, I thought to myself, I'll show 'em, and I started a boot sale instead. It's only been going a few months but people are coming from all around. And if the lane is gridlocked, it serves 'em bloody right.'

'Right. OK. Erm…' Owen wasn't sure how he was supposed to respond to that. 'Thanks for letting me camp in the other field,' he said.

The farmer's expression turned sly. 'You haven't got any friends with caravans who'd like to park up, have you?'

'No, sorry.'

'Pity. I could do with a few more paying guests.'

'Have you considered turning the field into a proper campsite?' Owen suggested.

'Nah, I'll have to set up toilet blocks and such, and I haven't got the cash to do that. Besides, those miserable lot in the village would probably put the kibosh on that 'n all.' He sniffed loudly, showing his displeasure.

Owen didn't like to say so, but he was glad that a supermarket wasn't going to be built in Foxmore. The village was quaint and unspoilt, with some lovely independent shops and businesses. A supermarket would change the whole vibe and, from what he had seen of Foxmore, people could already get pretty much everything they needed on a daily basis. He certainly could anyway: but then, his needs were simple. Food mainly, and occasionally toiletries. Which reminded him – he wanted to pay Sero a visit soon. He had noticed the refill shop when he'd driven into Foxmore nearly a week ago, and he had walked past it since but had yet to go inside. He was hoping they sold Castile soap, because he was almost out. The bar he was using was down to a sliver, and he needed to do a clothes wash shortly, otherwise he'd be out of clean socks. Plus, he wanted to put fresh sheets on his bed.

Out of nowhere, Owen had a vision of Harriet in his bed, her nut-brown hair splayed across his pillow. It was so unexpected, it made him gasp, and he shook his head to clear it.

Admittedly, he did fancy her, but he had fancied women in the past and never once had any of them invaded his thoughts the way Harriet had.

Owen put it down to having the *Don't Buy New* challenge on his mind over the last few days. Now that he knew Harriet was definitely going ahead with it, he had published the first post, in which he had outlined the challenge and introduced Dawn and her children. He had thought long and hard about changing the names, the gender, and maybe even the ages of Harriet's children, but he'd settled for giving them pseudonyms instead. So Sara had become Ava, and Bobby was Teddy. He'd also deliberately not included the location, although he had taken a photo of part of the church, one of the surrounding hills and the Celtic cross in the centre of the green, just to add some context. He had stressed that Harriet/Dawn was a normal mum, facing the same challenges that many other mums face, and emphasised that it might be more difficult for her to buy the things she needed because she lived in a small rural village. But that was it – the clues were there if one knew where to look, but no one would be looking so he was as sure as he could be that no one, especially Harriet, would realise who this family was or where they lived.

He was still thinking about her when she appeared in front of him, and his heart missed a beat.

'Oh, hi, you made me jump,' he said, to cover the confusion he felt at his reaction to seeing her. What was wrong with him? He knew she was going to be here, so he shouldn't have been surprised.

She gave him a curious look, so he added, 'I was miles away.'

He had just finished showing a couple of latecomers to their pitches and was back at the gate, daydreaming. He wasn't anticipating any more sellers arriving, as the boot sale had been in full swing for a good couple of hours, but he was hanging around just in case. Or that's what he told himself.

'Have I missed anything?' she asked, gazing at the busy field. 'I thought I'd be early.'

'Nine o'clock isn't early when it comes to a boot sale,' he said. 'Hi, Teddy.' He realised what he'd said when Harriet gave him another look. 'Sorry... Bobby. And hello to you, too.' He crouched down to pet the dachshund, using it as an excuse to cover his faux pas, and made a mental note to be more careful in the future.

Straightening up, he caught Harriet's eye and forced himself not to look away, even though he was sure his guilt must be showing on his face.

Gosh, she looked gorgeous. Her hair was loose and flowed over her shoulders, and she was wearing skinny jeans, green Wellington boots, a sweater in a shade of blue that matched her eyes, and a smart navy jacket over the top. Chic and sophisticated was what came to mind, and *waaay* out of his league.

Who was he kidding? Even if she wasn't, he was never in one place long enough to spark up a romance, and the days when he was into more casual flings were long gone. He knew deep down that if he wanted a proper relationship, he would have to stop travelling the length and breadth of the country. But the whole situation was a vicious circle – he'd not found anyone he wanted to stay in one place for, but it was unlikely he ever would find anyone special because he was never around long enough to get to know them properly.

Harriet was studying him. 'Are you OK? You don't have to accompany me. I'm a big girl – I think I can manage a boot sale on my own.' Her tone was sharp and he guessed he was coming across as a right prat.

'Sorry, I've had an early start. How about we grab a coffee before we look around?' Her hesitation had him adding, 'My treat. I'm sure T— Bobby could do with a drink. There's a stall over there that sells fresh juice: they make it while you wait.'

'Yes, please.' Bobby nodded enthusiastically, but when Harriet narrowed her eyes, Owen realised that by asking Bobby he had made it hard for her to say no. He'd also nearly slipped up again and called the boy Teddy. He'd have to be more careful.

'Or you could stop by the van later, and I'll make you a coffee? I've got apple juice in the fridge.'

'Perhaps that's a better idea,' she said. 'I want to get the shopping part out of the way first – if there's anything worth buying.'

'I'm sure there will be,' Owen said, not sure at all. He had no idea what girls Sara's age wore to parties. 'Are you looking for any particular style or colour?' He didn't know anything about style either, so he wasn't going to be much help. 'Shall we start at this end and work our way across the field?'

'You don't have to come with us.'

'I'd like to,' he said. 'I'm curious as to what you might buy.'

'You just want to make sure I stick to my vow,' she said, but she was smiling and he heaved a sigh of relief.

She was right in that he did want to accompany her to see what she bought, and he might also be able to take a surreptitious photo or two. He had already taken a few snaps of the boot sale itself and he would post them later, along with the narrative of how Harriet's party-dress quest went.

But he also wanted to walk around the boot sale with her because he enjoyed her company. Meeting new people was one of the things he particularly liked about being on the road, and Harriet fascinated him.

He was about to question why that was, when Harriet spied a rail of clothes. She was soon trawling through it, having handed the dog's lead to her son, who was beginning to look rather bored.

'Have you seen one of these before?' Owen asked him, spotting a wooden spinning top and launcher on the same stall. He picked it up.

'What is it?'

'It's a spinning top. You put it in the launcher like this, wind up the string, then pull and let go.'

Bobby was fascinated as he watched the top spinning upright on its pointed axis. 'Mam, look, it's a spinning top. Can I have it?'

'No, but you can have this,' his mum said, showing him a chunky black coat. 'Try it on. It says age 11–12, but it looks to be on the small side.'

Bobby tutted, and gave Etta's lead to Owen, who grasped it firmly with one hand while easing his phone out of his pocket with the other.

Bobby slipped the coat on and Harriet tugged at the sleeves, then made the boy turn around as she inspected it.

'It's a bit big, but not by much,' she said. 'At the rate you're growing, it'll be a perfect fit by Christmas. You can take it off now,' she told her son.

Owen was trying to work out how he could take a snap of the coat without Harriet noticing, when an idea came to him.

'Mind if I take a photo of it?' he asked, holding his phone up. 'I thought it might be a good idea to record what you buy and how much you pay for it, then you can compare it to what you would have bought if you hadn't made a pre-loved purchase. You'll be able to tell at a glance what you've saved – then perhaps it might make the challenge worthwhile.'

'Good idea,' she said, and his heart leapt, then immediately sank again when she said, 'Actually, there's no need, I can take a photo when we get home.'

Darn it! That scuppered his chance of obtaining an image to go with his narrative.

Or did it…?

Harriet had draped the coat on a trestle table as she gave it a final once-over, and as she checked it, Owen quickly pressed the camera icon. Before he could say 'cheese', he had taken a couple of shots, but because he was holding his mobile at chest height and was pretending to check his emails as he didn't want it to look like he was taking a photo, he had no idea whether he'd managed to capture an image of the coat or whether he had taken a photo of the sky.

Oh, well, he'd soon find out, and if they were dreadful, he would have to come up with something else.

Unfortunately, he had no idea what that something else might be.

–

'This isn't too bad at all,' Harriet said to herself as she paid for the coat Bobby had just tried on. It was a steal at four pounds, being a well-known make and one she knew other kids in Bobby's year group wore. Not only that, the stall Harriet had bought it from had several more items of interest and, before she knew it, Harriet had kitted her son out with two pairs of jogging bottoms, three T-shirts and a hoodie. Everything was a tad on the large side, but that didn't matter. Better too big than too small, and Bobby would soon grow into them.

As well as the price being great (she had bought the whole lot for under twenty quid), everything was clean and in good condition.

Feeling rather pleased with herself, she bundled her purchases into one of the tote bags she'd brought with her and grinned at Owen.

The poor bloke must have been bored witless watching her trawl through piles of neatly folded clothing, because he had spent most of the time on his phone.

Idly, she wondered what had held his interest for so long, but whatever it was, he'd been engrossed and she felt guilty for dragging him around the field. On the other hand, he had been quite enthusiastic when she'd bought something.

'How am I doing so far?' she asked, as they strolled past the next stall with barely a glance. It was full of knick-knacks and ornaments, and she wasn't on the lookout for that kind of thing.

'Brilliantly!' he cried.

'Are you going to say, "I told you so"?'

'I can if you want.'

Harriet laughed. 'There's no need. You were right – I do believe that buying pre-owned might be the way forward. However, I must warn you, I still haven't seen anything for Sara.'

'You will, I'm sure of it,' Owen replied, encouragingly.

Harriet wasn't so certain, but she'd keep looking, as they had only been around half of the field so far. She was surprised how many stalls there were, selling a diverse range of things such as furniture, plants, toys and household items. She also hadn't expected it to be so busy. Boot sales were clearly big business and attracted a lot of people, and she was beginning to wish she'd paid it a visit before now.

To be fair, though, Saturday mornings was when she usually caught up on her chores, so she rarely left the house before lunch, and if she did, she didn't come down this end of the village, as all the shops she needed were in the high street or on the green.

Today had been a real eye-opener, and she had Owen to thank for that.

Harriet glanced at him, about to tell him that very thing, and caught her breath as their eyes met. For a second, he held her gaze and she was transfixed by the intensity she saw there, then she hastily looked away, wondering at the sudden thud of her pulse in her ears and the way her tummy flipped.

It took her a moment to realise what had caused it, and when she did, she inhaled sharply. Pen had been right – she did fancy Owen. More than she had fancied anyone in a very long time.

'What about this stall?' he asked, breaking into her thoughts.

'Eh?'

'This stall?' Owen repeated.

Harriet, unable to meet his eye because she was worried what he might see in hers, looked at where he was pointing.

'Oh, right.' She made an effort to focus. 'Good spot! Do you mind if I take a look?'

'Not at all. I'm just here to keep you company. If you still want me to?'

She most certainly did. 'Only if you haven't got anything better to do,' she replied, trying to sound offhand.

'I haven't got anything planned.'

'Mam, can we go now?' Bobby asked. 'I'm bored.'

'Not yet. I haven't finished.'

'Aw…' He slumped, dejected, and Harriet wished she hadn't had to bring him with her. He never had liked shopping.

She was about to launch herself at the rail of colourful clothes, when a thought occurred to her that stopped her in her tracks.

What if she did find something she thought Sara might like? Bobby would probably blab that she'd bought it from the boot sale. As per Pen's suggestion, Harriet had been planning on buying Sara an outfit without telling her daughter where it had come from, but she couldn't do that without asking Bobby not to say anything, and that wasn't fair on him.

As she dithered, itching to get her hands on that rail of clothes because she had already spotted something she thought Sara might like, Owen came to her rescue.

'Bobby, what if you and I take Etta for a walk while your mum finishes up here?' he suggested. 'If that's OK with you, Harriet? We won't go far, just up the lane to the farm and back.'

'If you're sure…? I don't want to be any bother.'

'It's no bother at all, and I expect Etta could do with a run around,' he said.

'That's very kind of you. Bobby, be good for Owen.'

'I'm always good,' Bobby declared.

'That's debatable, cariad,' Harriet said with a laugh, and when she tousled his hair, he cried, 'Gerroff.'

'We won't be long,' Owen told her. 'Shall we rendezvous back at my van? Although, you might want to have my phone number, just in case?'

Harriet could have kicked herself for not thinking of that. With phone numbers swapped, she checked her mobile to ensure there weren't any messages from Kelly, then she turned her attention to the important task of trying to find something for Sara to wear to Darlene's birthday party.

The stall Owen had pointed out was manned by a woman in her late thirties or early forties, who was dressed up to the nines. Her hair was glossy and bounced on her thin shoulders, she had a full face of makeup, and was wearing an incredibly soft-looking cashmere sweater and pinstriped cord trousers. She was also driving a posh car, Harriet noticed with satisfaction. Although she was a total novice when it came to boot sales, Harriet had swiftly learned that checking out the person doing the selling might give her an indication of the quality and the condition of the goods on sale. And she had high hopes for this one.

What had drawn her eye was a rail of dresses, trousers and tops, all hung on wooden hangers and neatly spaced – not crammed on in a tangle.

Slowly and methodically, Harriet worked her way along the rail, liking many of the items, some of which were Sara's size, many of which weren't.

'Are you looking for anything in particular?' the seller asked.

'Um, yes, a dress for my daughter.'

'How old is she?'

'Eleven.'

'I've got some more girls' clothes over here,' the woman said, and Harriet noticed another rail on the other side of the large black Range Rover. 'How about something like this?' The seller held up a navy dress with small two-tone pink hearts dotted over it. 'My daughter wore it to a christening, so it might be over-the-top for everyday wear,' the woman added.

'It's for a special occasion,' Harriet said, staring at it. It was perfect – exactly the kind of thing she was looking for. The style wasn't too babyish, but neither was it too grown-up. 'May I?' She held out a hand.

'Of course.'

Harriet took it from her and turned it around, thinking furiously. Would Sara like it? Her daughter liked hearts and she loved this shade of bright pink in particular. The fabric was a sort of stiff satin, which gave the skirt some body, and was silky to the touch. The dress was finished off at the back by a row of pink heart-shaped buttons running from the neck to the waist.

'There's a little bag to go with it,' the woman said.

Oh, that clinched it! The bag was made out of the same fabric as the dress, with the addition of a gold chain for the strap and the buckle to hold the flap closed. The only drawback was that neither the dress nor the bag had a price tag.

'How much for both?' Harriet asked.

The woman pursed her plum-coloured lips. 'Well, they are designer and they were rather expensive new, so…' She paused and Harriet's heart sank. *Why come to a boot sale if you're trying to sell high-end items?* she thought.

'How about thirty pounds for the pair?'

'Make it twenty-five and you've got yourself a deal!' The words were out of Harriet's mouth before her brain had a chance to engage.

'Deal!' the woman echoed. 'I've got the box for it somewhere.'

'Oh, there's no need,' Harriet said, fishing another tote out of her shoulder bag. But she hastily changed her mind when she saw the box the woman was referring to – it had the same designer name across the top and must have been the one the dress originally came in. She said, 'I will take the box, after all.' And she was even more delighted when the woman took the lid off to reveal several layers of pink and navy tissue paper.

Harriet watched as the dress was carefully wrapped and placed inside the box, then she handed over the money. Clutching her purchases, she decided she was done for the day. The dress had cost rather more than she had intended to spend, but together with Bobby's clothes, she thought she'd done well.

Sara could still do with a wardrobe overhaul, though. Harriet had been shocked at how many of Sara's clothes no longer fitted, but she had enough to be going on with for the time being, even if she didn't see it that way.

Harriet left the field and strolled into the next, and was the first to arrive at the van, so she parked her bum on the edge of the old water trough while she waited, feeling so pleased with herself she could burst. The box was a brilliant touch. There was no way Sara would ever guess that her mam had bought it second-hand, not when it came in a posh box and was wrapped in tissue paper. And it was so nice of Owen to offer to take Bobby off her hands for a while, otherwise she never would have bought it.

She heard her son before she saw him, and she followed his chatty progress down the lane towards the gate. He and Owen were on the other side of the hedge, and she stifled a giggle as she listened to Bobby question Owen about the van.

'Can I use the toilet?' Bobby asked.

'You may, but I've got to warn you, it's a bit cramped.'

'What does "cramped" mean?'

'Small,' Owen explained. 'Closed-in.'

'I don't mind. I haven't peed in a van before.'

Harriet would never know what Owen was going to say to that observation, because just then they reached the kissing gate and Etta spotted her. She was pulling at the lead as usual, and when she saw Harriet, the dog pulled even harder, wagging her tail and uttering little whimpers of delight.

While Harriet greeted her and asked her son whether he'd behaved himself, Owen unlocked the van.

'Off you go,' he said to Bobby, and Bobby scampered up the steps. 'He needs a wee,' Owen explained.

'I know. I heard.' She beamed at him. 'Thank you so much for entertaining him for half an hour. It would have been a nightmare to buy anything for Sara with Bobby tagging along.'

'I thought he was very well-behaved.'

'He was, but if he'd seen me buy Sara's dress, he would have told her where it came from.'

'And that's a problem because…?'

'If she knew it was second-hand, she would probably refuse to wear it.'

Owen studied her for a moment. 'But isn't that the point? That the younger generation understands there is more to life than blatant consumerism?'

Wow, that got heavy fast, Harriet thought. 'Yes, it is,' she agreed. 'But there's no point in lecturing Sara – she has to find out for herself that second-hand can be as good as new.'

'Is that what I'm doing? Lecturing?'

'Just a bit,' Harriet conceded, smiling to show she didn't mind.

'I take it you managed to find a dress?' he asked, and his brow shot up when she took the box out for him to see.

Hastily, she shoved it back into the tote bag as she heard Bobby unlock the toilet door. 'I'll show you another time,' she said, meaningfully, hoping Owen wouldn't say anything in front of Bobby.

To her relief, he changed the subject. 'I think I promised you a coffee, didn't I? And an apple juice for scamp, here.'

'I'm not a scamp,' Bobby objected. 'That's what Mammy calls Etta when she's been naughty.'

'Is she naughty very often?' Owen asked.

'Sometimes. She ate my mam's shoes.'

'She was only a puppy,' Harriet said.

'You're so lucky having a dog,' Owen said.

'Why don't you get one?' Bobby asked.

'I never seem to get round to it. I know – how about a hot chocolate? It'll be Christmas soon.'

Harriet groaned. 'Don't remind me.'

'It's ages away,' Bobby said.

'Does that mean you *don't* want a hot chocolate?' Owen teased, and Harriet's heart swelled – he was so good with her son.

'I *do* want one,' Bobby said. 'Please,' he added as an after-thought.

'How about you, Harriet?'

'Yes, please, that would be lovely.' A hot chocolate did sound nice, and although she hadn't realised it at the time, because she had been so busy enjoying herself, it was rather cold out. Not surprising, considering they were now into October.

She watched Owen bring some oat milk to the boil on the hob, and marvelled at how cosy his van was. It was a home away from home, and he seemed to have everything he needed.

'Have you ever lived in a house?' she blurted, then clapped a hand to her mouth. 'Sorry, that was rude of me.'

'It's a perfectly reasonable question,' he said, getting a packet of cocoa powder out of an incredibly tidy and well-stocked cupboard. 'I lived in a house until I was twenty-one. After uni, I went backpacking around Asia and Australia, earning my keep as I went, and I sort of fell into the van-life out there. It seemed only natural to buy my own van when I returned to the UK.'

'Is this the same one?'

Owen chuckled. 'This is my third. The first was a VW camper called Freda, and I had great fun in her, but she was too small to live in on a permanent basis. So I bought a converted Transit next, and when that eventually gave up the ghost, I got this one.'

Once again Harriet wanted to ask him what he did for a living, because she was pretty sure vans like this weren't cheap, and she wondered how he financed his lifestyle. But she kept her mouth firmly closed and her curiosity to herself. Maybe if he stayed in Foxmore a while longer and she got to know him a bit better, she might bring herself to ask.

The thought sent a tingle down her spine. Not because she might ask him such a personal thing, but because he might stay. And Harriet was forced to admit that she did want to get to know Owen better. The question was – how much better?

Chapter 8

'It's gorgeous, Sara, bach,' Ginny said, as Sara did a twirl for her grandmother.

Harriet looked on with pride. Sara looked lovely and the dress fitted her perfectly. Harriet's heart had been in her mouth yesterday, wondering what her daughter would think of it.

Sara had returned from her trip to Dolgellau with Catrin not in the best of moods. She had complained to Harriet that she'd seen lots of things she'd wanted to buy, if only she'd had the money.

What she didn't say, and what Harriet had found out later when she'd phoned Kelly to thank her for taking Sara with her, was that Catrin hadn't been allowed to buy anything either. Certainly nothing for Darlene's party, which Catrin had also been invited to because she was in the same class as the birthday girl. According to Kelly, Catrin already had something suitable to wear and Kelly wasn't prepared to shell out for another outfit. *A woman after my own heart*, Harriet had thought. However, Harriet hadn't had much option other than to buy something for Sara, because most of Sara's clothes no longer fitted her.

'Take it off now,' Ginny instructed. 'You don't want to get gravy down it, do you?'

Sara looked horrified at the thought. 'Can you undo me, Mam?' She presented her back to Harriet for her to undo the buttons, then reluctantly wriggled out of it.

Harriet folded it carefully and placed it back in the box, along with the bag, which Ginny had also admired. 'Why don't you find Grandad and Bobby?' she suggested, knowing that her

87

mam would want to finish making Sunday lunch without Sara under her feet.

Harriet waited until Sara left, then started to count. She got to three before Ginny spoke.

'How much did that set you back? I thought you were trying to save money?'

'I am,' Harriet said. 'Twenty-five pounds.'

'And the rest,' her mam said. 'That's a designer dress, that is.' She jerked her head at the box.

Harriet knew: she had googled it and had been astonished when she'd seen how much it cost new. 'Honest, it *was* twenty-five pounds, cross my heart and hope to die,' Harriet said, wondering why she subconsciously reverted to acting Sara's age when she was in her parents' presence. 'Don't tell Sara, but I bought it from a boot sale. She thinks I ordered it online. Admittedly, I took a gamble, but she loves it, so it paid off. I got loads of stuff for Bobby, too – a coat, T-shirts, jogging bottoms and a hoodie. Some of it looks like it's hardly been worn.'

'That dress does look brand new,' Ginny agreed. 'Good for you. Did you go to the one in Foxmore? I heard it's really popular.'

'It is! I can't believe I haven't been there before now. It was busy and there were loads of stalls. I'll definitely be going back.' She stole a slice of beef, dancing back as her mum slapped at her hand.

'There'll be none left for lunch at this rate,' Ginny warned.

'Get off, Mam. You always cook loads.' She put her arm around her mam's shoulders and gave her a squeeze.

'I've never been to a boot sale,' Ginny said, patting Harriet's hand. 'I've never fancied it. What made you decide to go?'

Warmth invaded Harriet's chest as an image of Owen swam into her mind, and she could feel a flush spreading up her neck and into her face. 'Mind if I open a window? It's a bit stuffy in here with the oven on and all the cooker rings full blast.'

'Go ahead.'

Harriet opened the window and took a breath of cool air.

'Well?' Ginny was waiting for an answer. 'You do know you can ask us if you're struggling, don't you?'

Since Declan had buggered off, her parents hadn't been backward in coming forward when it came to offers of help, both physically (in terms of childcare) and financially. And although Harriet had been immensely grateful and had taken them up on the babysitting front (although she was careful not to abuse it), she had refused all offers of financial assistance. They were retired now, and even though they both had decent pensions, they weren't rolling in money. They had already paid their dues by raising her and Simon, and Harriet didn't think it fair for them to have to support her at her age.

'I know, Mam, but I can manage. And now I've discovered the joys of boot sales, I can manage even better. Owen—' She stopped.

'What were you going to say? And who is Owen? Is he a friend of Bobby's?'

'No, Granny, he's Mammy's friend,' Bobby said, and Harriet slowly closed her eyes, then opened them again.

Trust her son to come into the kitchen at such an inopportune moment.

Ginny raised her eyebrows. 'Is he?' she said, her voice full of meaning. She looked at Harriet, and her eyebrows rose higher when she saw the blush spreading across her cheeks. 'Tell me more.'

'What do you want, Bobby? A drink?' Harriet asked, stalling for time to formulate what she was going to say.

'Yes, please.'

'Blackcurrant squash?'

Bobby nodded. 'Can I take one for Sara? We're building a den in the leaves.'

'Of course you can. Den-building, eh? Is Grandad waging war on the fallen leaves again?' Harriet lifted a couple of plastic glasses down from the cupboard next to the sink.

Ginny said, 'You know he gets uptight about the state of the lawn this time every year. And stop trying to change the subject.'

'In a minute, Mam,' she said quietly. 'Here you go.' She handed the drinks to Bobby. 'Be careful you don't spill any.'

Bobby took one in each hand and turned slowly on his heel, a look of intense concentration on his face as he walked carefully out of the kitchen.

As soon as the door to the utility closed behind him, Ginny gave Harriet a look.

Harriet sighed. 'OK, if you must know, I met Owen in the cafe. He's a… he's um… a kind of traveller, I suppose.'

Her mother's mouth dropped open. 'A traveller? I don't like the sound of that.'

Harriet frowned: her parents could be quite narrow-minded at times. 'He's not what you think. He does live in a van, but he's an environmentalist,' she added.

'What does that mean, when it's at home?'

Despite herself, Harriet smiled. Her parents, her mam especially, were full of old-fashioned sayings. 'He's passionate about the environment.'

'So are a lot of people, but they don't all live in vans,' Ginny shot back.

'I think he goes where he's needed,' Harriet said, not entirely sure what she was talking about. Maybe if she knew what he did for a living, she might have a better idea; but she didn't, so what she was saying was mostly guesswork. 'He's recently lobbied the Welsh Assembly Government to close all open-cast coal mines.'

Ginny didn't look convinced.

Harriet carried on. 'Anyway, we got talking and he suggested I go to a boot sale to look for a dress for Sara.'

'Your dad and I would have paid for her dress,' Ginny objected.

'I know, but as I said – I can manage.'

'You're as stubborn as your father.' Ginny huffed and folded her arms. 'Like two peas in a pod, you are. And Sara's the same, so the next time you complain about her being pig-headed, take a look in the mirror.'

'Yes, Mam.' Harriet would much prefer to discuss her stubborn tendencies than to discuss Owen. But if she thought her mam was done with the subject, she was sadly mistaken.

'You met this man in the cafe, you say?'

'That's right.'

'You were at work?'

Harriet nodded.

'If that's the case, how come Bobby knows about him?'

'He – *we* – bumped into him at the boot sale.'

Ginny continued to stare at her, her foot tapping. 'And?' she demanded.

There was no fooling her mam, was there? 'OK, here's the lowdown. Owen came into Pen's Pantry and heard me moaning to Pen about Sara wanting something new for this damned party.' In her head Harriet had started referring to the event as the 'damned party' and it seemed to have stuck. 'I was carrying on about how she had loads of clothes and didn't appreciate what she had, and we got talking about consumerism and the throw-away society we live in, and he bet me that I couldn't go a week without buying anything new. I decided to go one better and told him I could get to Christmas.'

'What do you win?' her mam interrupted.

'Pardon?'

'If you win the bet.'

'I don't know. We haven't discussed it.'

'Maybe you should.'

Harriet gave her mother a keen stare. Is that all she could say? 'Anyway,' she continued, 'so far, it's worked out well. I've saved a fortune on a dress for Sara and bought loads of clothes for Bobby, plus I'm helping the planet at the same time. Owen's mantra goes something like… if you don't need it, don't buy it, but if you do need it, buy second-hand if you can.'

'This Owen sounds a bit of an odd bod to me,' Ginny said.

'He's not an odd bod!' Bobby was indignant, and Harriet blew out her cheeks. Her son seemed to be making a habit of overhearing conversations not meant for his little ears. 'Tell her, Mam – he's nice. I had a pee in his van.'

'Pardon?' Ginny gasped.

'It's a proper camper van, with a shower cubicle and toilet,' Harriet explained, trying not to laugh at the incredulous expression on her mother's face.

'I see,' Ginny said, faintly. 'Is it like those that you see on a proper campsite, then?'

'Were you imagining one of those colourful, horse-drawn, round-top waggons?'

'I was a bit,' her mam admitted.

'He's going to have a bath in our house, isn't he, Mammy?' Bobby had been listening avidly to the conversation.

'No, cariad, he's not.'

'But he hasn't got a bath.'

'He's got a shower, and that's perfectly adequate.'

'His shower is outside. He hung it off the side of his van,' Bobby informed his grandmother.

'Did he now?' Ginny was starting to look rather concerned.

'It's a solar shower, Mam,' Harriet said. 'He hangs it outside so the sun heats the water, then takes it inside to shower. He doesn't shower in the middle of a field.'

'Glad to hear it.' Ginny's expression was pained. 'I can't see it warming up much in the winter.'

'He's also got a proper shower inside, with a heater,' Harriet said.

'You seem to know an awful lot about him and his van, considering you've only known him five minutes.' Ginny's mouth was a straight line. She clearly didn't approve of Harriet's new acquaintance. Harriet wondered how her mam would feel if she realised Harriet fancied the pants off him, but consoled herself with the knowledge that her mam would never find out.

And thankfully neither would Owen.

–

Vegan Sunday lunches were usually hard to come by, but The Jolly Fox had two dishes on the menu. Admittedly, one was a nut roast (wasn't it always?), but the other was harissa roasted cauliflower, which sounded delicious.

Owen was sitting in Foxmore's one and only pub, drinking in the atmosphere as well as a pint of Guinness. It was busy, which he took as a good sign, and the aroma of cooking and wood smoke hung in the air.

He had found an empty table near the log burner, and he stretched his legs out towards it and eased his shoes off to warm his toes. He wasn't cold, despite the weather having taken a turn for the worse. Gone was the bright autumnal day they'd enjoyed yesterday and in its place was dank, dismal gloominess, and he guessed that winter was well and truly on its way. In just over two months the shortest day would be upon them, and Owen wasn't looking forward to it much. Although the van was cosy, the long nights meant less time spent outside and more time cooped up inside. It was then that he wished he had someone to share it with. Someone special.

Harriet's face swam into his mind, and he snorted.

'No, not her,' he said to himself. He might be attracted to her, but she wasn't his type. She didn't share his passion for the environment, for one thing – although he had to admit that she was making an effort. She had been delighted with her purchases yesterday, and he wondered how she'd got on with the dress and Sara. He had been hoping she'd have shown it to him, but he could understand why she hadn't. Bobby was a sweetheart, but he couldn't be expected to keep the origins of the dress to himself.

On impulse, Owen took his phone out of his pocket and sent her a text.

> Has Sara seen her dress yet? If so, what did she think?

A reply came back almost instantly.

> She loved it!!

> I'm so pleased. I've been thinking about you.

He hesitated before pressing send and, after a moment's thought, he deleted that last bit and instead typed, *Did it fit?* He knew that had been one of her concerns.

> I'll send you a pic of the dress later. At Mam's at the mo, for Sunday lunch.

Owen hissed, 'Yes!', earning himself a curious look from a man of the cloth on an adjacent table. 'Sorry.'

> Nice. I'm at The Jolly Fox for mine.

> Enjoy.

> You, too.

He would have liked to carry on the conversation, but he wasn't sure what else to say. At least he'd get a photo of Sara's dress out of it, so that was an unexpected bonus. He had been delighted to find he had several useable images from the photos he'd taken at the boot sale yesterday, and he had spent last night writing copy for the blog and uploading them. He noticed when he woke this morning that he was getting a fair bit of traction, with lots of comments, and he was pleased his instincts that this would be a good story for his blog were correct.

'Awright, butt?'

Owen looked up to see Aled Harris at his elbow. 'Hi, how are you? It was a good turnout yesterday, wasn't it?'

'You can say that again.' The farmer rubbed his hands together. 'I'm thinking of laying down some gravel ready for the winter.'

'It's a good idea if you want to carry on using the field when it's wet,' Owen said. 'But you'll need a fair bit.'

'Don't you trouble yourself about that. I've got loads of rubble from where the old barn had to be pulled down. Been wondering what to do with it.'

'Oh, OK.'

'Get a round in, and I'll tell you all about it.'

'Leave the poor bloke alone, Aled. It's you who should be buying him one. I saw him clearing up all the rubbish from your field.' This was said by an elderly gent in a flat cap, who was propping up the bar with an elbow. He had a Border collie at his feet, a pint of thick, dark ale in his hand.

'I paid 'im to do it!' Aled declared.

The man behind the bar called, 'Bet you didn't pay him much. I'm Dai, by the way, the landlord.'

'Owen. Pleased to meet you.'

'Likewise,' Dai said.

Aled huffed. 'I paid a decent wage for the job – didn't I, son?'

Owen smiled but didn't say anything, not wanting to be drawn into whatever this was. Aled appeared to be renowned for his parsimoniousness, but Owen didn't see that as a fault. He didn't like throwing money away either, and he had no complaint about how much he'd been paid. He had known what the going rate was before he had agreed.

'Are you the chap with the camper van in Aled's field?' the man sitting at an adjacent table asked, as Aled pulled out a chair and sat uninvited at Owen's table. The man was wearing a dog collar so Owen assumed he must be the local vicar.

'That's me,' he said.

'Are you planning on staying in Foxmore long?'

'I don't know yet.'

'I'm only asking because I do a mean service on a Sunday and I thought you might like to come next week.'

'To church?' Owen asked.

'Leave him alone,' his companion said with a roll of her eyes.

'I'm merely doing God's work,' the vicar replied loftily.

'You're doing work for the church roof,' the woman said. 'I apologise for my husband – Terry will grab any opportunity to drum up funds. It's in dire need of repair, you see.'

'Oh, I'm sorry. Let me give you a donation.' Owen reached into his pocket for his wallet. But at the same time as the vicar began, 'That's awfully good of you—' the woman said, 'Don't you dare. I won't let you be guilted into it.'

Owen hesitated, looking from one to the other.

'Seeing as you've got your wallet out,' Aled interjected, 'you might as well get some more drinks in.'

'I haven't finished this one yet,' Owen objected; besides, he'd only been planning on having the one.

The woman let out a loud tut. 'Aled, buy your own pint. Terry, wind your neck in. Honestly, this poor bloke has come in here for a quiet bit of lunch, and you two are haranguing him. I'm Betsan, by the way, and this lummox is Terry, otherwise known as the Reverend Terrence Pritchard. I take it you already know Aled, although I wouldn't put it past him to tap up a total stranger for a pint.'

Aled's face fell. 'You're like a bloody elephant, you are; you don't forget. It was only going to be a small supermarket, not one of those ruddy huge ones.'

'It doesn't matter how big or small it was supposed to be – Foxmore didn't want it.' The vicar's wife turned to Owen, who was rather bemused at the exchange. 'Not so long ago, Aled was trying to get a Cornerstone store built on his field without any of the villagers knowing.'

Owen wondered how that would have worked, because it wouldn't have been an easy thing to hide, but he didn't ask, fearing what sort of answer he might get.

With relief, he saw the landlord approaching with his meal: now he would have a legitimate excuse to not engage in conversation.

Aled had the grace to get up from the table to allow him to eat his meal in peace, but he did give him a parting shot. 'About that gravel, we'll speak later, when there's not so many nosy parkers around. There'll be something in it for you,' he said, but couldn't resist adding, 'I can't afford to pay you much, mind.'

'Ignore him,' Betsan advised, but she couldn't resist adding a little something of her own. 'If you're still in Foxmore and you fancy coming to the service on Sunday, we'd love to see you. We're a friendly bunch.' She glared at Aled's retreating back. 'Mostly.'

Owen, who had just popped a mouthful of piping-hot roasted cauliflower into his mouth, nodded an acknowledgement.

He loved places like this, full of odd characters and where everyone knew everyone else. It was comforting, somehow, and for the second time today he wished he had someone to share it with.

Unbidden, Harriet popped into his head again, and he slid his mobile out of his pocket.

Then slid it back in.

Harriet would not want to receive a message about his encounter with the vicar and his wife.

He didn't know whether she would want to receive another message from him at all.

But when his phone pinged a short time later with a WhatsApp notification, and he read who it was from and saw the photo accompanying it, his heart lifted and he spent the rest of the afternoon with a great big smile on his face.

Chapter 9

It was more than a week before Owen saw Harriet again, and when he spotted her outside the shop selling soaps and candles, his heart skipped a beat and his mouth went dry.

'Caught you!' he said, creeping up on her and making her jump.

She let out a squeal and whirled around to face him. 'Gosh, you gave me a fright!' She put a hand to her chest. 'For your information, you didn't catch me doing anything. I was just looking.'

'You were thinking about it,' he teased.

'I was trying to get some ideas.'

'For a present for the birthday girl?' he guessed.

Harriet nodded. 'I haven't a clue what to buy her. Sara says Darlene has asked for a Pandora bracelet.'

Owen wasn't particularly au fait with women's jewellery but even he had heard of Pandora and he knew it wasn't cheap. He raised his eyebrows.

'I know, right?' Harriet tutted. 'I wouldn't buy one for my own daughter, let alone a child that she's only just made friends with.'

'Haven't they known each other long?'

'Only since they started secondary school in September. Darlene is one of the "popular" girls.' Harriet air-quoted the word. 'If you ask me, she sounds like a right little madam, a real queen bee, and all the rest of the kids are buzzing around her.'

'And you don't want to risk Sara being singled out because she gave this girl a crappy gift – yet you also don't want to spend a great deal of money?' Owen guessed.

'Got it in one! And don't forget your challenge,' Harriet reminded him.

'There will be times when it won't be possible to stick to it,' he said. If she failed occasionally, it would add a certain piquancy to the blog thread. Not that he wanted her to fail, but it wouldn't be a disaster if she did. Owen suspected that anyone who set themselves this kind of goal would crash at some point, and he didn't want Harriet to beat herself up over it.

'But I want to stick to it,' she said. 'I'm not going to lie – it's saving me money.'

'Have you bought anything else since the boot sale?'

'Nothing,' she said, proudly. 'But then again, I haven't needed to. The crunch will come when I do.'

Owen smiled. She was right. Taking the high ground was all well and good until you were expected to act on it. 'How is the pre-loved enamel pot working out?'

'I haven't used it yet, but we're having a casserole tonight so I'll let you know.' She paused, and an expression that he couldn't read flitted across her face. 'Why don't you join us?'

'Um…' Wow, he hadn't expected her to say that! He desperately wanted to accept, but he was worried about what she was going to put in that pot.

Harriet must have sensed his concern. 'Oh, I forgot – you're a vegan, aren't you? Is that why I haven't seen you in Pen's Pantry lately – because you've sampled everything vegan on the menu?'

'Not at all. I've been earning a crust up at Aled's farm. He's had me moving tons of rubble from the farm down to the field, because he's hoping to be able to hold boot sales on it all year round.'

'I hope he's paying you,' Harriet said.

'Funnily enough, everyone asks that question.'

'Everyone?'

'I met the vicar and his wife in The Jolly Fox the other Sunday, and they wanted to know the same thing.'

'And is he? Paying you, I mean.'

'He is. Not much,' he added with a grin, then shrugged. 'But it keeps me in groceries, so I can't complain.'

He was aware of the curiosity on her face and guessed she was wondering if he had to rely on taking odd jobs for a living, but he didn't want to enlighten her as to where the majority of his income came from. In fact, just last night he'd completed an extensive article on regenerative farming, which he had sold for a tidy sum, although his idea of a 'tidy sum' was probably considerably less than most people's idea – but that was because he needed so much less to live on.

'I suppose I can do a vegan casserole,' Harriet said. 'I'm no stranger to vegetarian meals, so...'

'How about butternut squash casserole?' he suggested. 'I've got a squash in the van that I was going to make soup with, but if I do, I'll be forced to eat soup for every meal for the next three days so it doesn't go to waste. I've only got a tiny freezer compartment, you see.'

'I'm not sure... I've never made a butternut squash casserole before.'

'It's easy,' he said. 'I'll send you the recipe.'

'Why don't you come to mine early and you can help me make it? Bobby will be delighted to see you. He hasn't stopped talking about your van.'

'If you're sure?' Owen was thrilled, but he didn't want to put her out.

'I'm sure. Let me have a list of ingredients, though, in case I need to buy anything. What would I serve it with?'

'Rice is good.'

'I have some in my cupboard. What else do I need?'

'Sweet potatoes, garlic, an onion, tinned tomatoes... I can bring the sweet potatoes, as they were going to go in my soup, too.'

'Then I don't need to go shopping now,' Harriet said.

'When do you want me?'

He watched with interest as a spot of colour appeared on her cheeks, but he put it down to the keen easterly wind. They were now well into October and the weather was distinctly autumnal. Forecasters were predicting a harsh winter and Owen reminded himself that he needed to buy some more logs. He stored them in the roof box on top of the van, and he liked to ensure he had enough fuel for a couple of weeks at least, in case he got snowed in.

'Um… four thirty? The children come home at about half-three and I'll have to take Etta out before I start cooking.' She pulled a face. 'It's too dark to take her out afterwards.'

'I can take her for you, if you want? It'll give you a break.'

'I can't let you do that!'

'Why not? I don't mind and I quite fancy a stroll by the river.'

She was gazing at him quizzically and he wondered what she was thinking. He hoped he wasn't coming on too strong and giving her the wrong idea. He might be extremely attracted to her, but he had no intention of acting on his feelings, and he didn't want her to think he was hitting on her.

'That would be great, thanks. Sara hates coming in from school and having to go straight back out again to walk the dog, but she's not old enough to be left on her own just yet.' She chuckled. 'According to her, she's plenty old enough – she's eleven going on twenty.' There was pride in her voice. 'I'd better get a move on or I'll be late for work. Will you be popping into the cafe later?'

'I doubt it, but I'll see you at three thirty.'

'Three thirty it is. I'll send you my address.' She gave him a bright smile and then walked off down the pavement, leaving Owen staring after her, a warm glow in his chest.

–

Harriet didn't tell Pen she'd invited Owen for tea. She tried to convince herself it was because she couldn't take the ribbing, but the real reason was that she didn't want Pen to see how pleased she was. She was nervous too, and not entirely sure why she'd asked him in the first place, especially since she had no intention of this being anything more than a friendly gesture. Pen certainly wouldn't accept the explanation, as her boss had mentioned Owen so often during the past week that Harriet wished she'd never told her she had met Owen at the boot sale. And every time his name had passed her lips, Pen had given her a meaningful look.

Pen guessed that something was up, though, because she'd twice asked Harriet if she was all right.

'I'm fine,' Harriet said, when Pen asked her for a third time as she hurried towards the door, eager to go home. She wanted to change out of her work uniform of black trousers and a black shirt, and into something nicer.

'You *can* talk to me, you know,' Pen called after her.

'I know. Must dash! See you tomorrow,' she shouted back, then she was pelting along the street and hoping Owen wouldn't turn up until she'd at least managed to run a comb through her hair.

It was only when she reached her house that she slowed down and asked herself what she was playing at. This wasn't a date: this was merely an acquaintance popping around for a meal. She couldn't even refer to him as a friend yet, although she would like to. Telling herself that she had invited him because she wanted to thank him for introducing her to the benefits of not buying new, she hurried inside and dashed up the stairs, unbuttoning her work shirt as she took them two at a time. Kicking off her shoes, she unzipped her trousers, almost falling over in her haste to remove them, and yanked the clip out of her hair.

Finally in her underwear, she had just delved into her wardrobe when the doorbell rang, and Etta, who Harriet had yet to release from the kitchen, began barking madly.

Drat!

Grabbing the first thing she laid her hands on, Harriet dragged a knitted dress over her head and smoothed it down. With no time to tame her hair, she scurried back down the stairs and flung the door open.

Owen was standing on her step looking cool and collected, and very delectable.

Harriet swallowed nervously. 'Hi, come in. I was just getting changed.'

'I'm early. Sorry. Shall I leave and come back later?'

'Don't be silly.' Harriet moved aside to let him enter, and as soon as he stepped inside and had his back to her, she hastily ran her fingers through her hair, suspecting she had made more of a mess of it than it was already. 'Go through,' she said, her eyes on his behind as he went into the kitchen ahead of her.

Etta immediately launched herself at him, her whippy tail lashing from side to side. She ignored Harriet.

'Nice to see you too, Etta,' she said sarcastically, as the pooch whimpered and danced around Owen's legs. 'Just you remember who fills your food bowl every day.'

'She's so friendly,' Owen said, crouching down to pet her.

'If she carries on like this, you can have her,' Harriet muttered. 'Ungrateful hound.'

As though Etta understood, the dog turned her attention to her mistress, and Harriet scooped her up and cuddled her close, breathing in the familiar and comforting doggy smell. 'If you're still up for taking her for a walk, you might want to make a move before the kids get home,' she advised, 'because I'll bet my right arm that Bobby will want to go with you.'

'I don't mind taking him, if that's OK with you? He's good fun.'

Harriet groaned. 'When we were at my parents' house on Sunday, he told my mum that he'd peed in your van. She didn't realise it had a loo in it. You ought to have seen her face.'

Owen guffawed. 'That's priceless.'

'She also thought you had one of those old-fashioned gypsy vans and a horse to pull it.' Before she could say anything further, the door banged open and her son thundered in. 'Brace yourself,' she warned.

'Owen!' Bobby skidded to a halt, his coat flying in one direction and his bag in the other.

'Hi, sprout. Had a good day in school?'

'I told everyone I peed in your van.'

Harriet rolled her eyes. 'See?'

'Have you come to have a bath?'

Owen snorted and Harriet could tell he was trying not to laugh. 'Not today. I'm here to take Etta for a walk.'

'Can I come?' Bobby gazed hopefully up at her. 'Can I, Mam? I was good last time.'

'I know you were,' Harriet said. 'You can go if you want, but change out of your uniform first,' she yelled after him as he scampered into the hall. 'And pick your bag and coat up,' she added. Yep, Groundhog Day had nothing on her life.

Bobby was rushing upstairs to change as his sister sauntered in. Sara halted in her tracks when she saw Owen. She smiled at him but she wasn't as open, being more wary and reserved, and Harriet marvelled at her children's differing reactions.

'Sara, you remember Owen? We met him the other day when we were walking Etta.'

'Bobby hasn't stopped talking about him, Mam,' Sara pointed out. 'Hiya.' This was directed at Owen. The next words out of Sara's mouth were directed at her and were utterly predictable. 'What's for tea?'

'Butternut squash casserole and rice,' Harriet said. 'Owen is taking Etta for a walk, then he's going to help me make it. Bobby is going with him.'

Sara's eyes darted from her mother to Owen and back again. 'Just Bobby?'

'You can come too, if you like?' Owen offered, glancing at Harriet for confirmation.

Harriet nodded. 'You can, but I didn't think you'd want to. They're going down to the river. It's muddy,' she added.

'I want to.' Sara was firm.

'We could look for conkers,' Owen suggested.

'What are those?'

Owen's eyes widened. 'Have you never played conkers?' And when Sara shook her head, he added, 'You're in for a treat.'

Sara was about to ask more but Harriet stopped her.

'Hurry up and get changed,' she said, suddenly wishing she was going with Owen, too. Surprise that her daughter wanted to walk the dog after school caught her unawares and it took her a second to realise that Sara was envious of her brother. It took her another second to understand that both children craved male company. She knew they missed their father dreadfully, but his attention was sporadic and half-hearted, and they hadn't had any contact with him since before the summer holidays, so Owen must be a novelty for them.

'Thanks,' she said, when she and Owen were alone for a moment. 'And sorry for springing them on you.'

'I honestly don't mind. They're nice kids.'

'They are,' Harriet said, filling up with pride. Sara could sometimes be a bit of a handful, but she was no different to any girl who was rapidly approaching her teenage years, and trying to discover who she was and find her place in the world.

Within minutes the children thundered down the stairs, barging each other out of the way as they hurtled into the kitchen.

'Calm down, it's only a walk,' Harriet said, but her words fell on deaf ears. The kids were excited; Sara must have told Bobby that they were going to look for conkers and, even though neither child had any idea what conkers were, both of them were thrilled about it.

Harriet waved them off, then made the children a snack to come home to, before having a quick clean-up. The house wasn't untidy and neither was it dirty, but she felt the need to present it in its best possible light, so she gave the downstairs a quick once-over with the vacuum cleaner, picking up discarded and out-of-place items as she went, then hurried upstairs to make herself more presentable.

Guessing that a full face of makeup was over the top and so was getting out her curling tongs, she settled for a swipe of lip gloss and another coat of mascara. After tugging a comb through her hair, she checked her reflection in the full-length mirror and decided she'd have to do. She wasn't particularly pretty, she knew, but she was reasonably pleased with what she saw, and she hoped Owen would be too.

Wait a minute, lady…

Harriet quickly backtracked. There was no reason whatsoever for Owen to concern himself with the way she looked – and he probably didn't care anyway. So why was she so bothered?

'Oh, give it a rest,' she muttered. She knew exactly why – he was handsome in an understated way and she was seriously attracted to him. It was only natural that she'd want to look her best. It was a matter of pride. Nothing more.

Maybe if he wasn't constantly moving from one place to the next, they might have a chance; and give it another year or two, she also might be ready to start dating again. *If* he thought about her in that way. Which she was fairly certain he didn't.

So why invite him for tea? she could almost hear Pen ask. Pen would have said that a simple 'thank you' would have sufficed. And *that* was why she hadn't mentioned it to her boss, because deep down she knew Pen was right, and Harriet didn't want to hear it.

They were back, she realised, hearing the sound of her children's animated chatter and Owen's deeper tones, and she trotted downstairs.

'Did you have a good time?' she asked, giving the kids' wellies a pointed look to remind them to take them off. Owen made a face, his expression contrite, and he bent down to unlace his boots.

In stockinged feet, he stood there uncertainly as both children talked at once, and she smiled reassuringly at him. This level of loud chatter was quite normal, and he would have to get used to it if he intended to stay for tea.

Bobby held out a bobble hat stuffed full of shiny brown nuts. 'Look, Mam. Conkers.'

'So I see.' Gosh, this took her back. She'd never played conkers when she was a child (too scared of getting her knuckles rapped), but most of the boys used to, playing ferociously every break time and after school as well. Then it was banned by many schools, and no one played conkers at all any more.

'Crumbs, you've collected loads,' she said, picking up one of the smooth nuts and holding it in her hand. Seeing it reminded her of her childhood, and she smiled wistfully.

'I'm hungry,' Sara said, bringing her back to the present.

'Tea will be an hour or so yet,' she said, 'but there are cheese and crackers in the kitchen, if you want them, and you can have a flapjack each to tide you over.'

The children dashed off, leaving Harriet and Owen standing in the hall.

'I wish I had their energy,' he said.

'So do I!' Harriet's reply was heartfelt. 'They wear me out just looking at them.'

She led him into the kitchen, which was now mercifully empty, as the children had taken their snacks into the living room, and she emptied the hessian bag that Owen had brought with him earlier, placing the bulbous butternut squash on a chopping board. Several sweet potatoes followed.

'If you tell me what else we need, I'll get it out,' she said, and while she rooted around in the cupboard, Owen expertly peeled and chopped the vegetables.

It was odd having a man in her kitchen, she thought, as they stood side-by-side, cooking. Declan had never prepared a meal with her, unless opening a bottle of wine counted. But she realised she quite liked Owen being there. Occasionally, she would accidentally brush up against him, or he'd reach for something at the same time and their hands would touch. And every time they made contact, however fleeting, she would feel a shiver deep inside.

On the surface, the atmosphere appeared to be light and inconsequential as they chatted about this, that and nothing in particular, but Harriet didn't believe she was imagining an undercurrent of something she couldn't quite put her finger on. She wondered if Owen also felt it or whether it was just her overactive brain: that she had been without male companionship for so long, she was seeing things that weren't there and feeling a connection that didn't exist.

–

Owen hadn't had this much fun in ages, and collecting conkers had taken him right back to his childhood. Harriet's children seemed to have enjoyed themselves, too: Bobby full of bounce and eagerness (much like the dog), Sara a little more reserved at the start. But once he had led them to a spreading horse chestnut tree, it soon became a competition to see which of them could find the biggest conker.

The ground underneath the tree had been littered with the fallen nuts, some of them still firmly encased in their green spiky outer shell, but many had burst open to reveal the glossy brown seeds.

Because they looked like nuts, Bobby wanted to know if they could be eaten, and Owen had stressed that they most definitely couldn't. Although they probably wouldn't be fatal, the nuts were toxic, and he went to great pains to explain that they weren't like the chestnuts eaten at Christmas.

Without thinking, he had promised to take them foraging for sweet chestnuts and hazelnuts, before realising he should have run this past Harriet.

With the dog walked and a goodly number of conkers collected, Owen took the children back home to their mother, his pace quickening with each step. He was keen to return to Harriet, telling himself it was because he was hungry, and ignoring the suspicion that it was *her* he wanted, not the food.

Oh dear, he thought with dismay, he shouldn't have taken her up on her invitation. Not if he was beginning to have feelings for her. Purely carnal ones he could cope with – it wouldn't be the first time he'd felt sexually attracted to a woman and hadn't done anything about it – but this was different. He liked her a lot. He had liked her from the very first conversation they'd had in Pen's Pantry, when she had been as spiky as the casings on the conkers that he had helped her children collect today.

He admired her spirit in not only taking him up on his challenge (which he'd thrown down casually, never expecting her to go through with it), but also going two steps further. Christmas was still two months away and, considering there were presents to buy, she was going to have her work cut out. Still, this made the blog even more interesting, as his followers would want to read about how she coped. In some ways, Owen didn't envy her. He only had his brother and his family, and his parents to buy for. Children would be an added strain on her purchasing dilemma, and he was keen to see how she coped with it.

His heart had lifted when he saw her standing in the hall as he'd followed the children into the house. She'd looked delectable: her cheeks slightly flushed as though she had been rushing around, a hint of colour on her lips. Her hair was down and flowing around her shoulders, and the knitted dress she wore skimmed her curves.

She quickly put him to work, peeling and chopping, but if he had hoped that being busy would take his mind off her, he was sadly mistaken. He was acutely aware of every move she made and every word she spoke, and being in such close confines meant he could also smell her perfume – a subtle, floral scent that reminded him of summer meadows and sunny days.

Once or twice, their hands touched as they reached for the same knife or wooden spoon, and when that happened, his heart did a funny kind of skipped-beat thing that made him worry he might have a heart problem. Strange that it only happened when there was physical contact.

But when he glanced up from his butternut-squash dicing, caught her eye and almost coughed as his heart missed a beat, he wondered whether he did have a problem after all. This wasn't normal.

'Are you OK?' Harriet asked, and he realised he must have made some kind of noise. 'You look a little flushed.'

Was a red complexion one of the symptoms of an imminent heart attack? he asked himself, as he frantically tried to remember everything he had ever heard and read about heart issues. He probably knew as much as the average person in the street – a crushing pain in the chest, which he didn't have; numbness or tingling in the left arm, which he also didn't have. Breathlessness? Nope, not that either. And neither did he feel clammy, although he did feel a little hot under the collar, but the kitchen was rather warm, so that could easily be explained.

In desperate need of a moment to himself, Owen asked, 'Do you mind if I use the loo?'

'Of course not. There's a cloakroom just through there.' She pointed to a door, through which he could see an ironing board and a washing machine, and he guessed it was a utility room.

'Won't be a sec,' he said, and hurried out of the kitchen.

As soon as he closed the cloakroom door and locked it, he took a deep breath and studied his reflection in the mirror above the little sink. He did look a bit rosy but he certainly wasn't sweating profusely, and even as he watched, the colour subsided and his skin tone returned to normal once more.

Relieved, Owen splashed some water on his face and washed his hands, then took another look. He looked perfectly normal, he decided, and he felt it now, too. His heart had stopped skipping a beat, and when he put two fingers on his wrist and began to count, he found that his pulse was neither too fast nor too slow.

He'd better get back out there. Harriet would be wondering what had happened to him.

Whoa! The minute he thought of Harriet, his stomach cartwheeled and his insides tingled.

No skipped beat though, thankfully.

But that soon changed when he walked back into the kitchen and saw her stirring some onions in a pan. She was swaying gently as she cooked them, and he couldn't take his eyes off her.

Darn it, he had another palpitation, and it was then that the realisation hit him. It was *Harriet* who was causing this reaction: there was nothing wrong with his heart at all.

He became aware of music and realised she was mouthing the words of a song to herself, and he watched, fascinated. She had the cutest nose, slightly turned up at the end, and as he stood there, Harriet tucked her hair behind an ear and he was swamped by the urge to nibble the pale skin just beneath it.

She must have realised she was being watched, because she stopped singing and glanced over at him. 'OK?' she asked.

He cleared his throat. 'Fine. What can I do?'

'I've put the squash and the sweet potatoes into the oven to roast for ten minutes, while I caramelise the onions, and when that's done, we'll be ready to pop everything in the pot. Can you open a tin of tomatoes? There's some in the cupboard here.' She pointed to a cupboard next to the cooker.

It was also next to her legs, and he was careful not to touch her as he opened it and searched for the tin.

Hooking a finger through the ring pull, he peeled the lid off and plopped the tomatoes into the enamel pot, then almost dropped the empty tin when Harriet nudged him out of the way so she could spoon the onions in.

His whole arm was on fire where she'd touched him and it took all his self-control not to let her see his reaction. Taking a steadying breath, he stood back and let her finish preparing the casserole, keeping well out of the way until she eventually put the enamel pot in the oven.

He was wondering what they were going to do for the forty-five or so minutes until the meal was ready, when Bobby saved his bacon.

'Can we play with the conkers now?' he asked, and Owen leapt on the request.

'We'll have to prepare them first,' he said. 'Harriet, have you got a screwdriver I can borrow?'

'There should be one in here,' she said, opening a drawer. 'Yes, here you go.'

He took it from her carefully, making sure to avoid any contact. Just the thought of their hands touching made him shiver, and he debated the wisdom of staying for tea. He'd be better off going back to the van and having a cold shower.

This was getting ridiculous.

Wishing he hadn't started writing about Harriet and her challenge, Owen tried to focus on the job at hand – namely, piercing a hole through the middle of each conker and threading a piece of string through. Luckily, Harriet had some of that too, so with him doing the piercing and the children doing the threading (Sara hadn't wanted to be left out), the conkers were soon ready.

'Now what do we do with them?' Bobby asked, swinging one around above his head.

'Careful,' Harriet warned, leaning back to avoid being hit. 'You'd better go outside. I don't want bits of shattered conker all over my kitchen.'

Bobby's eyes widened and he looked at Owen, who nodded.

'Outside,' Owen said, grabbing the conkers as everyone trooped into the garden. It was almost dark already, but Harriet pressed a switch and the garden was immediately flooded with light.

He picked up a conker to show the children what to do. 'Wrap the string around your hand like this… Good… Then you stand there and Sara stands there…' He hesitated. 'It might be a good idea to watch your mum and me first. What do you say, Harriet? Are you up for a game of conkers?'

113

Harriet pulled a face. 'I know what to do, but I've never played,' she said.

Owen said, 'You can go first,' and he let his conker dangle. 'The purpose of the game is to strike the other person's conker with yours, and try to shatter it. You take it in turns, and the person who has a whole conker at the end wins. I must warn you, you'll probably end up with sore knuckles.'

Harriet didn't seem too enamoured of the idea of rapped knuckles but the children didn't mind, and soon there were conkers swinging everywhere, accompanied by whoops of joy and yelps of pain.

After a few goes, Harriet retreated to the kitchen, using the excuse that she needed to check on the casserole, and not long afterwards Owen joined her, having been soundly beaten by two children who had ganged up on him and broken the rules as well.

'I'll just wash my hands,' he said, as he stumbled, laughing, into the kitchen. 'I think I'll wear boxing gloves next time – your kids don't play fair.'

'Thank you for playing with them.'

Her voice was soft and it took him by surprise. 'I enjoyed it.'

'They did too.' She nodded towards the children, who were swinging their conkers with all their might, then skipping out of the way when one threatened to hit them. 'They miss their father.'

Owen slipped his stinging hands into the pockets of his jeans. 'Do they see much of him?'

'A bit, and not at all recently. They don't deserve to be treated the way Declan treats them.'

Owen pursed his lips, not sure what he was supposed to say to that. He wanted to know more but he didn't like to pry.

'I'll just… er…' He gestured to the downstairs cloakroom.

'Of course, sorry. And if you need any arnica cream, let me know.'

Yet another visit to the loo to compose himself, he thought, although this time he did have to wash his hands.

Once again, he checked his reflection and saw that his face was glowing. He put it down to being outside in the cold before coming into a warm kitchen.

It had nothing to do with Harriet sharing a confidence with him; nothing at all.

How Owen survived the meal was a question he would ask himself later. But if it hadn't been for the children diluting the increasingly charged atmosphere between him and Harriet (it wasn't his imagination, surely?), he might have exploded.

After an offer to wash the dishes, which Harriet turned down, and an offer of coffee from Harriet, which he turned down, Owen made his excuses and left. As soon as he was a safe distance away from her house, he hitched in a deep breath and let it out slowly, relief seeping through him.

The problem wasn't that he hadn't enjoyed her company, or that of Sara and Bobby – the problem was that he *had*.

And that was an issue because – fancying her rotten, aside – for the first time in his adult life he had caught a glimpse of another kind of existence. The kind of life he could have had if he had bought a house and not a van, if he had stayed in one place and hadn't become a nomad, if he had found a woman he wanted to marry and have children with.

He had done what he'd done, and not for one second had he regretted it.

Until now.

But was it this abstract idea of being married and settling down that had suddenly become so appealing, or was it the thought of being with *Harriet*?

Chapter 10

Will this do? Harriet wondered as she picked up a basket of toiletries wrapped in cellophane. It was brand new, so it must have been an unwanted gift, but the question was, would Darlene like it?

The boot sale was just as busy this Saturday as it had been the last time she was there – busier, if anything – so Harriet put the basket down and moved on. There must be something…

She wished she had Sara with her, but the children were with Granny and Grandad for the day, so Harriet was shopping alone. On second thoughts, if Sara had been with her there was no way Harriet would have been able to buy a birthday present for Darlene. Or anything else, for that matter; she had already purchased a couple of tops and some leggings that she hoped Sara would like, and all for less than a fiver. Result! But she wasn't having much luck with the birthday girl's present. Sara was beginning to get anxious and had been nagging to go shopping, even though the party was a couple of weeks away yet. This damned party was all she could talk about, and Harriet was dreading it. Thankfully, she still had time to find something, so she renewed her search with vigour, muttering under her breath. The not-buying-anything-new vow aside, Harriet would still have an issue with regard to present-buying, because she didn't want to spend a fortune and things cost so much these days.

Her phone pinged and, fully expecting it to be her mam, she wasn't prepared to see Owen's name come up. When she read his message, her pulse began to race.

Are you at the boot sale?

Yes. Are you?

I'm back at the van. Fancy a brew?

Would love one, but I'm present-hunting.

Still not found anything?

No.

Want some company?

Did she ever!

Yes, please. I'm standing next to a big white van with Union Jack bunting.

I know the one – it's here every week. Stay there, I'll come to you.

Harriet's heart was thumping and she swallowed nervously, hoping she didn't look as flustered as she felt and wishing she had made more of an effort with her appearance. She had been so eager to get going this morning that she'd not bothered with makeup, apart from a swipe of mascara, and had dragged her hair back into a ponytail. Consequently, she felt a right scruff.

Telling herself that Owen wouldn't care what she looked like (why should he, when she was just an acquaintance – although, maybe they could be classed as friends now?), she focused on the entrance to the field, hoping to see him. And when she did, she took a deep breath before letting it out slowly, because he looked yummy enough to eat.

He was wearing a navy beanie hat and he had the beginnings of a beard. His hands were stuffed into his pockets and he was scanning the field, and when he saw her, his smile made her heart leap.

She hadn't seen him since the meal, although he had messaged her to say thank you, and apparently he'd popped into the cafe last Monday, but Harriet hadn't been at work because Bobby's school had a teacher training day and she had stayed home to look after him.

Pen had teased her mercilessly, saying that Owen had looked quite crestfallen when Pen had informed him Harriet wasn't in, and she had begun the extremely unsubtle offensive of trying to persuade Harriet that having a bit of fun with Owen might be just the thing she needed. No-strings-sex was what Pen called it, claiming that it was the best of both worlds; Owen would move on sooner or later, so Harriet could 'cut her teeth on him' (Pen's words, not Harriet's) and use him as a practice run before diving into the dating scene again.

Harriet didn't agree. Dating didn't appeal to her because she wasn't interested in another relationship, and having a fling wasn't her style. Although seeing Owen stride across the field, wearing a beaming smile on his luscious lips, was almost enough to make her change her mind.

Taking him to bed and having her wicked way with him was rapidly becoming more appealing. No one would even know, and what harm would it do as long as she was discreet? Maybe Pen was right? Not because Harriet *wanted* a relationship, but because she *didn't*. She and Owen could have a bit of fun, then go their separate ways, without running the risk of either of them being hurt.

Or maybe not. Harriet blew out her cheeks. Let's not complicate things, she said to herself. Knowing her, she'd get too emotionally involved and it would be hard to say goodbye when Owen eventually moved on – which he would do, sooner or later.

Although she had been terribly upset, Declan hadn't broken her heart when he'd walked out – they had been drifting apart long before that – so she certainly didn't want to have it broken now. Because no matter how fervently she tried to convince herself that she wasn't going to fall for Owen, she suspected she might. He already occupied more of her mind than she was comfortable with. The last thing she needed was for him to occupy her heart.

'Hi.' He was grinning widely and gazing into her eyes, and she couldn't help but grin and gaze back, and as she did so, a wave of desire swept over her, leaving her feeling breathless and trembly.

It was quite a nice feeling and she would have enjoyed it immensely if she were a teenager. But she was rapidly heading towards forty and had two kids – she had responsibilities, and she shouldn't be lusting after a man she hardly knew.

Harriet cleared her throat. 'Hi. Had a good week?' There, that was suitably polite and friendly without being flirty or encouraging.

'Yes, thanks. You?'

'It was OK.'

'Where is everyone?'

'Sara and Bobby are with my parents, and Etta is at home. I'll take her for a walk later.'

'Tell them I said "hi".'

'I will.' She was still staring into his eyes, and when she realised, she hastily dragged her gaze away.

There was a second or two of awkward silence, then Owen said, 'Seen anything you like?'

Yeah, she thought, *you!* Oh dear… 'There was a basket of toiletries on a stall over there, but to be honest it's probably the sort of thing I would give to my mum, not to a twelve-year-old girl.'

'Shall we keep going? You might find something suitable.'

'I might not,' she replied gloomily, as they wandered to the next stall.

'Cup half-empty,' he teased.

'I'm not normally so negative,' she said, giving the stall a quick scan and not seeing anything.

'Hang on,' Owen said, as she began to walk away. 'What's this?' He was pointing to a brown cardboard box whose lid was propped open. 'It looks kind of girly.'

It certainly does, Harriet thought, and she peered at it closely. 'It's a milkshake-making kit.' There were four vials of powdered milkshake flavours, plus loads of packets of toppings. Her mouth watered just looking at the chocolate curls, mini marshmallows, white-chocolate stars and tiny pieces of fudge. She knew Sara would adore it if she received it as a gift, so Harriet suspected Darlene also might like it. After checking that everything was still in date, Harriet decided that if the price was right, she'd buy it.

'How much?' she asked, wishing sellers would put prices on things.

'Three pounds?'

'I'll take it.' Beaming at Owen, Harriet reached for her purse and dug out some coins. 'What a cute idea. Sara will adore it.' She sobered. 'Let's hope Darlene will,' she added, giving Owen a meaningful look. 'This is the child who asked for a Pandora bracelet, remember?'

'If she doesn't, then it's her loss,' Owen replied. He had been playing with his phone again, but he quickly put it away. 'Do you want to carry on looking around the boot sale, or do you fancy a coffee?'

'Bored already?' she teased.

'Not in the slightest.'

'Do you mind if we stay here for a bit? It's a treat for me to go shopping without the kids in tow, and I'd like to see if I can pick up a Christmas present or two while I'm at it.'

'Not at all. I love seeing what you buy.'

'You do?' Harriet was surprised. Declan had hated shopping, unless he had been buying something for himself.

'I like seeing things being repurposed, and I like it when people buy pre-loved stuff rather than new.'

'So you do,' she chuckled. She opened her tote. 'Look, I've bought some clothes for Sara. She's shot up recently, and most of what she's got no longer fits her.'

Owen craned his neck to see inside the bag. 'You'll have to show me later.'

'I will,' she promised.

She bought a few more things – a pair of jeans for Sara, a sweatshirt for Bobby, plus a brand-new duvet set that was still in its packaging, which would be one of Sara's Christmas presents. As soon as Harriet saw it, an idea came to her that she would redecorate Sara's room. Her daughter's bedroom hadn't been done in ages and was looking rather tired, as well as babyish. She would use the duvet set as a theme and see if she could pick up a few things to complement it.

She wasn't sure Owen would approve, though, because it didn't strictly fit in with this refrain of not buying anything unless it was needed. When she mentioned that to him, he was surprisingly sympathetic.

'You've got kids – you can't ignore Christmas,' he said. 'I certainly won't be ignoring it: I've got a mum, a dad, a brother and his family to buy for.' He smirked as he added, 'They don't always appreciate my choice of gifts, though.'

'Tell me more.' They were making their way out of Holly Field and towards the one where Owen had parked his van. Harriet was gasping for a cuppa and was also looking forward to a sit-down for five minutes.

Owen pulled a face. 'One year, I bought my mum a set of cotton mesh bags to take with her when she went grocery shopping. Bear in mind that this was before supermarkets started using paper bags or reusable plastic ones for you to put your loose fruit and veg in.' He laughed. 'I've mellowed a little since then. I now buy her a spa day, or a voucher for a wash and blow-dry.'

Harriet said, 'I'm not sure I'd appreciate mesh bags for Christmas, either.' Although that couldn't have been any worse than Declan buying her some shapewear. She'd not long had Bobby and was feeling self-conscious about her muffin top. To this day, she still wasn't sure whether he was trying to be thoughtful (she had been complaining about her flabby tummy a lot) or whether he was being judgy.

They were strolling down the lane and had almost reached Owen's field, when he paused. 'Are you hungry? I could do us a spot of lunch.'

'That's very kind of you but I have to get home to Etta. The poor dog's legs will be crossed. Just because you came to mine for a meal, please don't feel obliged to return the favour.'

'I don't. I just… never mind.'

'What?' Harriet was curious. He couldn't leave her hanging.

'Enjoy your company,' he finished, looking anywhere but at her.

Harriet was amazed. Did he really…? Or was he lonely? As far as she knew, the only people he interacted with were herself, her children and Aled. No wonder he wanted to spend time with her, if mean and miserable Aled was his only other option. 'Why don't I go home and drop these off—' she held up her bags '—fetch Etta, then come back?'

'You don't mind? I mean, if you've got something else planned…?'

'You're saving me from having to tackle the laundry,' she told him, knowing full well that all she was doing was delaying the inevitable. It would have to be tackled at some point. 'I'll be back in about half an hour, if that's OK?'

'Great!'

He looked so pleased, Harriet was glad she had accepted his invitation and she guessed her assessment that he was lonely was right.

Now, if she could keep a lid on her growing attraction to him and treat him like the friend he so clearly wanted her to be, everything would be fine.

–

Owen hurried back to his van, wondering what to make for lunch. He didn't want to look as though he was going out of his way to impress her, but he wanted to impress her nevertheless.

This past week he'd done little else other than think about her. It didn't help that she was constantly on his mind because of *Planet B*, but even if he weren't writing a weekly post about her, she would still have claimed centre stage in his thoughts.

Owen had come to a decision – one he hadn't taken lightly and had thought long and hard about – he was going to stay in Foxmore for the foreseeable future.

He liked the village immensely (he supposed he could even say he'd fallen in love with the place) but he liked Harriet more. And it was his growing attraction to her that was the main reason he didn't want to move on.

He was lucky he could work from almost anywhere, and although he might have to go to where the story was or do some research on site, that didn't mean he couldn't return to Foxmore. And to Harriet.

Shoving the key in the lock, Owen tripped up the steps and into the van, welcome warmth enveloping him. He had fired up the log burner last night and had fed the hungry black beast again this morning, not wanting the interior of the van to become too chilly, and the first thing he did now was to shove another log into its mouth.

A root around in the cupboard and the fridge gave him an idea for a tasty, quick and filling lunch, so he set about gathering the ingredients together to make creamy mushroom and spinach penne pasta, with freshly baked scones to follow. He had been planning on baking a loaf of bread anyway, so he'd make scones instead, with the idea that he could eat any leftover ones for breakfast tomorrow. They would go well with the jam he'd bought, and he could use the oat-based crème fraîche that he had originally planned to have with fresh fruit. Instead of the traditional sultanas, he had some dried cranberries, so he would put those in, along with a pinch of cinnamon and the zest of a whole orange. If he added a handful of flaked almonds, he could legitimately call them Christmas scones, although there was Halloween and Bonfire Night to get through first before Christmas arrived. Harriet was clearly in the mood for Christmas already, as her purchases today showed, so he hoped she'd like them.

He stared around his tiny kitchen area, wondering where to begin.

Scones first, he decided, as they would take the longest.

Owen loved cooking, and because he had been vegan for many years, he had become a dab hand in the kitchen. When he was a young chap, people used to look at him sideways when he said he didn't eat animal products – and there wasn't the variety of vegan products available now, so wanting to stick to his vegan guns and still eat well, he'd had to learn to cook for himself pretty sharpish. He often still baked his own bread, cakes and biscuits, and in the past he had been known to make his own hazelnut flour, although these days he preferred to go out and buy it.

The scone dough made, he rolled it out and cut it into circles, before lining a baking tray with parchment and popping it into the fridge for a quarter of an hour.

Then he set about making the sauce for the pasta, humming to himself as he worked.

His heart did that skipped-beat-thing again when he was abruptly reminded of watching Harriet at the stove. She had been singing softly along to the radio, and he remembered the way she had tucked a lock of hair behind her ear, exposing the soft, pale skin of her neck. He also remembered how he'd wanted to kiss that skin and nibble that ear, and he pushed the thought away.

He might think Harriet extremely lovely and sexy, but he didn't for one minute believe she felt the same way about him. She was just being friendly, and maybe she was a little bit grateful to him as well. He doubted she regarded him as anything more, so he knew he'd have to take things slowly. Even then, she might not be interested in him like that – but he intended to give it his best shot.

Owen didn't want a quick fling and he most definitely didn't want a one-night stand. For the very first time in his life, he wanted a proper relationship. He felt ready for it. Or… had he been ready all along but he simply hadn't met the right woman?

He would probably never know the answer to that, and it didn't matter anyway. What did matter were his growing feelings for Harriet, and that he seemed unable to keep them in check.

However, it wasn't just *his* feelings he needed to consider. How would Harriet feel about having another man in her life? She didn't seem to have had much luck with her ex-husband, and it might have put her off men for good. And there were her children to take into account: he understood that if he wanted a relationship with her, he would also have to have a relationship with Sara and Bobby.

As he poured boiling water on a handful of cashew nuts and a small amount of dried porcini mushrooms (a favourite of his and a staple which was always in his cupboard), he took a moment to reflect.

Did he really intend to stay in Foxmore and get to know Harriet properly?

It seemed so.

He heated oil in a pan and added a handful of halved chestnut mushrooms that he'd been planning on making soup with, along with a clove of garlic, but when the smell of frying food hit his nostrils, his stomach churned.

It wasn't too late to change his mind. He could leave right now, if he wanted. In three minutes he could be on the road. In ten he could be turning onto the A470 and heading towards the Llŷn Peninsula, as he'd originally planned. He could forget Foxmore, forget the challenge and forget Harriet.

But…

He removed the scones from the fridge and slid the baking tray into the oven, his mind whirling.

There was *Planet B* to consider. He could make something up as to why he couldn't report on Harriet's (or should he say, *Dawn's*) progress any longer, but it would be a lie. Besides, she was doing so well that he wanted to see her get to the end of it.

Then there was Harriet herself. She was the real reason he couldn't leave.

The thought of never seeing her again stabbed him in the gut, and he knew that running away wasn't an option. He had to see this thing out, to get to know her, to woo her – because he owed it to himself to try. If he didn't, he suspected he would regret it for a very long time. And if she didn't feel the same, then so be it. At least he would have tried, and he could go back to the way he'd lived for the past two decades – alone and on the road.

It wouldn't be the end of the world. He might suffer a bruised heart, but that would be it. He would make sure he ended the relationship long before he fell in love.

'Ha!' he grunted. What did he know about *love*? Apart from knowing that he'd never been in that state before. He wouldn't know love if it jumped up and bit him on the bum. He would just have to hope that if Harriet didn't want to get to know him better in *that* way, that he'd recognise when it was time to bail before he got hurt.

A knock on the side of the van brought him out of his reverie and he looked over his shoulder to see Harriet standing outside the open door.

'Something smells nice,' she said. 'I could smell garlic frying halfway up the lane.'

'Come in, take a seat. Hello, Etta.'

Owen crouched down to fondle the dog's silky ears, but in reality he was attempting to slow his heart rate down to a more acceptable level.

Bloody hell, the effect Harriet had on him was scary.

He had desired women in the past, he had lusted after them, had taken them to bed, and had totally and utterly enjoyed it, but never before had he been as besotted as he was now. He was behaving like a sixteen-year-old with a first crush fuelled by too much testosterone and unbridled emotion.

Straightening up, he smiled at her as she took a seat, and she smiled back. As his heart sang, he turned to the sink and washed his hands.

'What are we having?' she asked.

'Mushroom and spinach penne, with scones for dessert.'

'Mmm, sounds delicious.'

'It's almost ready,' he said, grabbing some cutlery and putting it on the table. He then got two bowls out of the cupboard and prepared to dish up. But first, he'd better check on those scones. He didn't want them turning out like rock cakes.

He was aware that Harriet was watching him with interest, and when she said, 'You didn't bake those yourself, did you?', a warm fuzzy glow lit him from within.

'I did,' he confessed, shyly. 'I do most of my own baking.'

'Wow! Good-looking and a good cook.' There was a sudden silence, then she said, 'Oops. I hope I haven't embarrassed you?'

She had, but only because he was well aware he was an average Joe when it came to looks. He had to admit, though, that as he aged, he appeared to be growing into his skin. The reflection that looked back at him these days was of a man who didn't put much store in the way he looked, so it was both flattering and unexpected that Harriet thought he was OK to look at. Or was she just saying that?

Um, no, he didn't think so. It had slipped out without her meaning it to, and her heightened colour gave him the impression that she was mortified at having said such a thing.

'I'm not embarrassed,' he fibbed. 'I could say the same about you.'

'Huh!'

'You are,' he insisted. 'I think you're beautiful.' Oh dear, now it was his turn to be discomforted.

'Thank you, but I was referring to my cooking skills.'

'Ah...' All he'd wanted to do was to reassure her that she was indeed gorgeous, and now he had made an utter fool of himself. 'You can cook, too,' he said, heat whooshing into his face. He concentrated on forking out the pasta into the bowls and wished he was anywhere but right there.

'I don't consider you having to show me how to make a butternut squash casserole as being a good cook,' she retorted.

Feeling on safer ground, Owen said, 'I seem to recall you telling me that you'd made the pumpkin soup in Pen's Pantry.'

'So I did.'

'And as I recall, it was delicious.'

'It was OK.'

'I make a lot of soups, and believe me, yours was lovely.' *You are lovely*, he wanted to add, but he'd said more than enough for one day. *Take it slow*, he told himself: he didn't want to frighten her off.

He placed two steaming bowls of fragrant pasta on the table and sat down. 'I hope you like it.'

'I'm sure I will.'

He waited anxiously for her to take a mouthful, and when she closed her eyes in bliss and murmured, 'This is sooo good,' he breathed a sigh of relief, despite not thinking that the way to a woman's heart was through her stomach. It couldn't hurt to try, though!

For the next few minutes there was very little talking as both of them ate, and as Owen's appetite was fully restored, he began to relax.

They chatted about the food they liked, and Harriet asked him for the pasta recipe, keen to try it at home, and she also wanted to suggest adding it to the cafe's vegan menu. Over the past couple of years there had been an increasing demand for vegetarian and vegan dishes, she told him, and they batted around a couple of recipes for a while.

Pasta consumed, Owen cleared away the dirty bowls, waving away Harriet's offer of help, and when they were stacked neatly on the side, he produced his scones with a flourish.

'There's crème fraîche and jam if you want it, or do you prefer yours buttered?'

'You can't have scones without jam and cream,' she said, taking a bite.

Once again, her murmurs of appreciation made him glow, but this time it wasn't because of the accolade, but because of the noises she made. They sent a tingle straight down his spine and he had a sudden vision of kissing her, his arms holding her close as she melted into him: she would be making those exact same noises...

'Coffee? Tea?' he grunted.

'Tea would be nice,' she replied around a mouthful of scone. 'What's in these? They're so unusual.'

'Dried cranberries, cinnamon, almonds and the zest of an orange. They're kind of Christmassy.'

'They're kind of delicious. I can't believe you made these yourself. You're a keeper.'

Harriet took another bite, her eyes on her plate, and he wondered what she'd meant by that. A keeper for whom? Her? Or was it just a figure of speech, and she didn't mean anything by it?

He busied himself making the tea, using a real teapot, complete with loose tea leaves and a tea cosy. Once again, he was conscious of her eyes on him, watching his every move, and he wondered what she was thinking. Actually, he could guess.

'I bet you think I'm old-fashioned,' he said.

'I don't. Although it does bring back memories of my great-grandma, who never used anything other than loose tea and always made it in a teapot. She used to say that the flavour was better. Mind you, she never drank anything other than Lapsang Souchong, so I'll take her word for it.'

'Funnily enough, it does taste better,' he agreed. 'But that may be more to do with the ceremony of it. Throwing a bag in a mug isn't the same, somehow. I also don't like using bags if I can help it, because most of them contain plastic and take years to decompose, if they ever do.'

'I don't think I've ever met anyone as serious about the environment before,' she said, as he gave the pot a final stir and poured them both a cup.

'I've only got oat milk, I'm afraid.'

'That's OK. I'll give it a go.'

'The crème fraîche you ate was made from oat milk,' he told her.

'Was it?' she sounded surprised. 'It was lovely.'

'Does it bother you that I'm a bit of a nerd when it comes to the planet?' he asked.

'Not at all. Someone's got to be. I wish I could do more.'

'You've made a start, that's the main thing,' he said. 'You can't be expected to change everything all at once. It takes time, and you've got to decide which changes you can live with and which ones you can't.'

Harriet finished her scone and sat back. 'I'm stuffed. That was wonderful – thank you.'

'It was OK,' Owen replied, modestly.

'It was more than OK. Have you ever thought about becoming a chef?'

He chuckled. 'I'm happy enough to cook for a friend, but the thought of cooking for a bunch of people I've never met scares the pants off me.'

'I can't imagine you being scared of anything,' Harriet replied.

'Believe me, I am.'

'Like what?' She cocked her head.

'The usual – climate change, global warming, drought, deforestation…' He got to his feet and began clearing away.

'That's quite a list. Anything else? Here, let me give you a hand.' She stood up.

'No chance! You're a guest. Anyway, it won't take me long. And in answer to your question, I'm not too keen on spiders.'

Harriet shuddered. 'Neither am I. So I'm not going to be able to rely on you to rescue me from a great big hairy beastie with long black legs?'

'Nope,' he said cheerfully.

'Then it's a good thing Bobby doesn't mind them, isn't it?'

Owen was aware of how close she was standing, although, to be fair, the van wasn't exactly roomy, so she didn't have a lot of choice. 'He's more of a man than I am,' he said, trying to keep the conversation light, despite the urge to lean in and kiss her. 'I'd never be able to rescue a damsel in distress.'

'Oh, I don't know…' Harriet's voice was soft.

The sweet floral scent of her perfume filled his senses with longing, and he wanted to nuzzle into her neck and smell her skin. Her eyes were luminous, the pupils large, and he felt himself falling into her gaze. And when her lips parted and she lifted her chin, he was lost. He had to kiss her.

Without conscious thought, his body acting without any instruction from his brain, he took one small step…

A high-pitched yelp made them both jump, and he looked down to see Etta sitting at his feet, holding up a paw.

Contrite, he dropped into a crouch. 'I'm sorry, little one. Did I tread on your paw? I didn't mean it.' He scooped the dog up and cradled her, checking her paw for any obvious signs of injury, hoping to goodness he hadn't done any permanent damage. He simply wasn't used to having an animal in the van, and he had been rather distracted.

'She's having you on,' Harriet said, reaching for her coat. 'She used to do this all the time when Declan and I…' she trailed off.

Owen looked at the pooch, who seemed to be wearing a pleased expression on her doggy face. 'No, I don't believe it,' he said.

'It's true. She gets so jealous. If you put her down, she'll have forgotten which paw you were supposed to have stepped on and she'll hold up the wrong one.'

Sure enough, when Owen gently put her on the floor, Etta immediately sat and held up her other paw. 'The sneaky madam!'

'It's odd, though, she never does it when the kids and I hug.' She blew out her cheeks. 'Thanks so much for lunch. I enjoyed it. You must come to us next time.'

'I'd like that.'

There was an awkward moment when Owen wondered whether he should try to kiss her again, but the mood had been well and truly broken, so he opened the van door instead and shrank aside to let her pass.

Etta, pleased as Punch with herself, jumped down the step after her mistress.

'Bye, and thanks again,' Harriet called as she strolled off, the dog at her heels, leaving Owen with the washing-up and a burning need to see her again.

Chapter 11

Blimmin' heck, it's autumn half-term next week, Harriet thought, as she hurried home from work on Tuesday. Where had the time gone? It seemed only yesterday that she was tearfully waving Sara off on the school bus for her first day in secondary school. Harriet had wanted to drive Sara the five miles herself, but her daughter had insisted she wanted to travel by bus and had been highly excited at the prospect.

Nowadays, Sara would give her right arm for her mother to take her to school, rather than endure the monotony of the school bus. Plus, in order for her to catch it and because high school started earlier than the primary, Sara had to get up a full hour before Bobby, which she thoroughly resented.

Oh, how the tables have turned, Harriet thought, remembering her daughter's pleas to be driven to school that morning. Sara would, however, have the luxury of a lift home, because today was Year 7 parents' evening, and Harriet had a number of appointments with Sara's teachers to discuss her child's progress.

Hastily, she barrelled into the house, fussed the dog for a few minutes, then scrambled up the stairs to change into something more suitable. As she was struggling to decide on an outfit (she didn't want to look too formal, but neither did she want to look as though she'd not made an effort), Bobby blew in through the front door in a wave of excitement. He was desperate to have a look around the school he would be attending when he was older, and was envious that his sister was already there.

Harriet wished he wasn't so keen to grow up. She was perfectly happy with him staying this age for a while. At the moment he was still her little boy and, having seen the abrupt surge in independence exhibited by her daughter since starting secondary school, Harriet wanted to hold him close for as long as she could.

'Bobby, can you let Etta out for a wee?' Harriet asked, hopping about on one leg as she tried to stuff the other into her skinny jeans and almost falling over.

She dragged them up her thighs and fastened the zip, then hunted in a drawer for a navy jumper to go over the white shirt she was planning on wearing. Teamed with a pair of soft leather boots that she'd had for years, and a suede jacket that was nearly as old as Bobby but luckily still fitted her, she thought she'd do.

'Sorry, my darling,' she said to the dog, who gazed at her with a mournful expression when she realised she was about to be abandoned again. 'We'll go for a walk later,' she promised, although they wouldn't go far because it would be dark by the time she got back. Thankfully, tea would be easy tonight – she had made lamb stew yesterday, in anticipation, so it would only need to be warmed through.

Bobby was bouncing around, urging her to hurry up, so she gave the dachshund a final pat.

'Here,' she said, handing Bobby a Tupperware box containing some snacks, knowing he would be hungry. 'You can eat this on the way, and there's a drink in my bag.'

'Mrs Anton says I'm the bestest speller in the class,' Bobby said, shovelling a handful of nuts into his mouth and chewing vigorously.

'That's fantastic. Well done!'

'She gave me a sticker.'

'I'm so proud of you.' Harriet blew him a kiss.

'I got another sticker for my poem. I'll read it to you when we get home because I can't remember all the words, but it's about Owen.' Bobby suddenly looked anxious. 'Will he be cross that I made up a poem about him?'

'I shouldn't think so. Would you be cross if he wrote a poem about you?'

'If it was nice I wouldn't,' Bobby replied reasonably.

'Fair point. Is yours nice?'

He nodded. 'Can I read it to him?'

'I expect so.'

'When will we see him again? I like him.'

Harriet liked him too. More than she thought was wise, considering he was a nomad and wouldn't be around forever. But then again, Declan hadn't been a nomad and he'd buggered off, so where someone lived and what they lived in seemed to be of little consequence when it came to the longevity of a relationship.

Had Owen been about to kiss her? she wondered for about the hundredth time since Saturday. Etta had seemed to think so. The dog used to be incredibly jealous whenever Declan came anywhere near her, not that he'd done so very often in the last few months they were together – and the dog had displayed the same reaction right at the point when Harriet thought she and Owen might have kissed.

Etta, you are an excellent method of birth control, Harriet thought, then let out a strangled cry.

'Mam?'

'Sorry, got a frog in my throat.' Harried fake-coughed to prove the point.

Dear God, had she just been imagining something more than a kiss?

She had, hadn't she? My, my…

Instead of the idea sending her running for the hills, the thought of spending the afternoon making love with Owen, cocooned in the bed over the van's cab like their own private love-nest, made her go all peculiar.

The disappointment she had felt at Etta's untimely interruption had been acute, and although she'd tried not to show it, she had gone home in a fog of unsatisfied hunger – which hadn't had anything to do with the wonderful meal he'd cooked.

Over the past few days since their non-encounter, she hadn't been able to stop thinking about him, and every thought was coloured by the kiss that never was.

But lack of kiss aside, she had enjoyed his company and had been surprised to discover just how good a cook he was. She had guessed from the butternut squash casserole that he was competent in the kitchen, but those scones had been to die for!

Good-looking, sexy, thoughtful… and a fantastic cook – what was not to like?

Her feelings for Owen ran a little deeper than liking, though, and she had to admit it worried her somewhat. The last man she'd had deep feelings for had been Declan, and that hadn't turned out too well.

Now she was being silly! She fancied Owen and she liked him, but that was as far as it went. She had no intention of falling for him.

'There's Sara!' Bobby yelled, making her jump.

Harriet had driven most of the journey from their house to the school on automatic pilot, and she was shocked to discover she had just driven through the school gates and was currently trundling past the main building, heading towards the car park.

She found a space and pulled into it, feeling a little shaken. It was time she concentrated on the matter at hand, rather than daydreaming. Anything could have happened.

Sara was peering out of one of the downstairs windows and waving madly.

Harriet waved back, as Bobby leapt up and down.

'Is that a classroom?' he demanded as they went inside. 'They've got a proper sports hall and a room where you can cook. And they have Bunsen burners with flames and everything.'

'Someone's happy to be here,' Kelly observed. She was standing in the reception area, looking lost. 'Do you know where we're supposed to go?'

'The main hall, I think.'

'Sara!' Bobby squealed, as his sister appeared.

'Shh!' Sara glanced around nervously.

'It's OK, we won't show you up,' Harriet assured her. 'I promise I won't say anything to embarrass you.'

'Is Catrin around?' Kelly asked.

'She's in the library. I'll fetch her.' Sara lowered her voice. 'She's worried you're going to tell her off because she forgot her PE kit and she's been given detention.'

Kelly smiled. 'Thanks for the heads-up. I'm not going to tell her off – having detention is punishment enough.'

While they waited for their respective daughters, Kelly said, 'A little bird told me that you're on a mission not to buy anything new from now until Christmas. How's it going?'

'Pen?'

Kelly nodded. 'I think it's a marvellous idea. Got any tips?'

'The boot sale on Holly Field is fab. I've got several nice things from there. But I'm not buying stuff just for the sake of buying it,' Harriet added. 'I'm only buying things that I need. Or that the kids need. Clothes, mostly. I can't believe how fast Bobby is growing.'

Kelly was giving her a knowing look.

'Spit it out,' Harriet said.

'Pen also mentioned a certain man who lives in a camper van? She said he was instrumental in this not-buying-new mission.' Kelly smirked. 'She also says you've got the hots for him.'

'Pen says far too much,' Harriet grumbled, blushing furiously.

'What's *the hots*, Mammy?'

'Oops.' Kelly looked contrite. 'It's when you get too close to a fire, Bobby,' she explained.

That was a good analogy, Harriet thought. Owen was the flame and she was the moth. She needed to be careful he didn't burn her to a crisp.

Bobby seemed to accept the explanation and wandered over to a cabinet filled with trophies, running his hand across the glass.

'Sorry, he was so quiet that I forgot he was there,' Kelly said.

'That's OK.'

'What's this guy like then? Pen said he was seriously good-looking.'

'He is, in a nerdy kind of way. He's more Clark Kent than Superman… if you like that sort of thing,' Harriet added.

'You clearly do,' Kelly retorted. 'I'm going to have to take a walk over to Aled's field and check him out.'

'Don't you dare!'

'Ooh, want to keep him all to yourself, do you?' Kelly teased, keeping her voice low.

'Certainly not!'

'Have you seen the inside of his van? What's it like? I can't imagine living in one all year round in our climate, can you?'

'Actually, I can. It's very cosy.'

Kelly raised her eyebrows. 'How cosy is cosy?'

'Get your mind out of the gutter. I had the kids with me.' Harriet wasn't going to tell her the whole story, or that she had been in it by herself without the kids. 'It's incredibly compact, but he's got proper kitchen space, a shower and loo cubicle, and he's even got a mini wood-burning stove.'

'I don't think I could be bothered setting up the bed every night. We had to do that last year when we rented a caravan. It was a pain in the backside.'

'He's got a bed over the cab,' Harriet said, then blushed again as she thought of him in it.

'I think you fancy him more than you're letting on,' Kelly began, but just at that moment Bobby let out a shout as Sara and Catrin appeared, and Harriet was saved from any further grilling.

Kelly had a point, though – Harriet did fancy him. Far more than was good for her.

'You're not closing yet, are you?' Owen asked, pushing through the door to the zero-waste shop and hoping he wasn't too late. His cupboards were looking decidedly empty, as was his fridge, although he would probably have to go to the supermarket to find vegan milk and cheese.

'You've got a few minutes,' one of the women behind the counter said, and Owen recognised her as the vicar's wife. Another woman was standing next to her, poring over a tablet.

Owen smiled his thanks and began to peruse the shelves. Good, they had porridge oats and wholemeal flour, and he scanned the baskets of nuts and seeds, pleased to see they had a good selection.

He took some containers out of his bag and popped them on the counter.

'Shall I weigh them for you?' Betsan asked.

'If you don't mind, that would be great. I love your shop, by the way,' he said, gazing around in satisfaction. There should be more shops like these on Britain's high streets.

'It's not mine, per se,' Betsan said. 'It's a co-operative. It belongs to the village as a whole, in a way.'

Owen had heard of co-operatives but he didn't know a great deal about them. 'Sounds interesting,' he said. 'And worth-while.'

'It is! Although if Cornerstone had built a supermarket on the outskirts of Foxmore like they were planning, our little shop probably wouldn't exist due to the competition.'

'Supermarkets have their place,' he said diplomatically, 'but I'm glad your shop is here. I always buy zero waste when I can.'

The other woman, who had so far not said anything, looked up from the screen. 'You wouldn't like to buy into it, would you? We have some shares available.'

'Rowena! You'll scare him off. At least let him buy stuff first.' Betsan laughed. 'Anyway, this is the bloke I was telling you about – the one who is camping in Aled's field. I doubt he'll be staying in Foxmore long enough to want to buy shares in Sero.'

'Oh, I don't know…' Owen mused. 'I might hang around for a bit.'

Betsan grinned. 'I know someone who'll be pleased to hear that.'

'Who?' Rowena asked.

'I'll tell you later,' Betsan replied, tapping the side of her nose. Then she hissed, 'Pen's been blabbing.'

Suddenly, Owen knew who Betsan was referring to – or he hoped he did – and a warm feeling spread through his chest.

Trying not to give anything away, he carried on adding to his supplies. 'Have you got any veg?'

'Sorry, no. We can't find a local supplier. You'll have to go to the convenience store down the street – although their range isn't particularly good. We're continuing to look, though, so if you're still here in a couple of weeks…' Betsan shrugged.

Owen wandered over to the household section and examined the toothpaste tablets, wondering whether he should get some more, and as he stood there, trying to remember how many he had left, a thought came to him.

He had written several articles on zero-waste shops in the past, so he didn't want to write another on the same topic, but this was a zero-waste shop with a difference. The co-operative angle was new, and one that many readers might find interesting as a way to keep small independent businesses alive. Combined with the backstory of the supermarket chain, it might make for a good article. It would also raise the profile of the shop, if Betsan and Rowena were interested.

'Excuse me,' he said. 'Can you tell me more about the co-operative side of your shop?'

'What do you want to know?' Rowena asked.

'Everything.'

Owen paid for his pint and propped himself up at the bar. The pub had a fair number of customers, and he was slowly coming to realise that The Jolly Fox was never empty.

He had visited the establishment a few times since his initial Sunday lunch, usually in the evenings when he fancied some company, and it had always been busy. But this evening was busier than he had expected. There were some faces he recognised, Aled amongst them, but he had yet to see Harriet on any of his visits and he wondered whether she ever came in here.

With difficulty, he turned his thoughts away from Harriet and onto the article he had sent to an online magazine. It hadn't taken him long to write – he'd emailed it the same day he'd interviewed Rowena. His contact there had been delighted with it, and he'd heard that it was going live tomorrow. Owen was also delighted because he had expected to have to send it to any number of publications before one of them bought it. The resultant fee would keep the wolf from his door for a while longer, and it was also why he was treating himself to a pint by way of celebration.

'It's quiz night,' Dai told him. 'If you don't want to be roped into it, you'd best sit in the snug. I've got a nice fire going.'

'I'm fine here, thanks,' Owen said to the landlord. 'I might grab a table, though.'

'Better hurry, we're about to start.'

No sooner had he sat down, than he was accosted by Pen and two more ladies, and his heart leapt. Maybe he would see Harriet after all.

'Before you ask, Harriet won't be joining us,' Pen said.

'I wasn't going to,' he replied. Which wasn't an outright lie: he might have been hoping she would, but he hadn't had any intention of asking.

'Mind if we sit here?' Pen didn't wait for an answer, and he watched in bemusement as she pulled out a chair and plonked herself down on it. 'This is Dee – she and her husband own the estate agent on the green – and this is Mrs Moxley. She helps out in the charity shop three days a week, and in Sero for one day. I've no idea what she does on the other days.'

'I've been playing bowls with Bernie Williams,' the elderly lady announced. 'I beat him last week. Oh, and I get my hair done on one of the other days.' She patted her lavender-tinted perm. 'On Sundays, I go to Janet's for my dinner. She's my daughter.'

'I see,' he said, faintly.

'Are you any good at pub quizzes?' Mrs Moxley demanded.

'I don't know. I've never tried.'

The three women exchanged looks. 'You have now,' Pen said. 'Right, ladies?'

'It depends if he's any good,' Mrs Moxley retorted. 'We don't want him if he isn't.'

Dee said, 'What's your general knowledge like? Are you any good at sport?'

'Er, fine, I think. But I don't follow sport much, sorry.'

'That's not a problem, because Mrs Moxley does. She's brill at it. How about literature?'

'OK, I guess.'

'History? Art? Music? How about the natural world? Physics?' Mrs Moxley was leaning forward, her hands on the table as she grilled him.

'Let's just see how he gets on,' Pen said. 'If he's useless, we don't have to have him next week.'

'Agreed!' Mrs Moxley cried. 'Now get the drinks in. Dee, it's your turn. I bought the final round last week.' She lowered her voice. 'Do we ask him—' she jerked a thumb at Owen '—if he wants one, only he looks like he's not got two pennies to rub together.'

Owen hastily got to his feet. 'Ladies, let me get these.'

Mrs Moxley puffed out her lined cheeks. 'Go on then, if you can afford it. But don't think this means you'll be part of our team next week. You've got to earn your place.'

Owen laughed. 'Understood.'

'Dee, go with him. You know what everyone wants.'

Dee shot him a pained look. 'Sorry,' she said, when they were out of earshot. 'Mrs Moxley can be a bit too forthright for her own good, and Pen is nearly as bad.'

'Does she have a first name?' he asked, as they waited to be served.

'It's Pen, short for Penny.' Dee pulled a face.

'Mrs Moxley,' he clarified.

Dai butted in, 'I've only ever known her as Mrs Moxley. I think "missus" might *be* her first name. What can I get you, Dee? The usual, is it?' The landlord looked over at Owen's table. 'I did warn you,' he said to Owen.

'I honestly don't mind.' The more time he spent in Foxmore, and in The Jolly Fox in particular, the more enamoured of the village he was becoming. There was such an eclectic mix of characters and quirky personalities that there was never a dull moment. And although he found it disconcerting everyone knowing everyone else's business, it was also comforting.

As Dee helped him carry the drinks back, she whispered in his ear, 'Mrs Moxley's first name is June, but don't let on that I've told you.'

He sat down and had only just taken a sip of his drink when Dai announced that the quiz was starting.

'We call ourselves "Team Macbeth",' Mrs Moxley stated, getting a pen out of her handbag.

'Am I Duncan?' Owen asked.

Mrs Moxley let out a loud cackle. 'There's hope for him yet,' she chortled. 'I had to explain it to Dai.'

'I would never have thought you were in any way witch-like,' Owen said, gallantly.

Mrs Moxley eyed him. 'I can see why Harriet likes him. He's not just a pretty face, is he?'

Owen could feel heat stealing into his cheeks.

'Aw, you've made him blush.' Pen giggled.

'Can we have silence, please!' Dai yelled. 'We'll be here until last orders at this rate.'

Gradually, the bar fell silent and Dai cleared his throat. 'Question one. Which sport uses a ball that weighs between five and six ounces?'

Mutterings travelled through the room as the various teams put their heads together.

'I know this,' Mrs Moxley said in a low voice. 'It's cricket.'

'Are you sure?'

'Definitely. Owen, would you agree?' Mrs Moxley jabbed the pen at him.

'I've no idea,' Owen admitted. 'I told you, I'm no good at sport.'

'We'll stick with cricket, then,' the old lady decided, and she wrote the answer down.

Dai said, 'Question two: who developed a vaccination for smallpox in 1796?'

Owen was fairly certain he knew the answer, but he held back and took a mouthful of Guinness while he waited for one of the others to say something.

'That's Edward Jenner, isn't it?' Pen said, and there were nods all round, and Mrs Moxley wrote that answer down, too.

The answer to question three – the county in which the series *Downton Abbey* was set – passed him by.

'It's Yorkshire,' Mrs Moxley said witheringly. 'Everyone knows that.'

'I don't watch TV much,' Owen said. He did watch the occasional film, though.

'Psst,' Pen said, giving Mrs Moxley a nudge. 'I don't think he's got a telly.'

'You've been in his van?' Dee's eyes widened.

'No, but Harriet has.'

'Ooh, I say!' Mrs Moxley sent him a meaningful look.

'I don't need a TV,' Owen said, keen to divert the conversation. 'If I want to watch something, I watch it on my laptop.'

'Can I have silence!' Dai cried, giving their table a glare. 'Next question. What type of animal is an oryx?'

'Antelope,' Owen said quietly.

'I've never heard of it.' Pen frowned.

'I have. It was on some nature programme or other, but I can't for the life of me remember what the damned thing looked like.' Dee was running a finger around the rim of her glass as she thought.

'Antelope,' he repeated.

'Do you know, or are you guessing?' Mrs Moxley demanded.

Blimey, Owen thought, *this old lady is a right dragon*. 'I know.' To his relief, she wrote his answer down, and Owen found he was enjoying himself immensely. He didn't think he was a particularly competitive person, but he really wanted his team to win.

By half-time, he had given the answer to another couple of questions and felt he'd conducted himself reasonably well so far. A twenty-minute break was long enough to get another round in, and by the time Dai called for silence once more, Owen's teammates had filled him in on some of the other people taking part. It seemed that quiz night was one of the highlights of the week for many, and the results were sometimes hotly contested.

Owen took a sip of his drink, then cracked his knuckles as the questions came thick and fast once more.

It was on question eighteen that Owen realised he was now an acknowledged member of Team Macbeth, when Dai asked, 'How is a permissive footpath represented on a map? Green dashes, a red dotted line or a yellow line?' and none of his teammates had a clue.

Owen said, 'Red dotted line,' and mentally fist-pumped the air when Mrs Moxley accepted his answer without quibbling.

Unfortunately, Team Macbeth didn't win, but they came a perfectly respectable second, let down by none of them knowing the name of Jacob and Leah's eldest son in the Bible. When Dai informed them that the answer was Reuben, Owen was none the wiser.

'I enjoyed that,' Owen said, once all the excitement had died down.

'You can come again next week, if you want,' Mrs Moxley said, her tone offhand.

Pen whispered in his ear, 'That's high praise indeed. She must like you. She's not the only one,' Pen carried on. 'If I'm not mistaken, Harriet's also got a soft spot for you.' She had her head tilted to the side and was peering at him intently, waiting for his reaction.

Owen thought for a moment, knowing that whatever he said would probably be reported back to Harriet, then said, 'I like her too. Very much.'

There, he'd done it, he had laid his cards on the table. All he hoped was that he wouldn't regret it.

Chapter 12

'I met a certain handsome chappie in The Jolly Fox last night,'
Pen said as Harriet filled a little jug with milk and placed it on
a tray.

'Idris Elba? Henry Cavill?' Harriet guessed, laughing.

'I wish! No, this man is much closer to home. Do you want
to guess again or are you going to give up?' Without waiting
for an answer, Pen carried on, 'It was Owen. Did you know
he's rather good at pub quizzes?'

'I didn't.' But then, why would she? She had never even been
to the pub with Owen, let alone joined him in a pub quiz.

'Mrs Moxley took a real shine to him. She told him he could
come again next week if he wanted.'

'Crumbs, she must like him!' Mrs Moxley was well known
for being nosy and cantankerous, although she had a heart of
gold, but nothing was more sacred to her than the pub quiz. She
was very particular about who was on her team, and for years
the three witches hadn't allowed anyone else to join them – not
even when quiz night had changed from Friday to Thursday
and there had been a danger that Dee would have to drop out
because it clashed with her Pilates class. Mrs Moxley had kicked
up such a stink, it had forced Dee to change to another class
so she could carry on with the quiz. Mrs Moxley could be a
stubborn and determined so-and-so when she wanted to be.
Owen was honoured!

'She's not the only one,' Pen said, smirking. 'I think you've
got a soft spot for him too. I told him as much.'

'Pen! You didn't!' Harriet was appalled.

'Do you want to hear what he said about you?'

'I don't know. Do I?' Harriet was still reeling.

'I think you do. Here, take that over to table three,' she said, placing a teapot on the tray alongside the milk.

Harriet did as she was asked and hurried back. 'Well, what did he say?' she demanded.

Pen wiped the coffee machine, paying particular attention to the nozzles, and Harriet waited impatiently for her to answer, knowing that her boss was enjoying every second.

'He said he likes you a lot.' Pen gave Harriet a 'what are you going to do about it?' look.

'He said that?'

'I'm not making it up. Anyway, any fool can tell he's head over heels.'

'He's not!' Harriet argued, but the thought that Pen might be telling the truth sent a shiver of excitement right through her. 'We haven't even kissed yet.'

'Isn't it about time you did? You know, try before you buy? You can tell a lot about a man in his kiss.'

'That's a song, isn't it? Cher?'

'Yeah. She knew a thing or two, did Cher.'

'I don't think she wrote those lyrics herself,' Harriet said, and Pen snorted.

'Stop trying to change the subject. He admitted he likes you a lot. I'd go one further and say that he's smitten, just like you are.'

'As I said, we've not even kissed, so how could either of us be smitten?'

'Mark my words, lady, you'll see that I'm right.'

Pen's words swirled around her head throughout the rest of the day, until Harriet couldn't think about anything else, not even the assorted Halloween things that she had picked up in the charity shop on the way to work that morning. The kids broke up for half-term today, and she was planning on spending the weekend making the costumes for Halloween, which was on

Monday. The kids always loved trick-or-treating, although she wasn't too keen on it herself; but just because she was dreading tramping around the streets, and the accompanying sugar hit afterwards, didn't mean she wouldn't take them.

She was fully anticipating Sara asking if she could go with her friends, but Harriet had already had a conversation with Kelly and neither of them was prepared to let their eleven-year-old girls go wandering around Foxmore in the dark, no matter how safe the village was. And Bobby was far too young to go on his own anyway.

Harriet didn't intend doing all the work when making the costumes. She would make sure Sara and Bobby helped. Both children loved arts and crafts (although she would do most of the sewing) and she couldn't wait to see them in their outfits. She must remember to send a photo to Owen, she thought, because surely this could count towards her pre-loved challenge. In the past, she would probably have bought a cheap outfit from one of the supermarkets, something that would have fallen apart within half an hour of putting it on. Her own efforts might not be much better, but it would be far more fun, and she loved doing things as a family.

She was hurrying home at the end of her shift, her eyes automatically scooting to the left as she passed shop window after shop window, when she glanced ahead and saw a familiar figure about to step into Sero.

'Owen!' she called, waving when he looked around.

The smile that lit up his face sent her pulse soaring. He looked thrilled to bits to see her, which did wonders for her self-esteem. It wasn't doing much for her heart rate, though, and she took a deep breath to steady herself.

'Off home?' he asked.

'Yes, I've just finished at the cafe. Thank God it's Friday, although I won't be quite so happy next week when the kids are off school. I love having them at home, but it can be a bit wearing.'

'If you need me to distract them, just give me a shout,' Owen said.

'I might take you up on that.' Harriet grinned at him. They may only be making small talk, but she felt as though something of far greater significance was taking place.

Owen was grinning back. 'What have you got planned for the weekend?'

'Making Halloween outfits.' She held up her bag of charity-shop goodies. 'All bought from the second-hand shop,' she announced.

'That sounds fun,' he said.

'Why don't you join us?'

'I think I'm a bit old to dress up for Halloween.'

Harriet giggled. The sound was so unlike her usual laugh, it took her aback. Gosh, she was flirting with him, wasn't she? She'd be batting her eyelashes and twirling a strand of hair around her finger next.

She said, 'I don't expect you to dress up, although you can if you want. I'm sure we could find something suitable. I wondered if you wanted to join us tomorrow for some arts-and-crafts fun? I could cook pizza?' She waggled her eyebrows at him.

'How can I resist? Pizza does it for me every single time.' He looked at her earnestly. 'Would you like me to bring my own?'

'I thought you might say that,' she said.

'Why don't I make pizza for everyone?' he suggested.

'This is getting to be a habit,' Harriet said. 'I feel as though you are doing all the cooking.'

'It's only fair, considering I'm the one with the pernickety dietary requirements. In fact, what if I bring all the ingredients for the bases and the kids help to make them? And I'll bring my own vegan cheese, if you sort out Sara and Bobby's toppings. Deal?' He held out a hand.

Harriet took it, and a bolt of desire so strong that it stole her breath shot through her at his touch. She inhaled sharply, and quickly let go of his hand.

She wondered if he'd taken offence at her reaction, because he looked quite shocked, but she thought she must have imagined it when he said, 'That's settled then. I'm looking forward to it.'

So was Harriet. And she wasn't able to get him out of her mind for the rest of the day.

–

His hand still tingling, Owen almost staggered into the zero-waste shop. What the hell had just happened? He occasionally experienced static electricity, but nothing like that. It had given him quite a shock and had sent his pulse racing.

To be honest, he didn't believe it had been static electricity. He might as well admit that what he had felt had been sheer unbridled, unadulterated desire. He knew he was in denial, because he was worried that if a single touch of her hand could do that to him, what would happen when they did kiss? He had a feeling there would be fireworks, and it made his heart race just thinking about it.

'Are you all right?' Rowena was standing at the far end of the shop, rearranging the contents of some shelves.

'I think so,' he replied, gathering his scattered wits and trying to focus on the reason he was there. Ah yes, the article, that was it.

He got out his phone. 'I want to show you something.' He flicked the screen on and turned it around for Rowena to read.

She took it from him, scanning it quickly, then looked up, her eyes gleaming. 'Is this what you wrote?'

'Uh-huh.' He nodded.

'It's brilliant! Thank you so much. When are you going to send it?'

'If you scroll up to the top of the page, you'll see that I already have. It was published today.'

'It's out there *already*? That was quick. I expected it to take weeks.'

'That's the beauty of digital publication,' Owen said. 'It's almost instantaneous. If they like something, it's just a few clicks and it can be on their website in minutes. This site doesn't have a very big readership,' he warned, 'but it's a foot in the door of getting you noticed.'

'Everything helps,' she said. 'Business is pretty brisk, but I wouldn't say no to more people coming into the shop. We're thinking of doing a website and selling online,' she added.

'When you do, let me know and I'll write something up about that, too.'

'I know you said you didn't want any payment, but…?' she trailed off.

'And I still don't. I got paid when I sold the article.'

'Can you send me the link? Betsan will be delighted, and so will the rest of the shareholders.'

'Of course, but please do me a favour and not mention my name.'

Rowena looked confused. 'OK, I won't; not if you don't want me to.'

'You want to know why, don't you? Let's just say I like to be anonymous.'

'In that case, of course I won't.' She was still holding his phone, and she scrolled up to the top of the article. 'Planet B,' she said, reading the byline. 'Is that you?' And when he nodded, she asked, 'Does that stand for anything in particular?'

'It does. There is *no* planet B.'

Rowena thought about it for a moment, then she got it. 'There isn't, is there?' she agreed. 'This is the only planet we have. We've all got to do our bit, and this is mine.' She gestured around the shop. 'Are you sure I can't pay you? I feel awful, you doing this for us for nothing.'

'Please don't. It was my pleasure. While I'm here, can I have a kilo of strong white bread flour? Looks like I'll be making pizza tomorrow.'

'Of course you can, but—'

'If you're going to say that I can have it on the house,' he warned, 'I won't shop here again.'

Rowena pulled a face and shook her head. 'You are one stubborn man,' she said to him.

'I've been called worse,' he laughed. 'The very first day I was in Foxmore some chap called me a tree hugger because I was handing out leaflets.' He smiled at the memory. That was the day he'd met Harriet, the day he had bet her that she couldn't last a week without buying something new, and she had gone one better and issued a counter-bet that she could make it to Christmas. So far, she was winning.

As he strolled down the lane towards his van, he idly mused that neither of them had decided on a forfeit.

He would have to ask her about that. He knew he'd never collect on the bet if she lost, but it was the principle of the thing. Although, in reality, he had already lost because he strongly suspected he'd lost his most precious possession – his heart.

–

'What do you think?' Harriet urged Bobby to stand up. He was wearing a man's overcoat with the buttons done up and his head was poking through them at about chest height. The rest of the overcoat stood to attention above his mop of curls, so it looked like he was carrying his head in some fake hands, which were actually a pair of men's gloves stuffed and pinned to the coat. His real hands and arms were inside the coat itself and couldn't be seen.

Owen squinted. 'Not too keen on that monster's face,' he said. 'It's a bit scary.'

Bobby squealed. 'I'm not scary! You are!'

'I totally agree,' Owen said, leaping to his feet and making growling noises, holding his hands in the air like claws as he pretended to stalk him.

Harriet smiled indulgently. The children were getting on so well with Owen, it made her want to cry. She could see how much they missed having a male role model in their lives, and although her dad did his best, he was their grandad and they had a totally different relationship with him to that which they were experiencing with Owen. Owen was always up for a laugh, always happy to spend time with them, and although her dad did all of those things without complaint, she was aware he wasn't getting any younger, and she guessed that sometimes he found them too lively.

Owen didn't seem to mind how lively they were, Bobby especially. Sara was more reserved around him, but then she had never been much for rough-housing and had never been as full of beans as her brother. Bobby was a tornado, a whirlwind of irrepressible energy, and he'd found his match in Owen, leaving Harriet and her daughter watching amused from the sidelines as Owen chased Bobby around the kitchen, into the garden and back again, Etta hot on their heels and yapping excitedly.

'Boys,' Sara huffed, earning herself a laugh from Harriet.

Sara's costume had been trickier to make. She wanted to be Wednesday from the Addams family, which had involved creating a black dress out of an old tunic, stitching a white collar and cuffs into it from a shirt with bleach stains that Mrs Moxley had been intending to throw out because it couldn't be sold in the charity shop, and cutting the arms out of an ancient stripey T-shirt of Harriet's to use as stockings. The hard part had been making a black wig out of yarn. That had been Owen's job, and Harriet had been impressed with the way he hadn't baulked at the idea but had set to with enthusiasm, stitching the yarn onto an old bobble hat.

Sara had to show him how to plait, and Harriet had a lump in her throat as she watched the two heads bent over the impromptu wig: Sara playing the role of teacher, Owen listening intently and following the child's instructions.

He would make a great dad.

The thought took her by surprise, but now that it was in her head, it was there to stay. As he showed the children (and her) how to make pizza bases and encouraged them to spread the tomato sauce and sprinkle on their own toppings, her feelings for him grew.

The way to a man's heart might be through his stomach, as the old saying went, but the way to a mother's heart was through her children. It didn't hurt that he was also drop-dead gorgeous (and wasn't aware of it), thoughtful, kind and fun to be with.

All in all, he was the perfect man.

Did she love him? Maybe a little, and the more time she spent in his company, the harder she was falling for him, until very soon he would own her heart completely.

After pizza, the children wanted to watch TV. It had been a busy day and Harriet thought they could do with some down-time, so she and Owen left them in the sitting room while the adults retired to the kitchen with a bottle of wine.

'You must be so proud of them,' Owen said, his eyes jerking towards the sitting room door.

'I am. They're good kids.' Her heart swelled with love and pride. They *were* good kids, despite Sara continually pushing the boundaries. That was what kids did, it was part of growing up, and she fully expected Bobby to do the same when he got to Sara's age.

The thought of her children becoming less and less dependent on her filled her with sadness. What would she do when they had grown and flown? Would she be on her own with just Etta for company? As loving and as cuddly as the dog was, Etta wouldn't fill the hole in her heart.

But Owen might.

Then again, Owen mightn't want to. Harriet came with children, and no matter how much he liked her or how good he was with them, it wouldn't be an easy task to step into a ready-made family.

But she was getting ahead of herself. As she had said to Pen, they hadn't even kissed yet, and here she was planning a future in her head with him very much in it.

Let's see what Christmas brings, she said to herself. If Owen was still in Foxmore when the festive season was done and dusted, maybe she would believe that a proper relationship with him was possible. In the meantime, she would enjoy getting to know him better, and prayed that he would eventually snog her, because she didn't know how much longer she could keep a lid on this desperate need to feel his lips on hers.

Chapter 13

Owen wasn't a fan of Bonfire Night and hadn't been for many years, so he usually stayed well clear, but seeing as a firework display had been organised on the very field he was camping in, unless he upped sticks and moved his van, he could hardly avoid it. Not only that, Aled had got him to shift a great quantity of rotten timber into the field and pile it up in the middle. Having never built a bonfire before, Owen hoped he had done it right and that it would burn properly.

But as darkness began to fall, he found he was looking forward to the event, although he suspected his enthusiasm had more to do with seeing Harriet than the prospect of waving a sparkler around.

The display was due to start at seven p.m., with the bonfire being lit at seven thirty, and as people started to arrive, Owen kept a lookout for Harriet and the children.

He soon spotted her, and his heart clenched with anticipation and nerves. She looked incredibly cute, bundled up in a scarf and knitted hat, her cheeks rosy from the chilly air. The temperature had dropped sharply over the past few days and winter was well and truly on its way. Owen was also dressed warmly, in a worn but still serviceable donkey jacket and a beanie on his head, and as he hurried over to her, he wished he had thought to wear his gloves.

'Hi, guys.' Owen addressed his greeting to the whole family, but it was Harriet he was looking at, and as their eyes met, a jolt shot through him.

He held her gaze for several seconds before Bobby distracted her by tugging on her sleeve.

'Can I have a hot dog?'

'You can't be hungry already,' Harriet objected. 'You haven't long had your tea. I swear to God this child has hollow legs.'

The aroma of frying onions wafted through the air, and even Owen's mouth watered, despite him knowing that the hot dog stand would be unlikely to serve anything vegan. Along with the frying onions, he could also smell doughnuts, coffee and hot chocolate.

'You can have a hot dog after the fireworks,' Harriet promised her son, as the four of them strolled across the field towards a cordoned-off area behind which the display would take place.

'I love fireworks, don't you?' Harriet said. 'To me, Bonfire Night is the start of the Christmas season.' The children skipped on ahead, and Harriet smiled indulgently. 'To be honest, I wasn't looking forward to Christmas this year, but I'm starting to get into the spirit of it now. Last year was a bit grim.'

'Oh?' Owen gave her a sideways look.

'Declan,' she sighed. 'It was our first Christmas since he left, and the divorce had only just come through.'

'It can't have been easy.'

'It wasn't.' Her expression was sad for a second, then she brightened. 'This year should be so much better, and some of it is partly due to you.'

'*Me?*' Owen felt a surge of hope. Did that mean Christmas would be better this year because *he* was around?

Harriet whispered, 'Pre-loved,' in his ear. 'Buying presents was such a struggle last year, but I've already bought loads of stuff for a fraction of the cost of buying them new.'

'Oh, that.' Owen's spirits sank.

'What do you do for Christmas?' she asked suddenly.

'I usually spend it with my parents.'

'Pen said you're from Narberth originally. Is that where they live?'

'Yep. Still there. And my brother, his wife and their kids live just around the corner from them. It's a bit chaotic when we're all together for Christmas lunch.'

'Good. I'm glad you've got somewhere to go. I would hate to think of you on your own. I was going to suggest you come to us for Christmas dinner – if you are still in Foxmore.'

'I'll still be here,' he said, catching her eye, and for the second time that evening he was lost in the depths of her gaze. 'I'll visit my parents for the holidays, but I will be back.'

'Promise?'

'I promise.'

Harriet seemed flustered. 'To be honest, I didn't imagine you would stay in Foxmore as long as you have.'

'Someone's got to make sure you don't renege on your challenge.'

'Is that the only reason you've stayed? The challenge ends at Christmas,' she reminded him. 'There's no reason for you to stay after that.'

'Yes, there is. *You.*'

Bonfire Night was forgotten. The crowds, the noise, the cold, all faded into the background. Harriet filled his senses, and the world around him ceased to exist.

A terrific bang overhead, followed by a shower of sparks, brought him abruptly back to earth, and he glanced up at the sky.

'I think the fireworks have started,' he said.

Harriet held his gaze. 'They certainly have,' she said, and he drew in a sharp breath as he realised what she meant. She said, 'Would you like to walk me home later? You could come in for a nightcap.'

He searched her face. 'I'd like that.'

'We'd better find the kids,' she said, and the charged atmosphere dissipated, leaving him wondering what had just happened. Did walking her home simply mean escorting her to her house and having a quick drink as a thank you, or did it mean something more?

God, he hoped so. Once again, they had come so close to kissing, and his pulse was racing so fast that he thought he might have a heart attack. He was breathless with wanting, and when Harriet slipped her glove off and placed a warm hand into his cold one, the contact sent heat surging up his arm and into his chest.

With the fireworks lighting up the night sky, he turned his gaze towards the heavens, thinking they were nothing compared to the fireworks going off in his head. Because Owen realised something quite extraordinary: he was totally and utterly bewitched. And he loved it!

–

Guilt was an emotion Harriet was quite familiar with: she suspected most mothers were. She had felt guilty when Declan had left, as though she had been the one to blame for his leaving. She felt guilty about not being able to grant her children's every wish, even though she knew it would be bad for them if she did. She felt guilty about not making them eat more vegetables, allowing them to stay up later than their bedtime, and a hundred and one other things. Guilt also hit her hard about having to leave Etta on the days she had to work, and she beat herself up about not being able to take the dog for longer walks at this time of year during the week because it was too dark in the evenings. On the other hand, she hated herself for having to drag the children out to go on those walks, because there was no way she was leaving them on their own in the house, even for half an hour.

And now here she was, giving herself something else to feel guilty about – namely, her rampant desire to take Owen to bed.

Was it such a good idea to invite him back to her house this evening? She had practically spelled it out to him that there was more than a nightcap on offer. Her children would be there, for goodness' sake – not that she'd do anything while they were still awake, but that was beside the point.

But, good grief, did the fact that she was a mother mean that she had to behave like a nun for the rest of her life – or until they had moved out, at least? And when would that be? The way house prices were rising, they might still be living with her when they were in their thirties!

Would she be a bad mother if she made love to Owen, knowing that he probably wouldn't be in Foxmore forever? That there was little chance of this being any more than a fleeting romance?

She didn't want to make a habit of sleeping with just any man who took her fancy, but neither did she want to live without love for the foreseeable future. Declan didn't have the same qualms. From what Harriet had heard, he was embracing single life with complete abandon and bedding any woman who was daft enough to be seduced by his smooth patter and dimples. But what was good for the gander wasn't necessarily good for the goose, and if Declan didn't give two hoots about their children, Harriet most certainly did. There was no way she was going to subject them to a series of 'uncles'. Therefore, if she was going to kiss Owen, she had better make sure the kids never found out. Which also meant not telling anyone, especially not Pen, who would be delighted for her but couldn't be trusted to keep the news to herself.

'Is it over?' Bobby asked, after a particularly loud volley of bangs, the sky fading to black as the last firework died.

'It looks like it,' she said, surreptitiously removing her hand from Owen's. 'I think they're going to light the bonfire now. Shall we watch?'

'I want a hot dog,' her son insisted.

'Me too,' Sara chirped. 'And can we have some doughnuts? Pleeeaaase?'

If there had been a firework display last year and her children had asked the same question, Harriet would have had to refuse. Money had been incredibly tight back then because she had been saving so hard to buy them Christmas presents and hadn't had any spare cash for treats like this. But this year, she had already bought some gifts, and although she still had a way to go, she was confident she could get the rest of them without bankrupting herself.

'Go on, then,' she said, although she wouldn't have anything herself because she still had to be careful with money. 'Can I get you anything?' she asked Owen.

'No, thanks. I'll wait here, while you join the queue.'

Hot dogs and doughnuts bought, Harriet was touched when she returned to the spot where she'd left Owen to find him holding a hot chocolate for each of them.

'You didn't have to,' she cried, feeling guilty – she should have thought about a drink.

'I wanted to,' he said.

'Thank you, it's very thoughtful.' She accepted it gratefully, sipping at the hot liquid. It was delicious and she suddenly began to feel Christmassy.

The bonfire had taken hold and was burning merrily by the time the children had finished eating, and the four of them enjoyed the warmth for a while, watching the flames and listening to the crackle and snap as the wood was hungrily consumed. Sparks drifted skywards and Harriet's gaze followed them, mesmerised.

Eventually, though, the children grew bored and it was time to head home.

'I need a wee,' Bobby announced. 'Can I go in your van?'

Harriet closed her eyes and shook her head, before opening them again. 'He's fascinated with your van, the loo especially. Anyone would think he's never seen one before. You can wait until we get home,' she told her son. 'We'll be there in fifteen minutes.'

'I want to go *now*,' Bobby protested, crossing his legs to prove a point.

'I don't mind,' Owen said. 'We'll be walking past the van anyway, so he can easily pop in.'

'Yay!' Bobby cried, earning himself a disgusted look from his sister.

'You're such a freak,' she said, but Sara didn't sound as though she meant it, and Bobby stuck his tongue out at her.

Miraculously, now that permission had been given to use the loo in Owen's van, Bobby no longer appeared to be quite as desperate, and he skipped around the adults, still full of beans, despite it being close to his bedtime.

'Be quick,' she warned, when Owen opened the door and Bobby darted inside.

It wasn't long before he came back out, and Harriet could immediately tell something was wrong.

'It doesn't work, Mammy.'

'What doesn't?'

'The toilet. It won't flush. I didn't do anything, honest! I just had a wee, then pressed the button, but nothing happened. It's not my fault.' He was close to tears.

'I'll go take a look, shall I?' Owen said. 'I'm sure it's nothing to worry about.'

Harriet put her arm around Bobby's shoulders while they waited for Owen to reappear.

'Bet he's broken it,' Sara taunted.

'Haven't!' Bobby protested. 'I didn't break it, Mam.'

'Of course you didn't. Sara, what's got into you lately? You never used to be so mean to your brother.'

Sara hung her head. 'Nothing. He's lame, that's all.'

'I'm not! *You're* lame. Lamey, lamely, lamey,' he chanted.

It was definitely time to go home. Both children were becoming fractious, and she was relieved when Owen eventually appeared in the doorway. He'd been in there longer than she had expected.

'Everything OK?' she asked.

'Fine,' he said, but she could tell he was fibbing and she hoped to goodness that Bobby hadn't broken anything. 'Let's get you two home, shall we?' he said to the children.

'Are you coming with us?' Sara asked Owen as they walked through the gate and onto the lane.

'I'm going to make sure you get home safely,' he said. 'It's dark and cold, and there could still be a ghost or two hanging about.'

'Halloween was ages ago,' Sara retorted, but she glanced around nervously nevertheless.

'It was only Monday,' Owen said.

'It's Saturday now,' Sara pointed out.

'Six days is no time for a ghost. They can wander the earth for ages.' He uttered a ghostly moan, and she giggled.

'You're silly,' she said. 'Ghosts don't sound like that.'

'They don't? What do they sound like?'

'They go wooooowoooowooo,' Sara yodelled, and all the way home she and Bobby competed to make the ghostliest noises possible.

'You're good with them,' Harriet said, as the children trotted ahead.

'You mean, considering I don't have any of my own?'

'You're putting words in my mouth.'

Owen's gaze shot to her mouth, and she felt his eyes linger on her lips, as tangible as a caress.

'Tell me, honestly, did my son break your loo?' she asked, keen to distract herself from her lascivious thoughts.

'No, he didn't.'

'That's a relief, because for a minute there I thought… Wait up, there's something you're not telling me. What has he done?'

'Nothing. It isn't his fault.'

'Ha! So there *is* something wrong!'

'Sneaky,' Owen said, nudging her gently with his elbow. 'OK, I admit, there is an issue with the toilet, but it's nothing to do with Bobby. The pump is kaput. It's been playing up for a while.'

'Does that mean you've not got a working loo?'

'That's exactly what it means.' He sighed.

'Can it be fixed?'

'It can, but I can't do it myself. I'll get straight onto the nearest garage on Monday.'

Harriet fished her keys out of her bag. 'Right kids, it's nearly bedtime, so I want you in your pyjamas with your teeth brushed, and your hands and faces washed, in five minutes. Chop, chop.' She clapped her hands, the noise accompanied by groans from both children.

'Can't we stay up?' Sara asked.

'I think nine o'clock is plenty late enough, although you can both read for a while if you want. But lights out at ten.'

As she waited for the children to go upstairs, Harriet held a hand out for Owen's coat, popping it on a free peg when he slipped out of it. 'They won't settle down for ages,' she said. 'They think I'm mean, making them go to bed at nine on a Saturday, but I do like to keep them in routine.' She knew that if she let them stay up late tonight, they would be tired and grouchy tomorrow, and as they were back in school on Monday, she wanted them as fresh as possible.

Harriet was right, it did take her children a while to settle. She left Owen nursing a glass of wine on the sofa with Etta curled up next to him while she went upstairs to check that teeth had been brushed and hands and faces had been washed, before she tucked them in and gave them a kiss. By that time it was nine thirty, which she thought was a perfectly reasonable time for her children to be in bed.

Sara had other ideas. 'Can we say goodnight to Owen?'

'I don't think so,' Harriet said. She knew it was a delaying tactic, an attempt to go back downstairs and linger for a while.

Bobby, who had been listening, yelled, 'Goodnight, Owen!' at the top of his voice, and Owen called back, 'Goodnight, Bobby; you too, Sara. Sleep tight and don't let the bedbugs bite.'

'Bedbugs? What are they?' Sara wanted to know.

'It's just an old saying,' Harriet told her.

'Yes, but what are they?'

'Tiny little insects that bite people. A bit like mosquitoes or midges.'

'I don't get it,' Sara insisted.

Harriet kissed her on the forehead. 'Remember, lights out at ten. What are you reading?'

'Michael Morpurgo, *Private Peaceful*. We're reading it in school.'

Harriet was impressed that her daughter appeared to be doing homework at this time of night on a Saturday. 'Is it a good story?'

Sara nodded, opening the book and removing her giraffe bookmark. 'It's really good,' she said. 'If it wasn't I wouldn't read it.'

'Not even for school?'

'I would have to read it in school, silly,' she said. 'But I wouldn't read it at home. My teacher says he's written lots of books. Do you think I could have some for Christmas?'

'I'm sure Santa Claus can manage to pop one or two in your stocking,' Harriet said. She got up off the bed and went to the door.

'Darlene says he's not real,' Sara said. 'Is he real, Mam?'

Harriet had known this was coming, but she'd hoped to have another year or so of her eldest child still believing in Father Christmas.

'What do you think?' Harriet asked, not wanting to get into this conversation right now.

'I'm not sure.' Sara was frowning. 'I suppose it depends on whether you believe in magic or not, because Santa Claus would have to be magic to be able to visit every child in the whole wide world, wouldn't he?'

'Do you believe in magic?'

'I think so.'

'Well, then,' Harriet said. 'Night, cariad. Love you.'

'Love you, Mam.'

Harriet pulled the door almost closed, leaving just a sliver open, and went into Bobby's room to repeat the ritual.

But Bobby wasn't reading. Bobby wasn't even in bed. Her son was crouched down on his bedroom floor, Lego spread out around him.

'It's too late to be playing with Lego,' Harriet said. 'Come on, get into bed. I said you could read, not play.'

Bobby gave a huge sigh and reluctantly stood up, and when she saw his face, she realised something was bothering him. 'What is it?' she asked.

'I did break Owen's toilet, Mammy.'

'Owen said everything was fine,' Harriet hedged.

'He was fibbing. It wasn't fine. It didn't flush. When Owen went inside, he didn't flush it. I know because I was listening – it makes a grumbly noise when you press the button. How can he live in the van without a toilet, Mammy?'

Her son had a valid point. How *was* Owen going to manage without a functioning toilet? She supposed it would be fine if he was on a proper camping site where they had a toilet block, but he was in Aled's field, and she didn't like the thought of him having to go outside for a quick pee.

'Can it be mended?' Bobby still looked very concerned.

'I'm sure it can,' Harriet said. 'Owen thinks it might be the water pump, but you didn't break it,' she insisted. 'These things happen. Remember when my car wouldn't work?'

Bobby nodded uncertainly.

'Was that Mammy's fault?' she asked.

Bobby wrinkled his nose. 'I don't think so.'

'It wasn't,' she insisted. 'If you use things a lot, they eventually wear out and need replacing.'

'Like my old rugby ball?'

'Exactly like your old rugby ball.' It didn't matter how many times Harriet had pumped it up, the ball hadn't stayed pumped for very long, the air leaking out of it faster and faster each time, until eventually she'd been forced to buy him another one.

'Stop worrying,' she told him, 'and go to sleep.'

'You said I can read.'

'You can, but only until ten o'clock, then it's lights out, OK?'

'OK. Night, Mammy.'

'Night, Bobby bach. Love you.'

She watched for a moment to make sure that Bobby was indeed snuggling down with his book, then she went back downstairs.

'Let me freshen that for you,' she said, seeing that Owen's glass was almost empty. He handed it to her and she refilled it, pouring herself a glass of white at the same time.

She made sure to sit in the armchair and not join him on the sofa, because she didn't trust herself. She wasn't quite sure why she had invited him back. She badly wanted him to kiss her but there was no way that was going to happen with the children upstairs wide awake, and she knew full well that they probably wouldn't go to sleep until Owen had left. Like her, they weren't used to having a strange man in the house. Since Declan left, the only men who had visited were Harriet's dad and the bloke who'd serviced the boiler. Until Owen.

'How are you going to manage?' she asked abruptly, Bobby's question playing on her mind.

'Manage what?'

'Your loo situation.'

'Oh, that. I'll be fine. I can always pop up to the farm and ask Aled if I can use his, if I need to.'

If he needed to, Harriet huffed to herself. Of course he would need to. 'How long do you think it will take to get it mended?'

'It depends on how soon the garage can fit me in and how long it takes for a pump to be delivered. Assuming they could fit me in on Tuesday, they'd have to order the part, so maybe another day. Thursday?'

'That could be five days without a toilet.' Harriet was horrified.

Owen shrugged. 'It'll be fine,' he said.

'It won't be fine at all. You'll have to stay here.' As soon as the words left her lips, Harriet wanted to take them back. What was she thinking? Where would he *sleep*?

'Thanks for the offer, but I'll manage,' Owen said.

The very fact that he had refused made Harriet all the more determined. 'Nonsense, I insist. As long as you don't mind sleeping on the sofa, you're welcome to stay.'

'It's very kind of you,' Owen said, 'but you don't want a great big hulking man kipping in your living room.'

'Am I right in assuming that if your water pump doesn't work, not only have you not got a toilet, but you've also not got a shower?'

'True. But I can manage, honestly.'

'What with?' Harriet scoffed. 'Don't tell me you're going to use that solar shower contraption. In case you haven't noticed, there isn't a great deal of sun at this time of year to warm it up.'

'It's not as though I don't have any water at all,' Owen said. 'Don't forget there's a standpipe in the field.'

'That water will be freezing,' Harriet pointed out. She had no idea why she was being so insistent. Washing in cold water for a couple of days wasn't going to kill him. And he was right about being able to manage not having a loo. As he said, he could ask Aled or he could go to the pub. It wouldn't be convenient, but it wouldn't be the end of the world.

'I've washed in cold water before,' Owen told her with a smile.

'I still don't like the idea of you not having a loo. Please stay, just for tonight, at least. You can have that bath Bobby was on about.'

Owen didn't answer her for such a long time that she thought he wasn't going to, but when he said quietly, 'I'd like that,' the pleasure that coursed through her took her by surprise.

All she had to do now was stop herself from sneaking down in the middle of the night to accost him while he slept.

Owen had slept in some truly uncomfortable places in his time, but Harriet's sofa wasn't one of them. So why was he finding it so difficult to drop off?

The sofa was a long one, which meant that his feet weren't sticking out over the end, thankfully, and it was lovely and squidgy. Harriet had found him a pillow and a spare duvet, so he was all warm and snuggly, but sleep continued to elude him.

Who was he kidding? He knew exactly why he couldn't get to sleep. It was the thought of Harriet in bed upstairs, just a few vertical feet above his head.

He hadn't taken her up on the offer of a bath; although the thought of immersing himself in hot bubbly water sounded divine, it didn't feel right somehow. He might have a quick shower in the morning, but that would be more functional than pleasurable; he simply couldn't see himself lying full length in the bath with the children and Harriet just outside the door. He wouldn't be able to relax.

He wasn't able to relax now, though, was he? So maybe he should have had a bath. It might have soothed him enough to allow him to drop off. Restlessly, he pushed the duvet back and sat up, reaching for his phone. He didn't want to lie there, staring up at the ceiling, so he might as well do some work.

As a matter of habit, he googled *Planet B*, just to check that everything on the website and the blog looked OK. No matter how careful he was, sometimes things didn't look quite as good on a mobile as they did on a laptop, so he always checked it on a daily basis. Not only that, he wanted to see if there were any comments, because if there were, he liked to respond to them as soon as possible.

He noticed with satisfaction that many of his followers were getting into the spirit of not buying new and there seemed to be a lively discussion around the subject, with many readers offering hints and tips. There were several comments about the designer dress that Harriet had bought her daughter to wear to the party, with most people applauding the purchase, although one person had completely missed the point and wanted to know where they could buy the exact same dress.

Owen responded by saying that people needed to be more fluid in their purchasing decisions and not go out of their way to look for a specific item, brand or colour, but to see what was available and how they could use that instead. Keeping an open mind to possibilities was his message, and he signed off feeling pleased with how the blog was going. It was by far the most popular subject he'd written about that year, and he was chuffed he had thought of it. Although, in the back of his mind, a part of him wondered whether he was taking advantage of Harriet and her situation, and he debated coming clean and telling her about it. But things were going so well between them that he didn't want to jeopardise it, despite knowing he was probably betraying her trust. He should have asked her permission, and although he had considered it at the time, it was too late now.

He told himself no one in Foxmore was ever likely to read it, and Harriet certainly wouldn't. Although she had accepted the challenge and was doing remarkably well, she was by no means as dedicated to reducing, reusing and recycling as he was. She was just someone who was trying to do her bit to the best of her ability. It was only diehards like him who followed his blog, despite concern about the environment having grown steadily over the past few years, and gradually gaining more traction along with more interest from mainstream publications and websites; he had even sold an article or two to *The Times* and *National Geographic*.

Sighing, he put his phone on the floor and settled down, pulling the duvet up around his shoulders, and tried once more to get to sleep, but it was no use. He was too strung up, too conscious of Harriet's relative nearness, and every cell of his body burnt for her. He couldn't stop thinking about her, and he realised too late that staying tonight was a bad move. He should have gone back to the van, where he wouldn't have been surrounded by the very essence of her. He could smell her perfume in the air, hear echoes of her in the creaks of the house settling, feel her in the softness of the pillow under his head. And when he closed his eyes, he could see her face in his mind.

God, how he wanted her. Not just her body, he wanted her heart, too.

He stared unseeing into the darkness, marvelling at how daft he was. He hardly knew her, yet she seemed to have touched him more deeply than any woman had before, and he was definitely falling for her. The question was, how far would he fall and would she be there to catch him? He still wasn't sure how she felt, despite Pen telling him that Harriet had a soft spot for him.

But one thing he did know: he was going to hang around in Foxmore until he found out.

Chapter 14

'Owen, Owen, why are you asleep on our couch?' Bobby was shaking him, and when Owen opened his eyes, he found the boy's face was inches from his own.

He blinked owlishly and turned over to lie on his back, trying to remember where he was and what he was doing there.

'What time is it?' A small furry body jumped onto Owen's lap and attempted to lick his face. 'Get off, Etta,' he groaned, pushing her away. It was dark and he wondered whether it was still the middle of the night. He felt stiff, his right knee was aching, and his brain felt muzzy and slow.

'Half-six. I can tell time really good,' Bobby said. 'I'm hungry. What's for breakfast?'

'I don't know, you'll have to ask your mum.' Good grief, this child had an impressive appetite.

'She's asleep. So is Sara. They won't be up for ages.'

'Why are you up?' Owen asked.

'I like snuggling on the sofa with Etta,' the boy said. 'And I want to watch telly.'

'Are you allowed?'

Bobby nodded emphatically. 'Yes, Mammy says if I'm awake and I want to come downstairs I can, as long as I'm quiet. Would you like to watch cartoons?'

'Er, OK.' Owen hadn't watched cartoons since he was a kid.

'Goodie! Can I have some juice?' Bobby aimed the remote control at the TV and threw himself into a chair.

Owen assumed he was supposed to fetch the child a drink, and he pushed the duvet back and swung his legs to the floor.

'Do you need a wee?' Bobby asked, not taking his eyes off the screen and flicking through the menu with practised ease.

Owen stifled a laugh. 'Not right now.'

'OK. Juice?'

'Coming right up,' Owen said, shuffling into the kitchen. It didn't feel right delving into Harriet's fridge, but he located some apple juice and a glass, and poured Bobby a drink. Then he noticed Etta waiting by the back door and guessed the dog needed to be let out.

What a surreal start to the day, he thought, as he returned to the living room, a grateful dachshund in tow.

'Here you go, sprout.' He handed Bobby his drink and sat back down, his eyes drawn to the lurid colours on the TV screen. If this was a cartoon, it was nothing like the ones he used to watch when he was a kid. He remembered programmes like *SuperTed*, *He-Man and The Masters of the Universe*, which were far more 2D than this.

'Why do you call me sprout?' Bobby asked.

'I dunno. My grandad used to call me sprout when I was little.'

'Do you like *Doc McStuffins*?'

'Who's that?'

'Her.' Bobby pointed to a figure on the TV. 'She's called Doc and she helps make toys better. She's kind.'

'I'm sorry if Bobby woke you,' Harriet said from the doorway, and Owen wondered how long she had been standing there.

His breath caught in his throat. She looked delectable in a pair of pink fluffy pyjamas, with her hair unbrushed and a rosy glow to her cheeks. He wanted to take her to bed and make slow, leisurely love to her for the rest of the day.

'I was awake,' Owen said. 'Kind of.'

'You weren't,' Bobby said. 'You were snoring.'

'I don't snore.'

'He does, Mammy. Not as much as Daddy, but he does snore a bit.'

'That was the dog you heard,' Owen said, flashing Harriet a grin.

'It was not! Mammy, can I have some breakfast? I asked Owen and he said I had to ask you.'

Harriet frowned. 'Why didn't you just go and get it yourself? You know where the cereal lives.'

'I want scrambled eggs and I can't make it myself.'

'OK, buster, scrambled eggs it is. Would you like some?' Harriet asked Owen. 'Oops, sorry, I forgot. I'm not sure I've got anything you can eat,' she said apologetically.

'That's OK, I'm not hungry.' Just then his tummy rumbled loudly enough for her to hear, and she cocked her head and raised her eyebrows.

'See, Mam, he's a liar.'

'It was only a little white lie,' Owen said. 'Have you got any fruit?'

'I've got bananas, apples and grapes,' Harriet said.

'Then you *have* got something I can eat,' he told her.

'I'll have to get some vegan stuff in,' she said, locking her gaze with his, and he nodded slowly. 'I can't have you staying here and not being able to eat anything.'

'Is he staying here because of his toilet, Mammy?' Bobby asked.

'That's right. Have you let Etta out?'

'I did,' Owen said.

'Thanks. I'd better feed my hungry son,' she said, and went into the kitchen.

Owen followed her under the pretence of fetching a banana, but in reality he wanted to look at her some more. He didn't think she realised how incredibly lovely she was. Declan had been a fool to let Harriet go. Owen would never have let her slip through his fingers.

By the time he'd eaten his fruity breakfast and had drunk a cup of black coffee, he felt more himself and was grateful to take Harriet up on her offer of a shower before he left.

'You could have a bath,' Bobby suggested.

'I don't think so, sprout. A hot bath might make me all sleepy and then you'd have to tiptoe around me while I snored on the sofa,' he teased.

It was quite a novelty being in a proper bathroom. He had become so used to cramming his tall frame into a cubicle barely larger than a wardrobe that the oodles of room seemed positively decadent, as did the copious litres of hot water gushing from the power shower. Not wanting to waste water or to outstay his welcome, Owen made his shower brief, wishing he had a change of clothes and a toothbrush.

Harriet must have read his mind, because as he was getting dressed, he heard a knock on the bathroom door and she called, 'There's a new toothbrush in the cupboard under the sink. Is there anything else you need?'

Only you, he thought, and stamped down on it. 'I'm good thanks,' he called. 'I'll be out in a tick.'

True to his word, a few minutes later Owen was downstairs and preparing to thank her for her hospitality. She was still in her pyjamas and was cleaning the kitchen, Etta dancing around her feet.

Owen had an idea. 'Why don't I take Etta for a walk? It's the least I can do.'

'Please don't feel obliged,' she said. 'I'm sure you've got other things to be getting on with.'

'I haven't got anything planned for today and a walk would do me good.'

'Can I come?' Bobby asked.

Owen looked at Harriet, who shrugged and nodded. 'I'm getting a feeling of déjà vu,' she said.

'Except this time I won't be coming back and making butternut squash casserole,' he laughed.

'What *are* you doing for lunch?' Harriet asked.

'Er, I hadn't thought about it.' Owen had enough food in the cupboard and the fridge to last him for a while, so he was pretty sure he could rustle something up.

'Would you like to have lunch with us?' she asked.

Owen would, but… 'I don't want to put you out any more than I already have.'

Harriet snorted, a most unladylike sound. 'You're not putting me out: we are going to The Jolly Fox. It's Pen's birthday and she's invited us for a meal. You're more than welcome to join us.'

'Will she mind me tagging along?'

Harriet grinned. 'Not at all. She'll be delighted.'

Owen had a feeling he knew what she was referring to. Pen struck him as a bit of a matchmaker. 'In that case, I'd love to come. I'll take Etta for a walk, then pop back to the van to get changed and meet you there. Is that all right?'

'Perfect,' she said.

It was, he thought. It really *was* perfect.

–

Pen's eyes are as round and as large as the plate in front of her, Harriet thought, when her boss saw her walk into The Jolly Fox with Owen at her side.

'What's he doing here?' she hissed out of the corner of her mouth when Harriet leant over to give her a kiss on the cheek and present her with her gift. 'You shouldn't have. Thank you. Boot sale?' she quipped.

'No, actually, I bought it ages ago, so it's brand new.'

'I wouldn't mind if it wasn't,' Pen said. 'I think what you're doing is great. I've decided to have a go myself, but there's this gorgeous pair of shoes I've seen and…' She let out a sigh. 'Still, it is a damn good idea. Having to stop and think about whether you really need to buy something or not is sensible. It certainly prevented me from buying a hideous blouse the other day, just because it was reduced to less than half price. I asked myself whether I needed it and of course the answer was no, because I've got tonnes of clothes. Then I asked myself why I was buying it, and the reason was that it seemed like a bargain. But that's false economy, isn't it?' she said to Owen.

'Happy birthday,' he said. 'Yes, it is. Buying something you don't need, don't want and don't particularly like, just because it's a bargain…' He ground to a halt.

'But those shoes,' she drooled. 'I'll open this later, shall I?' she said, referring to Harriet's present. 'I think we should order before Dai runs out of roast beef.'

'I thought I'd give the borlotti and red wine pie topped with kale mash a go,' Harriet mused.

'Please don't do that on my account,' Owen said. 'If you want the beef, have the beef.'

'No, I think I will have the borlotti pie. I've been doing a bit of research on environmental issues, and I've read that a vegan diet is better for the planet.'

'That's true,' he said, and she could tell he was surprised. She could also see he was pleased.

Harriet had no intention of giving up meat completely, but as she'd lain in bed last night, thinking of Owen just a few feet below her – sprawled on the sofa, so near yet so far – she had arrived at the conclusion that if she wanted a relationship with him (she did, she really did), it might be an idea to delve a little further into the way he lived his life.

Of course, that was assuming the relationship would continue past Christmas. Heck, she hadn't even kissed him yet, although they had come close on a couple of occasions. Besides, she had been seriously impressed with how tasty vegan food could be, and if it got the kids to eat more vegetables, she was all for it.

All through lunch she was conscious of Pen's eyes on her and the questions they held, and she knew she was in for a grilling as soon as her boss got her on her own. She was also very aware of Owen's presence. It felt so natural and so comfortable to have him by her side; it seemed as though he had always been there, and she warned herself not to get too accustomed to it. He claimed he would stay in Foxmore, but there were no guarantees that he would. He might go to visit his parents at Christmas and decide he wouldn't come back. It was a risk she would have to take if she wanted him in her life.

'Ready for school tomorrow?' Pen asked Sara and Bobby, as they were eating their dessert.

Neither child looked enthusiastic – Sara even less than Bobby. 'I've got maths,' she said.

'Don't you like maths?' Owen asked.

'She loves maths,' Harriet said, wondering why Sara seemed so down. Her daughter was a bright child, equally good at the humanities and the sciences. The only subject she didn't seem to like was PE, but Harriet suspected that had more to do with the fact that Sara had had swimming the previous term, and hadn't liked getting her hair wet and then having to go to class afterwards.

'I hate it. And I hate school,' Sara announced.

Uh-oh, this was new. 'I thought you liked school?' Harriet said.

'Not any more. It's stupid.'

Pen said, 'You have to go to school to get a proper education so you can do whatever job you want when you leave. What do you want to do when you grow up?'

Sara pulled a face. 'I want to be famous.'

'For doing what? You can't just be famous for the sake of being famous,' Harriet pointed out.

'Darlene says the Kardashians are. I want to be a Kardashian.'

'Do you actually know who the Kardashians are?' Harriet asked her.

'Darlene showed me on her phone. When can I have a phone?'

Oh dear, not this again. 'I told you, you're too young for a phone.'

'I'm nearly twelve. You said I could have a phone when I'm twelve.'

'You'll just have to wait until then, won't you,' Harriet told her. That would be another expense she wasn't looking forward to. Neither was she looking forward to her daughter having access to so much of the internet. But on the other hand, she couldn't prevent Sara from growing up, and she knew that even if Sara didn't have a phone of her own, other children in her class did: children who would be more than happy for her daughter to see things that Harriet would prefer she didn't. Like the Kardashians, for instance. Not exactly good role models, were they?

'I wanted to be a detective,' Owen said.

'A policeman?' Bobby asked, licking ice cream off the back of his spoon.

'No, a detective like Sherlock Holmes.'

'Who's he?'

'He's a fictional character who used logic and clues to solve cases. Or a pilot. I wanted to fly planes.'

'I want to be a dog walker,' Bobby said. 'I like dogs, and I could take Etta with me. She'd have lots of doggy friends.'

'You'd have to walk them in all kinds of weathers, and in the dark,' Harriet warned. She turned to Owen. 'I have dreadful trouble persuading these two to go for a walk after school. They just want to come home and chill. But poor Etta needs a walk.'

'I could take her for you?'

'I like going for a walk with Owen,' Bobby announced. 'He knows stuff. He showed me where snails hide in the winter. They sleep under leaves and rocks, and Owen said they seal up their shells until it gets warm again.' He paused, then added, 'Owen snores.'

Pen's eyes widened and her mouth dropped open.

Before her boss could jump to the wrong conclusion, Harriet said, 'The water pump in Owen's van is broken, so he slept on my sofa last night.'

'I see.' Pen's tone was full of meaning.

'It'll hopefully be fixed tomorrow, or the day after,' Owen said.

'Or maybe not.' Pen shot Harriet a look, and Harriet groaned silently. She was in for it tomorrow at work – the questions and the teasing, not to mention the innuendoes, would be unbearable. However, Pen appeared to be delighted for her, because she was grinning from ear to ear, and Harriet couldn't help grinning back.

Harriet endured the rest of the meal as best she could, and when it was finally time to leave, she was so relieved that she allowed Pen to get the bill. She hustled the kids into their coats, leaving Owen to deal with Pen's insistence that she'd pay for his meal too.

'I never would have agreed to come if I thought Pen would be paying,' Owen grumbled after they'd left.

'Me neither. Don't worry, I'll settle up with her tomorrow.' Harriet had been saving up for this for ages, knowing that Pen didn't have much in the way of family, although she would go to her brother's this evening for a little birthday celebration. 'I only agreed to come on the strict understanding that I'd pay for myself and the children,' Harriet told him.

'Let me give you my share,' Owen said, and Harriet was about to object, when common sense kicked in. She couldn't afford to pay for his meal too, and the way he was looking at her suggested that he wouldn't take no for an answer anyway.

'Does Owen have to go home?' Bobby asked.

'I don't know what he's got planned,' Harriet said. She would love to spend more time with him, but she was conscious that they had been together for nearly twenty-four hours and he might very well have had enough of her and the children.

'What did you have in mind, sprout?' Owen asked. 'Do you want to take the dog for another walk?'

They were strolling along the road encircling the green, and as they came to the high street, they paused. Harriet lived in one direction and Owen's van was in the other, so parting company here was the logical thing to do.

However, Harriet felt anything but logical. 'Do you have to go back to the van? Only…' She hesitated. 'I think you should come back to ours and spend another night with us. I still don't like the idea of you not having a working toilet.'

'I'm sure you've had enough of me for one day,' Owen said, but there was a flash in his eyes that led Harriet to believe he would very much like to spend another night at her house.

'Please, Owen,' Bobby pleaded, and to Harriet's surprise, Sara joined in with the begging.

'We like having you here, don't we, Mam?' Sara said.

'We do.' Harriet's voice was an octave higher than she would have liked, and she wondered if she sounded as desperate for his company as her children.

Owen ruffled Bobby's hair and went to do the same to Sara, who ducked out of reach, giggling. 'You only want me because you don't want to go back out into the dark,' he said.

'True.' Harriet was relieved to hear that she sounded more normal.

'Is dog walking my payment for borrowing your sofa?' he teased. 'How many dog walks equates to one night's kip?'

'Several, I think,' Harriet laughed.

'Tell you what, I'll come back to the house with you, grab Etta and pay a quick visit to my van. This evening I'd like to sleep in pyjamas.'

Harriet felt heat surge into her cheeks as she wondered whether he had slept in the buff last night. He had been fully clothed when she'd got up, and it hadn't occurred to her that he hadn't had any nightclothes. The thought of him lying on her sofa naked, with only a duvet to cover him, made her go weak at the knees.

'Good idea,' she said. 'Sorry, I should have seen if I had anything you could wear.'

'I don't think I would have fitted into your fluffy pyjamas,' he said, twinkling at her and sending her heart rate soaring.

Dear God, this man was going to be the death of her.

–

It had been a battle to get the kids to bed, and at one point Harriet had regretted asking Owen to stay another night. Bobby had wanted to sleep on the sofa with Owen, and Sara was adamant that she didn't want to go to school and had ended up having a bit of a paddy.

Harriet was at the end of her tether by the time both children were safely tucked up in bed, and she slumped onto the sofa with a groan.

'I don't know what's up with Sara lately,' she said. 'She used to love school. I thought she had settled into high school but she keeps telling me she hates it.'

'Do you think it's because she's had a week off?' Owen asked.

Harriet huffed. 'I don't know; she was never like this before. Maybe she's finding the work too difficult, although there wasn't any indication of that when I went to the parents' evening the other week. Her teachers seemed pleased with her progress.'

'It's a big leap from primary to secondary school,' Owen said. 'I used to love primary, but I wasn't too keen when I went up to the big school. There were too many new faces, and the whole routine was different. Maybe secondary school was a novelty at first, and now that it's wearing off, she's not enjoying it as much?' he suggested.

'I hope you're right. What are you watching?' She turned her attention to the TV, not wanting to talk about the children any more. She was far too conscious that there was only a foot or so between her and Owen, and she could smell his woody aftershave. His nearness made her feel quite giddy.

'It's a documentary about Mars.'

'Do you like that kind of thing?'

'I'm interested in anything to do with nature and space, but please watch whatever you want,' he said. 'I don't want to interfere with your routine.'

Too late for that, Harriet thought. 'By this time on a Sunday evening I'm normally so frazzled I fall asleep in the chair, so I don't watch anything anyway,' she said.

'Don't let me stop you. If you want to fall asleep, fall asleep.' He patted his shoulder. 'I don't mind being used as a pillow.'

Harriet sensed a sudden change in the atmosphere. It had become charged, sending tingles through her. His eyes scanned her face, rested on her mouth for a moment, then met hers.

This was it, this was crunch time. She could either laugh it off and shuffle away, or she could move closer and let him kiss her.

Scooting closer, she caught her bottom lip between her teeth and gazed deeply into his eyes. The desire she saw in them made her catch her breath, and she let it out in a soft sigh of longing.

It was all the invitation he needed.

With a muffled groan, he reached for her, wrapping his arms around her waist, drawing her towards him. She could feel the tension in his muscles, the solid cage of his arms enclosing her, and his warm breath on her cheek as his mouth came down on hers.

This was no soft, gentle kiss. This was hard and urgent, and his tongue flicked between her open lips, hungry and demanding. She met his desire with equal passion, her hands roaming up and down his back as he buried his fingers in her hair.

Gently, he pulled her head back, breaking the kiss, and for a second she was bereft, but then she felt his lips on her neck and her collarbone, and when his hand slipped underneath her sweatshirt, Harriet nearly melted with desire.

It was Owen who drew away first, and she almost cried out with frustration.

'Not here,' he said, his voice ragged and hoarse. 'It's too risky.'

She knew it was, but for a fleeting moment she hadn't cared. She had wanted him, more than she had ever wanted any other man in her life. She still did. She was burning for him, desperate for his touch, wanting him to claim her as utterly and as thoroughly as she knew he would.

But he was right. Not here, not now.

Feeling guilty that she had so nearly got carried away, she sat up and straightened her sweatshirt. Her lips were throbbing, her skin smouldered where his mouth had lingered, and she was trembling – so fired up, she was scared she might burst into flame.

'You're beautiful, and I want you so much it hurts,' he said, stroking the side of her face and tucking a strand of hair behind her ear. The longing in his eyes nearly undid her again, but she fought it.

It was one of the most difficult things she had ever done – because she now knew without a shadow of a doubt that she was in love.

Chapter 15

'Do a twirl for me,' Harriet instructed. Sara was standing in the middle of Harriet's bedroom, a big grin on her face. She looked absolutely gorgeous in her party dress.

Sara slowly turned around, twisting her head so she could watch her mother's reaction. 'What do you think? Do I look OK?'

'You look beautiful,' Harriet said, pride swelling her heart so much that she thought it might burst. Although Sara had tried the dress on before, it had just been a quick check to make sure it fitted. Today, though, was Darlene's birthday party and Sara was fully kitted out with navy ballerina pumps on her feet, and holding the bag that went with the dress. Her hair was gathered up on the top of her head with little strands falling softly around her face, and Harriet choked up as she thought how lovely her daughter looked, and how grown-up. Sara had suddenly gone from being a little girl, to almost being a teenager. It was thrilling and terrifying at the same time.

'Yes, but do I look OK?' Sara asked again.

Harriet knew what she meant. 'You'll fit in perfectly. It's not too babyish but it's not too grown-up either, and it's dressy enough to wear to Deri Castle.'

'Do you think I should have my hair down?' Sara was looking in the mirror, the beaming smile replaced by a frown.

'Not to a makeup party. It's best to keep your hair out of your face.'

Sara nodded, the frown disappearing. 'That makes sense.'

Harriet pressed her lips together to hold back a laugh. 'Come on, let's get a move on. You don't want to be late.'

'Are you going to go like that?' Her daughter glared at her.

'Why?' Harriet asked. 'What's wrong with what I'm wearing?' Harriet had on jeans, trainers and a sweatshirt. She thought she looked perfectly respectable.

'Everyone else's mam will be dressed up.'

'That's as maybe, but I've no intention of coming in.'

'Why not?'

Harriet wrinkled her nose. She wanted to tell Sara she couldn't afford it and the prices in that place were astronomical, but it wasn't fair to lay that kind of burden on her daughter's young shoulders. 'I thought I'd sit in the car and read my book, or if it's not too cold I'd take a walk around the grounds.' Being the middle of November, it probably would be too cold, so she would most likely remain in the car.

'You'll look like a weirdo.'

'Thanks.'

'You know what I mean. Everyone else's mam or dad will be inside. You can't just wander around – they'll think you're odd.'

'I don't care what anyone else thinks—' she began, but before Harriet could say any more, Sara leapt in with, '*I* do. Please, Mam.'

'Oh, OK. If you insist.' Darlene's mother was laying on some refreshments, so Harriet would just have to make a single cup of coffee last a couple of hours. She could maybe stretch to buying another if she had to. But only the one. And she usually kept some biscuits in her bag in case the kids got a bit peckish when they were out, so she could always have one of those. 'What do you suggest I wear?'

'Yay! Wear a dress,' Sara instructed.

'I'll have time to change, but I'm not going to be able to do anything with my hair or put any makeup on,' Harriet warned as she got off the bed and opened her wardrobe. She had a few nice dresses, although they were several years old, and she grabbed one at random. 'Will this do?'

Sara nodded. With the embarrassing-mammy crisis over, she quickly lost interest, and turned her attention to what was in her bag. 'I'm taking tissues and deodorant,' she announced. 'Do you think I'll need anything else?'

Harriet didn't think she'd need even those things, but she didn't say so. 'I think you've got it covered,' she said. 'Can you do my zip up, please?' Harriet swept her hair to the side and turned her back so Sara could do her up. 'There, will I do? Wait a sec, I need to put on my shoes.' She wrestled her way into thick woollen tights and stuffed her feet into a pair of ankle boots. 'I'm ready. Don't forget the present and the card.'

'I won't.' Sara rolled her eyes.

'Right, let's go.'

Harriet went downstairs, grabbed her winter coat off the peg in the hall, and picked up the car keys. She wasn't looking forward to this little outing at all. Once upon a time she might have been thrilled to visit Deri Castle, because it would have been a right treat and she would have enthused over it for days. But all she could think about now was how many weekly shops she might be able to do with the amount of money that Darlene's mother was spending on her daughter's birthday party. Harriet didn't know the exact amount, of course, but she had been on the venue's website and she had seen the starting prices for wedding packages, and she had also taken a look at the prices of rooms and the lunchtime menu. It had made her eyes water.

As she slid into the car, her phone pinged, and she smiled when she saw it was a message from Owen.

Hope you have a good time today.

> What are you doing?

> Not sure yet. I miss you.

She missed him, too. Last weekend had been magical, despite not managing to share another one of those magnificent kisses. She had left him on the sofa and had taken herself off to bed, thrumming with passion and brimming with longing, and had lain awake for hours, listening to the house settling around her and wishing she had the courage to go downstairs and make love to him.

But he was right – they couldn't risk it, not with the children in the house – so she had spent a restless and frustrated night alone. And the rest of this week hadn't been any better. To her dismay, the garage had been able to mend the van's broken water pump on the Monday, so there had been no excuse for him to spend another night at her house.

Mind you, she wasn't sure she would have been able to resist him if he had, so maybe his return to the van had been a good thing. Or it might have been, if she could have wrangled some time alone with him – time that could have been spent in his arms.

She would just have to wait, and hope that the waiting would make their eventual lovemaking even more spectacular.

'Mam! Let's go.' Sara was getting impatient.

> Sorry, gotta go. Speak later?

A smiley face and a red heart were Owen's reply, and Harriet's own heart soared in response. That kiss…

'Mam!'

'Sorry.' Harriet started the engine, pushing thoughts of Owen and their kiss out of her mind. Easier said than done, though, because he was the last thing she thought about before she drifted off to sleep at night, and the first thing she thought about when she woke. And most of every day as well! However, this afternoon she would concentrate on Sara and the party, and do her best to keep lustful thoughts at bay.

Deri Castle was situated about fifteen miles away from Foxmore. It wasn't a castle as such, more a country house or manor, but it was certainly very grand. It had extensive grounds and a long sweeping drive bordered by large trees, the majority of which now sported a considerable number of bare branches.

When the building came into view, Sara let out a gasp and bounced up and down in her seat with excitement. Harriet wished she could share her daughter's enthusiasm. She had to admit that the place was incredibly impressive. It had an enormous porch on the front, built out of stone, with four immense stone columns holding it up. The doors on the main entrance were three times the normal size and were standing wide open, giving a glimpse into the hotel's elegant interior. There was even what Harriet could only describe as a bell tower on one side of the building, and she wondered if in the past the former owners might have had their own chapel. It was certainly quite old, possibly built in the eighteenth or nineteenth century, and she could see how it would make an ideal setting for a wedding. But it was far too over the top for a child's birthday party.

The inside was just as imposing, and Harriet guessed that much of the decor might have been original, as were the furnishings.

Sara was hanging back a little, forcing Harriet to slow down as she walked through the large hallway with a grand staircase at the far end. There was a sign next to it that said 'Happy Birthday, Darlene', and the words 'Snowdon Suite' underneath, with an arrow showing the direction.

Harriet bit her lip. God help it if any of those children broke anything, and her stomach clenched at the thought of Sara knocking over a vase. She hoped the hotel had adequate insurance.

Sara's eyes were huge, and for once she was dumbstruck. Harriet could tell she was overwhelmed, because she slipped her hand into her mother's and clutched it tightly. 'You won't leave, will you, Mam?' she asked worriedly.

'I said I wouldn't,' Harriet assured her. 'I'll be wherever the other parents are.'

'I don't think I want this for my birthday,' Sara said, and Harriet didn't like to tell her that even if she had wanted it, she wouldn't have got it.

'Why not?' she asked instead.

Sara's brow creased and she whispered to her mother, 'It's too grown-up.'

'I thought that's what you liked about it,' Harriet said, surprised.

Her daughter shook her head. 'It's for old people.'

Harriet had to agree. She'd had a quick glimpse into one of the rooms and it had indeed been full of people who were rather on the elderly side. There wasn't anyone under sixty in sight.

'So, then, a sleepover at our house it is,' Harriet quipped.

'And the cinema,' Sara added.

'We'll see.' If Sara only wanted a couple of friends, then the cinema was doable. Any more than three and it would start to get expensive. 'Here we are.' Harriet drew to a halt outside a door marked 'Snowdon Suite'.

It was half open and she could see a gaggle of girls inside, flitting around like so many colourful butterflies. She gave Sara a gentle push. 'In you go,' she said.

For a heartbeat Harriet had a feeling that her daughter was going to ask to be taken home, but Sara straightened her shoulders and lifted her chin. With a smile plastered on her face, she walked into the room, and Harriet was left standing in the corridor alone.

She hesitated for a moment, wondering whether she should go in and ask where the other parents were, or go back to the hall and ask at the reception desk. As she dithered, she was aware of someone else approaching and she turned to see Kelly and Catrin walking towards her.

'The party is in there,' she said, nodding towards the door.

Kelly bent down, gave Catrin a kiss on the cheek and handed her a large gift bag. 'Off you go. Have a wonderful time,' she told her daughter. 'I'll be with the other mams and dads, if you need me.' Kelly looked at Harriet. 'Do you know where we're supposed to go?'

'Haven't got a clue,' Harriet said. 'I'd be tempted to sit in my car for the duration, but I promised Sara I'd stick around.'

'You can't sit in your *car*,' Kelly said. 'Have a drink, at least. I fancy gin. It's a shame I'm driving.'

'Me too,' Harriet said, her voice heartfelt. 'I haven't been looking forward to this.'

'Whyever not?'

Harriet didn't feel like telling Kelly the truth – that she was intimidated by the sheer luxury of the place and that the prices scared her. 'I don't know,' she hedged. 'It's a bit over the top for a kiddies' party, don't you think?'

'Ladies, are you with the birthday party?' a well-modulated voice asked, and Harriet looked over her shoulder to see a woman stalking down the corridor, her high heels sinking into the carpet and her hips swaying with every step. She was made-up to the nines and wearing an outfit that wouldn't have looked out of place at Ascot or a royal garden party. All it lacked was a hat.

'We are,' Kelly said. 'Do you know where we are supposed to go?'

'And whose mummy are you?'

'I'm Kelly, Catrin's mam, and this is Harriet, Sara's mam.'

'How wonderful! I'm Amanda, the birthday girl's mum. I think you are the last to arrive, so if you'll excuse me, I'll have to love you and leave you. No doubt I'm wanted inside. There's a room just down here on the right, reserved for any parents who would like to stay. Feel free to help yourselves to some refreshments. I'm sorry, non-alcoholic only. Lovely to meet you, bye.'

And with that she breezed into the room and closed the door firmly behind her.

Harriet stared at Kelly. 'Wow, so that's Darlene's mum?' She kind of hadn't expected anything less. But something niggled at her; for some reason she had the impression she'd met the woman before, but she couldn't think where. She frowned, racking her brains, trying to remember, but gave up. It wasn't important, and no doubt it would come to her eventually. 'Shall we get a drink?' she suggested.

'Why not? And afterwards, do you fancy having a quick gander? I'm dying to have a look around this place.'

Glad that she wasn't on her own, Harriet followed Kelly, feeling a little self-conscious as she walked into a room where over a dozen other parents were seated.

She looked around for somewhere to sit and found two chairs next to each other, with a little table in between. There was no sign of any refreshments, though, so after they sat down, Harriet immediately began to fidget. She could see other mams and dads – and a grandparent or two – with drinks, and she wondered if there was a bar they had to order from, but then she saw a lady in an old-fashioned maid's outfit, complete with a white pinafore, approach.

'What can I get you?' the woman asked. 'We have tea or coffee, or you can have a soft drink. I highly recommend the cordials.'

'Tea for me, please,' Harriet said, and looked at Kelly.

Before Kelly could give her order, the waitress said, 'Would that be English breakfast tea, Darjeeling, Earl Grey, Lapsang Souchong, Rooibos? Or we have a selection of herbal teas.'

'Breakfast tea, please, with milk.'

'Certainly, madam. And for you?'

Kelly asked for coffee, strong and black.

Harriet waited until the waitress was out of earshot, before saying, 'That's some outfit she's got on. I'm glad Pen doesn't expect me to wear anything like that. I think I'd tell her where to get off.'

'It is in-keeping, though. Talk about Downton Abbey! Look at that fireplace – it's huge. I wonder if they ever light it. Have you seen the chandelier?'

Harriet looked up at the ceiling. 'Good grief, it's huge! Do you think it's made of glass?'

'I expect so. I don't think they'd have a plastic chandelier in a place like this.'

Harriet was just about to say that she hoped it was secured firmly, because it must weigh a tonne, when Sara burst into the room.

'Mammy!' she cried. Her face was bright red and tears were streaming down her cheeks.

'Oh my God, what's wrong?' Harriet leapt to her feet, knocking the small table over in her haste to reach her daughter.

Sara threw herself into her mother's arms and sobbed. 'I want to go home.'

'What's happened?' Harriet glanced at Kelly. 'Sorry,' she said, 'I'm going to have to go.' With an apologetic look at the rest of the people in the room, Harriet hurried Sara into the corridor, worry making her feel sick. 'What's wrong?'

The only answer she got was a hiccupping sob.

The door to the room where the birthday party was being held was firmly closed, and Harriet was tempted to barge in and demand to know what was going on, but Sara tugged her hand, dragging her into the hall and outside.

'Get in the car,' Harriet said, and Sara, sobbing so hard that it made Harriet's heart ache to hear it, clambered in. Harriet got into the driver's seat, but before she started the engine, she turned to her daughter. 'I'm not leaving until you tell me what happened.' If someone had hurt her daughter, by God she'd go back in there and—

'It's *your* fault!' Sara cried.

'Excuse me?'

'It's your fault,' she repeated. She had a flinty look in her eye and her chin jutted out. 'I hate you.'

'Why? What have *I* done?'

'My dress.' Sniffing loudly, Sara reached into her bag for a tissue, pulled out the packet, then threw the bag at Harriet. 'How could you?' Sara twisted away, refusing to look at her. 'You ruined my life.'

Harriet froze. *Oh, God.* She suddenly knew where she had seen Darlene's mother before.

'I didn't know,' Harriet said in a small voice. How could she? Because the last person Harriet would have expected to see at a boot sale was Darlene's *mother*.

–

'It was awful, Pen.' Harriet jammed her mobile between her ear and her shoulder as she poured herself a large measure of wine. This was her second of the evening.

'It sounds it. Poor Sara, and poor you. Is there anything I can do to help?'

Harriet took a deep glug of her wine. 'Wind the clock back?'

'How could you know something like that would happen?'

'I keep telling myself that, but it doesn't do any good.' She took another gulp and swallowed hastily. 'I might have known it was too good to be true.'

'Have you been drinking?'

'Yes, I have. What of it?' The last thing Harriet needed was a lecture from Pen. She'd had a bloody awful day as it was, without that.

'Good. I was going to suggest you had a glass or two. It won't change anything, but it might help dull the pain for a bit. I was only asking because you seem a little… out of focus, shall we say?'

'I wish I was,' Harriet retorted with feeling. 'Unfortunately, everything is in very sharp focus indeed.'

'What a cow.'

'I wouldn't go as far as to call Darlene a cow. That's a bit harsh; she is only twelve.'

'I was referring to her mother. What a horrible way to treat a child. She should be ashamed of herself.'

'It wasn't Darlene's mother who said anything about the dress, it was precious little Darlene herself.'

Pen gasped. 'How did she know it was *her* dress? You could have legitimately bought it from the same place her mother bought it. What a cheek to assume that she's the only one to own a dress like that. Does she think she's that much of a queen bee that other people can't afford to buy designer dresses?'

Harriet finished her wine and poured herself another. She didn't normally drink much, never more than a glass or two, and only when she was out or with friends. But on the way back from Deri Castle she had called into the corner shop, her hands shaking and nausea roiling in her stomach, and had come out with two bottles of wine and a big bar of chocolate.

She was already beginning to feel the effects of the alcohol, because things were starting to get fuzzy around the edges. Good. She needed all the fuzziness she could get, in order to drive the image of her poor distraught daughter out of her mind. But she had the feeling that no matter how much she drank, she would never forget.

'Darlene knew it was her dress because of the buttons,' Harriet said. 'It seems the dress originally came with buttons that were covered in the same fabric as the dress itself. One or two of the original ones had come off and couldn't be found, so Darlene's mother had bought pink, heart-shaped buttons and had replaced them all.' Harriet closed her eyes in despair. 'What are the odds?'

'Blimey, you couldn't write this stuff, could you?'

'No, and I wouldn't want to. Sara cried all the way back, and as soon as we got home, she went straight upstairs and shut herself in her room and hasn't come out since. I took some food up to her, but she didn't touch it. Bobby's been trying his best to cheer her up, but she keeps yelling at him to go away and leave her alone. Apparently, I'm the worst mother in the world. She hates me, she never wants to see me again, and she's going to live with her father.' Harriet let out a sob.

'She doesn't mean it,' Pen said soothingly. 'Give her a chance to calm down. I'm sure she'll come round.'

'It doesn't end there.' Harriet groaned, biting her lip to stop herself from bawling. 'Darlene said the card Sara made for her was lame, and she hated the present we got her because she's allergic to milk and she doesn't eat chocolate.'

'It sounds like she's allergic to good manners,' Pen muttered. 'What kid doesn't eat chocolate? What's the matter with her? It's one of life's great joys!'

'She told Sara it's fattening,' Harriet stated, flatly.

'Good grief! She's twelve! A kid that age shouldn't be worrying about her weight, unless she scoffs pounds of the stuff. Everything in moderation, I say.'

Harriet eyed the bottle of wine, which was already two-thirds empty, and topped up her glass. She'd have a hangover from hell tomorrow, but she didn't care.

'I wish I'd never seen the damn dress!' Harriet cried. 'I should have just bought one from a shop. I can't believe I was so stupid.'

'How were you to know?' Pen repeated.

'I should never have agreed to that stupid challenge.'

'But look how much money you've saved.'

'Look how much grief it's caused,' Harriet shot back. 'Bloody Owen,' she muttered, and just as she said that, her phone pinged.

It was from Owen. It was the third message from him that evening and she ignored it, the way she had ignored the others.

'I hope you're not blaming Owen.' Pen sounded cross.

Pen was right. 'It's not his fault,' Harriet agreed. 'He didn't force me to do it. But if I'd never met him this never would have happened.'

Chapter 16

The next morning, Harriet was sitting in her kitchen with her head in her hands and groaning. She had made inroads into the second bottle of wine when Kelly had phoned to ask if Sara was all right, and to tell her that the party had been a bit of a flop. The other girls had felt so awful about the way Darlene had treated Sara that the atmosphere had been subdued and not in the least bit celebratory. Catrin had demanded to go home and so had one or two others. According to Kelly, who had got it from Catrin, Darlene was more feared than liked, and Harriet was worried that Sara might be picked on in school tomorrow.

'Serves you right for drinking so much,' her mother told her, plonking a glass of water down on the table, along with a blister pack of painkillers. 'I've not got any sympathy,' Ginny added, as she rooted around in the fridge and brought out a packet of bacon. 'You need something to settle your tummy.'

'I can't face eating anything,' Harriet said, looking up. The movement made her head hurt worse than ever and she let out another groan. Her mam's actions belied her words, and Harriet knew she was concerned about her.

'You need some food inside you,' Ginny reiterated. 'I bet the children would like a bacon sandwich, too.'

Her mam had phoned earlier in the morning but Harriet hadn't been in any fit state to speak to her. Bobby had, though, and what he had said to his granny had sent her hotfooting it to Harriet's house.

'Thanks, Mam.'

'Do you want to tell me what's going on? Bobby didn't make a great deal of sense. He said something about a dress and Sara threatening to go and live with her dad.' She snorted. 'As if that would ever happen. Has he actually had any contact with his kids recently?'

'No. They've not heard a peep out of him for months.'

'I thought as much. She's just trying to make you feel bad. Bobby also said you had been sick. If I'd realised you were suffering from a hangover, I mightn't have called round.'

Harriet gratefully swallowed the painkillers and washed them down with the water, draining the glass; then she wished she hadn't, as she struggled to keep it down.

Ginny stopped what she was doing and turned to face her. 'It was that posh birthday party yesterday, wasn't it?'

'It was.'

'Didn't Sara enjoy it?' Her mam narrowed her eyes. 'Where is she?'

'In her room.'

'Bobby!' Ginny yelled, making Harriet wince. 'Tell your sister to come down. I want to speak to her.' She gave Harriet a look. 'What's she done?'

'It's what *I've* done, more like. Remember the dress I bought for her to wear to the party? I only went and bought the very same one that used to belong to Darlene.'

'So? Is that any reason for her to have a paddy? I once went to an event that your dad's firm held, only to find I was wearing the same dress as the MD's wife. I'm not sure who was the most embarrassed. These things happen. It's not the end of the world.'

'You don't understand,' Harriet groaned. 'It was Darlene's *actual* dress. Her mam sold it to me at the boot sale.'

'Yeah, thanks, Mam,' Sara said, banging open the kitchen door and crossing her arms sullenly. 'Everyone's laughing at me. I hate you. Hi, Granny.'

'Hello, Sara, bach. Come give your granny a kiss.' Ginny held her arms out and Sara walked into her grandmother's embrace.

204

Ginny held her for a moment, then pulled away and studied her. 'Do you want to tell me about it?'

'No.' Sara hung her head. Harriet noticed that her face was blotchy, and guessed she had been crying again this morning.

'If you don't tell me, how can I help?' Ginny asked, reasonably.

Sara shrugged. 'I want to live with Dad.' She shot Harriet a venomous glance from underneath her brows, then resumed staring at the floor.

'I don't think you want to do that,' Ginny said.

'I do! He wouldn't have bought me a cast-off.'

Harriet drew in a breath. 'Is that what Darlene called it?'

Ginny's eyes widened. 'Is that such a bad thing?'

Sara gave her an incredulous look. 'Duh!'

'Listen up, young lady – Bobby, switch the telly off and come here. He needs to hear this too,' Ginny said.

'Mam…' Harriet warned. She had a horrible feeling she knew what her mother was going to say.

'I know you want to protect them, but sometimes it's better to know the truth,' Ginny told her.

'I'm not adopted, am I?' Sara asked.

'No, silly, you're not adopted,' her granny said. 'Who wants a bacon buttie?'

'Me! Me!' Bobby yelled. 'I had to get my own breakfast.'

Harriet pursed her lips. 'You often get your own breakfast!' she pointed out, saying to her mother, 'He's perfectly capable of pouring some cereal into a bowl and adding milk.'

'I wanted toast.'

'Tough.' Harriet wasn't in the mood for this. She watched her mam put a few more slices of bacon under the grill, and sighed. What a shitty weekend this was turning out to be.

Ginny wiped her hands on a towel. 'Right, I want the pair of you to listen carefully to what I'm about to say.' She gazed at them solemnly. 'Your mother isn't made of money.' It was said with a kind of flourish and Harriet rolled her eyes.

'Is that it?' Sara asked. Bobby simply looked confused.

'OK, let me explain,' their grandmother said. 'Since your dad left, your mam hasn't found it easy to cope, financially.'

'What does that mean?' Sara interrupted.

'Money has been tight,' Ginny said. Harriet opened her mouth, but Ginny held up a hand. 'It's about time they knew the truth. You can't keep it hidden from them forever.'

'Keep what hidden?' Bobby looked as though he was about to cry.

'Your dad gives your mam some money to help pay the bills, buy food, and so on, but it's not enough.'

'But Mam's got a job.' Sara stuck her chin out.

'A part-time job that fits in around your school day. It doesn't pay a lot.' Ginny looked at Harriet for confirmation, but Harriet ignored her. Ginny carried on, 'To make sure you have all the things you need and continue to do all the things you used to do before your dad left, your mam has had to be very careful with money. That means if she can buy clothes and things second-hand, she does.'

Sara was horrified. 'All those clothes you just bought me used to belong to *someone else*?'

'Not all of them,' Harriet said. 'Just some.'

'Yeah, like the dress.' Sara scowled darkly.

'Owen says it's better for the planet if people reuse stuff and don't buy new,' Bobby said.

'Whatever.' Sara clearly didn't give a hoot about the planet.

In an attempt to make the family's financial shortcomings less worrisome, Harriet said, 'That's not the only reason I've been buying pre-loved things—' pre-loved sounded so much better than second-hand or used '—Owen has set me a challenge.'

Ginny sighed and shook her head. 'That man has a lot to answer for,' she muttered.

'Shh, Mam. As I was saying,' Harriet continued. 'A few weeks ago, Owen bet me that I couldn't last until Christmas without buying anything new, so I took him up on it.'

'That's so lame.' Sara's scowl deepened.

'I think it's cool.' Bobby bounced up and down on his chair.

Sara stuck out her tongue at him. 'No one says cool any more. Chump.'

'I'm not a chump.' Bobby wore a hurt expression. 'Tell her I'm not a chump, Mam.'

'Don't call your brother names,' Harriet scolded.

Sara muttered something under her breath which Harriet didn't catch and didn't intend to pursue.

Harriet said, 'Have you seen the adverts for Vinted on the telly?'

Sara narrowed her eyes. 'Yeah… So?'

'Vinted is a pre-loved site. Loads of people use it. There's nothing to be ashamed of. You get to have new stuff without paying new-stuff prices, and it *is* better for the planet. It's really hip to be so environmentally conscious.'

'Hip?' Ginny snorted. 'You should say lit or sick, or even dope – hip is what your gran used to say in the Sixties. What century are you in?'

Harriet stared at her mother. 'Since when have you been so with-it?'

'You've got to keep up with the youngsters—'

'Mam!' Sara cried. 'Can we get back to my dress?'

'Oops,' Ginny said. 'Sorry. Got a bit carried away there. It was unfortunate about your dress, but it says more about that other girl than it does about you. You should hold your head high and not let mean-spirited, over-entitled people stop you from doing what's right.'

'Eh?' Sara wrinkled her nose.

'I might not approve of Owen's way of life but he does have a point,' her granny said. 'We should all be buying second-hand when we can.'

Harriet blinked.

'It's my planet too, you know,' her mother told her. 'Just because I won't be around to see how bad it might get doesn't mean to say I don't care. I want my grandchildren to—'

207

'Why don't you like Owen?' Bobby interjected. 'He's nice. He had a sleepover at our house.'

'*Oh?*' The word was loaded with meaning as Ginny turned a beady eye on Harriet.

'His loo broke,' Harriet explained. 'He slept on the sofa,' she added. 'It was only for two nights.'

'*Two* nights?' Ginny pursed her lips.

'The kids like him.'

'How about you? Do *you* like him?' The question was loaded with meaning.

Harriet did, but she wished she didn't. 'He's OK,' she said.

Ginny gave her the kind of look that meant she didn't believe her, but thankfully she let it go. 'I'd better get off. Your dad wants to go to the garden centre.'

'It's November; surely he's not thinking of buying plants?'

'He wants to stock up on seeds for the spring, so I told him he could treat me to a cuppa and a cake. You should come; a bit of fresh air will do you good.'

'I'll have all the fresh air I can handle when I take Etta out,' she moaned. It was the last thing she wanted to do right now.

Or next to last, she thought sadly, when her phone pinged again with another message from Owen. A message which she ignored, like the last three. At some point she was going to have to speak to him.

–

There must be something wrong, Owen worried, when yet another message went unread. He could tell it had been delivered, but the double-tick had yet to turn blue. And she hadn't answered his calls, either. He debated whether to pop around, but felt it might be bordering on stalking. She would speak to him in her own good time.

Unless something was wrong…

And he was back in another cycle of wondering whether he should go and see her, before talking himself out of it once more.

He hadn't heard from Harriet since yesterday morning, and he wanted to know how the party had gone, as well as wanting to hear her voice for the sake of it. Surprised by how much he missed her, he picked up his phone again. Nope, she'd still not read his messages.

Had he done something to upset her? Was she ghosting him? His heart plummeted.

Nah, she wouldn't do that to him. Would she?

He didn't think she would. He hoped that she would tell him to his face if she didn't want to see him again. She wouldn't leave him hanging.

But what if there was something wrong?

No one would think to let him know – apart from Pen, maybe.

Pen! That was it! He would call into Pen's Pantry, which had just started opening on Sundays in anticipation of the high street being busy in the run-up to Christmas, and ask her if she knew whether Harriet was OK. He'd have a camomile tea to soothe his nerves while he was there.

The cafe was busier than he had expected, and so was the high street and the shops around the green. With only six weeks to Christmas, festive buying was ramping up – which reminded him, he needed to get a move on in that regard, and he wondered whether he should give Harriet and the children something. Would it look odd if he did? Would it look mean if he didn't?

He would ask Pen's advice. It would be a good excuse to talk to her.

He found a free table and shrugged off his coat. The inside of the cafe was warm and steamy, the coffee machine belching out clouds. The chiller was filled with cakes and sandwiches that would normally have tempted him, but right now he was too tense to eat, even though it was nearing midday and he hadn't had any breakfast. He should be hungry, but all he felt was sick.

'Hi, Pen, a camomile tea, please.'

Pen gave him a weak smile and nodded, and he knew instantly that something was most definitely wrong. The cafe owner couldn't look him in the eye.

He followed her to the counter, and she jumped when she realised he was behind her.

'Sit back down, I'll bring it over,' she told him.

'Actually, I wanted to pick your brains. I'm not sure whether I should buy Harriet and the kids a Christmas gift. I think I should, but I don't want her to feel awkward. Maybe if I just got the children a little present? What do you advise?'

'Um, I'm not sure.' Pen turned away, busying herself with some plates. 'Did you want a sandwich to go with your tea? I've not got any hot food today, sorry.'

'Nothing to eat, thanks. Look, Pen, is Harriet all right?'

Pen's expression was pained. 'Er, you'd better ask her yourself.'

'That's the problem. I can't. I've been trying to get hold of her but she's not replying to my messages and she's not answering her phone.'

'Oh dear. She will. Give her some time.'

'Why does she need time?' Owen was genuinely perplexed.

'I shouldn't have said anything.' Pen was looking uneasy, which worried him even more.

'You know how I feel about her,' he said quietly. 'I was hoping she was beginning to feel the same way.'

'She does. I'm sure of it,' Pen said earnestly. 'But...'

'She doesn't want to take it any further.' Disappointment washed over him, swiftly followed by despair. 'It's OK, I can take a hint,' he said. 'My van's fixed so I'll be on my way.'

He was almost at the door, his heart heavy and a lump in his throat, when Pen called, 'Wait a minute.'

She hurried over. 'I shouldn't be saying this, but there was a bit of a problem at the birthday party yesterday. Sara wore the dress Harriet had bought from the boot sale, but – you're not going to believe this – it used to belong to the very girl whose party it was. The girl called Sara out about it. As you can imagine, Sara was terribly upset and Harriet is blaming herself.'

'I see.' Owen saw everything in a flash – the reason why Harriet was blanking him was because she blamed him for putting her daughter in this situation. 'It's my fault,' he said, accepting full responsibility.

He should have realised that in a small place like Foxmore, any item being sold locally might be bought by someone who knew the seller. He should have warned her this might happen, especially since he knew Harriet didn't want Sara to find out where she was buying her 'new' clothes.

When he said as much to Pen, she tutted. 'Although Darlene goes to the same school, she lives some miles away, so I highly doubt if the boot sale in Foxmore is the nearest one to her. And Harriet hadn't met either Darlene or her mother, so she couldn't have known she was buying the blasted dress off her.'

'Does she hate me?'

'No, she does not. She might be beating herself up because she put Sara in such a position, and she might wish she had never taken you up on the challenge, but she doesn't hate you. If you ask me, I think she's in love with you. I'm only telling you this because I think you're in love with her, too. There, I've said my piece. If you tell Harriet what I said, I'll deny every word. Go.' She pushed him towards the door. 'Talk to her. Sort it out. It's not the end of the world: she'll come round. This time next week, you'll be wondering what all the fuss was about.'

Owen left, his mind racing and his heart thumping.

No wonder Harriet was cross with him, but as Pen said, it wasn't the end of the world. If she cared for him as much as he cared for her, they could surely sort this out.

He was just about to knock on Harriet's door when he sensed someone behind him and he whirled around. A woman of around the same age as Harriet was regarding him curiously.

'Are you the infamous Owen?' she asked. 'We've never met but I've seen you around. I'm Kelly, a friend of Harriet's. Our daughters are in the same class. Have you come to give her some moral support?'

'Yes, I'm Owen,' he confirmed. 'I'll, um, go. I can call back later. I don't want to intrude.'

'I'm sure you won't be,' she said, and before he could object, she rang the doorbell and Harriet was suddenly standing in front of him. She didn't look happy.

'What are you doing here?' she demanded. 'Not you, Kelly. *Him.*'

'Harriet!' Kelly cried. 'He's come to give you some moral support.'

'If it wasn't for Owen, I wouldn't need any.'

Owen gave her a sad smile, his heart breaking. 'It's OK, I'll go. Sorry, Harriet. I'd give anything for this not to have happened.'

'You've heard then? I suppose it's all over the village,' Harriet snapped.

'Pen told me. I called into the cafe because I was worried about you. You hadn't read my messages and you didn't answer your phone.'

'She wasn't in any fit state to speak to anyone last night,' Kelly explained. 'You were a bit tipsy, weren't you, lovely? I bet you had a stinker of a headache this morning.' She held up a bag. 'I brought cake. Let us in and I'll put the kettle on.' Kelly pushed past her and trotted into the hall.

Owen hung back. 'I truly am so sorry,' he said. 'How's Sara?'

'Not speaking to me.' She sighed. 'You might as well come in now you're here, but don't expect Sara to be thrilled to see you. As far as she's concerned, I'm public enemy number one and you're number two.'

'She knows about the pre-loved stuff?'

'My mother told her. For someone who doesn't champion your way of life, she stuck up for you. Said the idea is a good one. Then she gave me a good telling-off for not coming clean to the kids in the first place. Bobby is all for not buying anything new ever again, but I'm afraid it'll take a while for Sara to come around to the idea.'

Kelly was already in the kitchen, getting the milk out of the fridge. The kettle was coming to the boil and several cakes sat in an open cardboard box on the table. She popped tea bags into three mugs. 'Catrin wanted to come, but she's got this ballet thing. Her dad's taken her.'

'I doubt Sara would have spoken to her if she had. She has already told me she's not going to school tomorrow. She's too embarrassed to face anyone.'

'She needn't be,' Kelly said. 'Nearly all the girls in her class stuck up for her. The only ones who didn't were those kids that used to go to Darlene's primary school, and Catrin reckons they only took Darlene's side because they're scared of her.'

'That's what worries me,' Harriet said. 'I don't want to keep Sara off school, despite her not wanting to go, but what if she gets picked on? I know she has to learn to stick up for herself, but kids can be very mean.'

Kelly patted her hand. 'That's why I'm here. I've been thinking about the reasons you aren't buying anything new if you can help it – cost aside – and I think they're sound. It gave me an idea. What if we hold a Christmas Fayre, just selling second-hand items? Nothing new whatsoever. I've got an attic full of clothes, toys and household things that I've been meaning to get rid of, and most of it is in jolly good nick. Some things are brand new – yeah, yeah, I know what I just said, but this is different.'

'You mean, we do a boot sale?' Harriet didn't look impressed.

'Yes and no. It'll be a Christmas-theme sale, specifically for pre-owned goods with an emphasis on toys and other items that can be given as gifts. I'm sure there are loads of people who struggle financially at this time of year, plus they'll also be doing their bit for the environment. And that's how we should pitch it. What do you think?'

Owen thought it was a brilliant idea, but he would, wouldn't he? This sort of thing was right up his street. Or right up his blog!

He didn't say anything, though, wanting Harriet to make up her own mind. After the dress debacle, the last thing she needed was him trying to influence her.

'I'm not sure…' she said after a while. 'Where would we hold it? On the green?'

'I was thinking of Holly Field.'

'But there's a boot sale there every Saturday anyway,' Harriet pointed out.

'That's why it's so perfect. It's already geared up for this kind of thing. I was thinking we could have it on a Sunday, a couple of weeks before Christmas, if Aled is willing, and we can make it a real village affair. It will be held *by* the villagers, *for* the villagers. We could have a cake stall – help yourselves by the way.' She pulled out a chair, sat down and picked up a cake.

Harriet followed suit, and Owen, not wanting to feel left out, also took a seat. He didn't bother with a cake, too het up to eat one even if they were vegan, which he highly doubted.

'What do you think?' Harriet asked him.

'You know I'm going to say it's a great idea, don't you?'

'I know, and it is, but I'm not sure it'll work.'

'Why not?' Kelly asked. 'If it's marketed right, people will buy into it.'

'Kelly used to work in marketing, if you hadn't guessed,' Harriet told him wryly.

'I was good at it, too. It's all about perception, which is why I don't think we should piggyback on the boot sale. Don't think *second-hand*, think "saving the planet" and saving money. Everyone likes to believe they're doing their bit and everyone likes to save money.'

'People will still buy the latest Lego set, or Xbox,' Harriet pointed out. 'If that's what their son or daughter wants for Christmas, they'll buy it for them.'

'Agreed,' Owen said. 'But even if they buy only a quarter of their Christmas presents from the Fayre, that's better than nothing.' He could see by her slow nod that she was coming around to the idea. 'If we remove the stigma – not that there is much of one these days, apart from snobs like Darlene – then Sara might not feel so bad. In fact, we might be able to convince her that she's spearheading the cause.'

'I'm not sure she'll go for it,' Harriet said doubtfully.

'We can try,' he insisted.

'I know Catrin would back us up,' Kelly said, licking the last crumbs from her fingers. 'She felt awful for Sara yesterday. OK, folks, I'm going to have to dash off. Gavin's got a rugby match this afternoon, and I need to make him lunch before he goes. Gavin is my fourteen-year-old,' she added for Owen's benefit.

Harriet saw her to the door, leaving Owen in the kitchen wondering whether he should go too. He rose and stood there awkwardly.

'I'm sorry,' he repeated. 'I didn't mean for this to happen.'

'I know you didn't. It's not your fault, it's mine. I knew Sara wouldn't like the idea, yet I still went ahead and bought the damned dress.'

Bobby poked his head into the kitchen. 'Can I come down now? Hi, Owen.' He hung back shyly.

'Hi, sprout.'

'Of course you can.' Harriet said to Owen, 'He's been hiding in his room since Granny left, in case Sara went off on one again.'

'Sara's silly. I don't care if my stuff used to belong to someone else. Even if you bought it from a proper shop, it will have belonged to them first.'

'That's one way of looking at it,' Owen said, ruffling the boy's hair as he moved to the table.

Bobby was eyeing the cakes. 'Can I have one, please?'

'Only if you promise to eat your lunch,' Harriet said.

Bobby tucked in with enthusiasm. 'Shall I tell Sara we have cakes?' he asked, around a mouthful of apple turnover.

'If you like, but I doubt she'll come down for one. She's not very happy with me at the moment.'

'She'll get over it,' Bobby said. He took his cake with him and Owen heard his footsteps thundering up the stairs.

'She will,' he said. 'You're her mum and she loves you.'

'It doesn't feel like it sometimes,' Harriet said sadly. 'I'm losing her. I thought I'd have a few more years before teenage angst set in, but it looks like Sara has started early. I wish she wasn't growing up so fast.'

'I don't want to grow up, Mammy.' Sara hovered by the door.

'Sara, cariad, have a cake. Kelly brought them. Catrin would have come with her, but she's got ballet.'

'I'm not hungry.' Sara looked so miserable that Owen wished he could turn back the clock. If he could relive the day he met Harriet, he never would have leapt into a private conversation. But if he hadn't, he wouldn't be sitting here now, falling in love with her, and that didn't bear thinking about.

Sara sidled closer to her mother and her chin wobbled. He could tell from her red eyes that she had been crying, and he felt so guilty. He was to blame for the fact that this girl was hurting. Him and his ideals!

'It's my fault,' he said to her. 'I'm so, so sorry. If I hadn't bet your mum that she couldn't go a week without buying anything new, you wouldn't be in this position.'

'It's not your fault,' Sara said in a small voice.

'No, it's mine,' Harriet sighed.

Sara looked up from underneath her lashes. 'Maybe a little, but Granny explained. I wish you'd said something, Mam. I would have understood.'

'Would you?' Harriet held her arms open and Sara rushed into them. Harriet gazed at Owen over the top of her daughter's head, her expression inscrutable.

'I would have *tried*,' Sara amended with a sniffle. 'Are we really poor?'

'How can we be poor when we've got each other?' Harriet told her, burying her face in her daughter's hair, her voice muffled.

Owen crept into the hall. This was a private family moment and he was acutely conscious he was intruding.

'Where are you going?' Harriet called after him.

'Er, I thought you might want to be alone,' he said, pausing mid-step.

'You're not leaving me to plan a Christmas Fayre all on my own! Get back here. We've got work to do.'

Owen's spirits lifted. 'You're going ahead with it?' He sidled back into the kitchen.

'*We* are. But I'm going to need help. Sara, how do you feel about helping me, Owen and Kelly hold a Christmas Fayre on Holly Field?' And when she told her daughter all about it, Owen was gratified to see the child's misery ease a little.

'I want you and Bobby to design some flyers. Do you think you can do that?'

Sara nodded.

'Off you go, then. Owen and I have a lot to sort out.'

Harriet waited until Sara had left, before saying, 'I'm glad you're here.'

'I thought you were ghosting me.'

'I was, kind of. I was just so mad – at myself, mostly – that I couldn't face speaking to you.'

'But you can now?'

She beckoned him closer. 'I can.'

He took a step.

'You'll need to come closer than that.'

'Why?' A smile was playing about his lips and his heart was beating faster.

'So I can kiss you,' she said.

'The kids are upstairs,' he pointed out.

'Just a quick one…'

'If you insist.' He closed the gap between them and gathered her into his arms. As he lowered his head to hers, he murmured, 'I thought I'd lost you.'

'Would that have been so bad?' she asked quietly.

'It would have been awful. I think I'm falling in love with you, Harriet.'

He felt her hesitate and hoped he hadn't scared her off. He hadn't meant to tell her, but he hadn't realised just how much she meant to him until he thought he had lost her. He wasn't *falling in love* with her – he had *fallen*. It was the most wonderful feeling in the world.

'I'm falling for you, too,' she replied. 'Now, shut up and kiss me, before someone can't find a pencil!'

Chapter 17

As Harriet and Owen pushed open the door to the hairdresser's, Lowri looked up from the permed curls of the woman whose hair she was combing out and did a double-take. 'Are you two an item now? I've heard rumours.'

What a surprise, Harriet thought in resignation: rumour was the energy source that kept the village going. She didn't mind, though. It was nice that everyone looked out for everyone else, and she was hoping this community spirit would be in evidence today.

'Kind of,' she said, shooting Owen a shy glance.

'We are,' he confirmed, putting an arm around her shoulders.

Harriet glowed. It was a novel experience having him by her side, and she was revelling in it, after having blagged Pen for an extra-long lunch break in order to get some flyers put up around the village. It was also an opportunity to introduce Owen to a few more people, because he was the one who'd be doing the lion's share of the work in organising the Christmas Fayre. As soon as he had left her house yesterday, he had popped up to the farm and asked Aled's permission to hold it on Holly Field, free of charge, and the farmer had reluctantly agreed. Now that they had a date, Harriet had added it to the flyers that Sara and Bobby had designed, and she had called into Powells Estate Agent on the way to work this morning to ask Dee if she would be kind enough to print some off.

Harriet couldn't believe she'd gone from suffering from a despairing hangover yesterday to planning a Christmas Fayre today. They had already achieved so much and it was only

Monday, although she did have a to-do list as long as her arm. She was hoping Kelly would take some things off her, and Owen would be responsible for the bulk of the remainder. After all, if it wasn't for him and his assertion that people shouldn't buy new if they could help it, holding a Christmas Fayre solely for pre-owned goods would never have entered anyone's mind.

'Can you put a flyer up?' Harriet asked. 'It's for a Christmas Fayre.'

Lowri held her hand out and read it. 'What a good idea! The baby is growing so fast, I can't keep her in romper suits. And you need so many of them. I might be able to pick up a few little dresses for her for Christmas, too. I resent spending a fortune on baby clothes when she's only in them for five minutes. Did your two spit up constantly, or is it just me who has a sicky baby?'

'They all spit up,' Harriet laughed. 'I had permanent yellow stains on nearly every top I owned.'

'What did you do?' Lowri asked.

'A lot of washing,' Harriet replied dryly. There had been mounds of the stuff. There still was. Bobby was always covered in mud from playing football or rugby, and Sara had lately made a habit of changing her outfit at least three times a day and putting what she had just taken off in the laundry basket, even though it was still clean. Harriet had started fishing her daughter's clothes out of the basket when she wasn't looking, giving them a blast with Febreze, and sneaking them back into her wardrobe, hoping the child wouldn't notice they hadn't been washed.

Thinking about her daughter led Harriet to wonder whether Sara was OK. Harriet had had a fight on her hands to get her to go to school today, and had been forced to threaten to take her to school in her PJs if she didn't hurry up and put her uniform on. Harriet might be sympathetic to Sara's fears, but the child couldn't stay at home for the rest of her school life. She had to bite the bullet and go back at some point, so she might as well do it today. Little would be gained by keeping her off school for a few days, and it would probably make the situation worse because the delay would give Sara more time to dwell on it.

All Harriet hoped was that the talk she'd had with her yesterday would be enough to enable Sara to hold her head high in school and not feel embarrassed about wearing a pre-loved dress.

'Crumbs, look at the time!' she cried. 'I'd better get back to work before Pen decides she can manage without me and gives me the sack!'

Planting a kiss squarely on Owen's lips, she whispered in his ear, 'Later,' and darted off, giggling at the shocked expression on his face and marvelling at how this man could make her feel like a teenager again.

–

Blimey, what a week, Owen thought, as he wrote the final sentence on the latest blog post. He had wavered about whether to incorporate the Christmas Fayre into his posts about 'Dawn' and her family, but decided to leave it out until after the event. It would make a good finale to the series and would also give his blog a Christmas vibe that had been sadly lacking in previous festive seasons. While the whole world was being showered with adverts for beautiful gifts and perfect Christmas scenes, he had preached restraint and advised people not to get sucked into the blatant consumerism.

He was like Mother Nature's Scrooge, full of bah-humbug and dire warnings, with the ghost of a dead planet hanging around his neck instead of chains. Only resolute environment-alists wanted to read that kind of stuff, so in recent years he had gone quiet on the blog front from the end of November until after the New Year.

This year was different, though. He was determined to impress on his followers, old and new (of which there had been a substantial number lately), that they didn't need to buy loads of stuff to have a brilliant Christmas, and he was looking forward to seeing what gifts Harriet had managed to find for her family. She had mentioned that she was redecorating Sara's room as part of Sara's Christmas present, and he hoped he could find something that the girl would like to have in it. He didn't know what yet, and he probably wouldn't until he saw it. Of course, it would have to be pre-owned, and he vowed to scour the stalls in the next two boot sales, hoping something would catch his eye.

Bobby was much easier to find a present for, and Owen had contacted an old mate of his who ran survival courses for both adults and children. He would have to ask Harriet about it first, and if she was happy, he could offer to accompany Bobby.

Thinking of Harriet's children brought a smile to his lips. They were great kids and he loved spending time with them. Despite having a niece and a nephew, Owen hadn't been around children a great deal, and now that he was seeing Sara and Bobby on a regular basis, he realised what he had been missing. Kids were *fun*. They brought out the child in him: through Sara and Bobby, he was reliving his own childhood.

But the biggest change since he'd come to Foxmore was undoubtedly Harriet. He simply couldn't imagine his life without her in it. She made his soul sing every time he saw her, and even when he wasn't with her, he thought about her constantly. She had crept into his heart almost without him realising, and it made him feel blessed, hopeful, scared and anxious all at the same time.

Owen, he said to himself, *you're an emotional mess*, but he wouldn't want it any other way.

A rat-tat-tat on the outside of the van door made him jump, and he hoped it wasn't Aled asking him to do some job or another for him. It was dark and cold outside, and all Owen wanted was to make himself a meal and settle down with a book.

With a sigh, he lurched to his feet and went to see who it was.

'Hi, what are you doing here?' he asked when he saw Harriet standing on the other side of the door. She had Etta with her and was wearing a mischievous smile.

'My mam and dad had the chance of some tickets to the panto in Dolgellau this evening, so they've taken the kids. They won't be back for ages.' She held up a bag. 'I've brought goodies.'

'You'd better come in.'

He held the door open, despite there not being enough room for her to squeeze past, and he used the enforced proximity as an excuse to kiss her deeply and thoroughly.

'What's in the bag?' he asked, when they eventually came up for air. To his continuing amusement, Etta was holding up her right paw and looking pathetic. The little dog still didn't approve of him kissing her human mum, although she didn't seem to mind if Harriet cuddled one of the children.

'Snacks,' she said. 'I thought we might be hungry later.'

'Later? I'm quite hungry now,' he said, eyeing the bag with interest.

'So am I, but the food can wait.' She caught her lip between her teeth and the desire in her eyes burned so hot, it seared his soul.

'Are you sure?' He didn't want her to jump into bed just because this was the first time they had managed to be alone. He wanted her to be certain she was ready to take this final step, because he knew in his heart that once they had made love, there would be no going back.

'I've never been as sure of anything in my life,' she whispered, her mouth against his. 'Take me to bed or lose me forever.'

'Isn't that a line from a film?'

'Stop talking,' she said, and funnily enough, he did…

—

'I need to go,' Harriet said, easing herself gingerly into a sitting position; the roof of the cab was only inches from her head and she didn't want to risk knocking herself out.

Owen's bed was very comfy and cosy, though, and she was surprised how warm she felt, despite being naked. Mind you, that might be because of the unaccustomed exercise she'd just had.

Harriet smiled. *Two* lots of exercise. She should be tired, but she felt invigorated and languid at the same time. It was a strange feeling, but one she definitely wanted to repeat – soon and often. Goodness knows when they would get the opportunity to be alone again like this, though. Maybe she could ask Kelly to babysit – but then she'd have to tell Kelly where she was going…

Oh, well, she reasoned, would that be such a bad thing? It was already obvious to everyone that she and Owen were an item, so it was only natural they would want to spend time together alone. And that could only be done at his place, or hers when the children were out. It was far too soon in their relationship to invite him to share her bed and stay overnight. Him sleeping on the couch was one thing; him sleeping in her bed, and the children knowing about it, was altogether different, and she wasn't sure she was ready for that level of commitment yet.

'I'll walk you back,' Owen said, swinging his legs over the side of the bed and dropping to the floor with a thud.

The noise woke Etta, who had been curled up on one of the seats on the other side of the van, her back to them in disgust. The dog hadn't been happy at the turn of events.

Harriet had, though. She had been ecstatic.

She still was. The glow from their lovemaking warmed her, inside and out, and she hugged herself in glee.

Owen held out his arms. 'I'll catch you,' he said.

Trusting him, she pushed the duvet back and scooted to the edge of the bed. It seemed a long way down, but she eased herself over the side and slid into his waiting arms.

Pressing hard against him, she wriggled seductively.

'I thought you needed to get back?' he murmured, his lips teasing her ear and making her squirm with pleasure.

'I do.'

'In that case you'd better stop doing that,' he warned.

Reluctantly, she pushed him away to find her clothes, which were scattered across the floor. Etta eyed her warily, as if expecting her mistress to resume her shenanigans.

Harriet would have loved to, but it was already nine o'clock and the children were due back in half an hour. Normally, she wouldn't have let them out on a school night, but the tickets had been gifted to her parents – something to do with friends of theirs not being able to go at the last minute and not wanting them to go to waste – so she didn't feel she could refuse.

But that hadn't been the sole reason. When she had realised that she would have a child-free evening, Harriet had grabbed some snacks and high-tailed it to the field where Owen's van was parked.

She had debated phoning him to let him know she was on the way, but hadn't, rationalising that if he was at home then it was meant to be. And if he wasn't, it was a sign from the heavens that maybe the time wasn't yet right to take their relationship to the next level.

But he *had* been home, and the time had most definitely been right.

Harriet didn't regret it in the slightest.

Owen got dressed and she gazed at him out of the corner of her eye, trying to commit his surprisingly muscly chest, trim waist and narrow hips to memory – not knowing when she would see him in all his glorious nakedness again, but praying it wouldn't be too long.

Her attention was caught by his hands as he tied the laces on his sturdy hiking boots, and she blushed to think how much she'd enjoyed them roaming over her body. Then she began to think about other parts of his anatomy, and her blush intensified.

Who knew making love could be so good? He had been more skilled and attentive than she could ever have imagined, and although she had only just risen from his bed, she couldn't wait to return to it. If they had more time, she would—

Behave! she told herself. She needed to stop the lascivious thoughts and put her sensible head back on, because in twenty minutes she would have to be mother to two tired children.

Finally clothed, Harriet clipped the lead onto Etta's collar. 'I don't want to go,' she said quietly.

'I don't want you to go, either,' he replied. 'I wish I could hold you all night.'

'Just hold me?'

'And more.' He took her in his arms and kissed her deeply.

'Oh,' she breathed, when he finally released her and she saw how much he still wanted her. 'I wish…'

'So do I, but there'll be plenty of other times to make love. Right now, I'd better escort you home.'

With a disappointed sigh, Harriet cast aside her seductress persona. He was right. They had all the time in the world.

Chapter 18

A couple of weeks later, Owen popped into Harriet's house after she had finished work for the day to find her busily drumming up trade for the Christmas Fayre while preparing the evening meal at the same time.

'No, there's no charge for the pitch,' Harriet was saying, her mobile wedged against her ear as she attempted to peel some carrots.

Even the simple act of slicing vegetables fascinates me, Owen thought, unable to take his eyes off her. He couldn't seem to get enough of her and had taken every opportunity he could to be with her since that glorious evening two weeks ago when he had taken her to bed.

'Just make sure everything you sell on your stall is pre-owned,' she was saying. 'We don't want to see a pile of ex-catalogue or warehouse clearance goods. This Fayre is for people who are clearing out their attics, not for professional sellers.' She waggled her eyebrows at Owen and blew him a kiss. Owen blew her one back and tried to ignore his libido, which had perked up at the sight of her luscious, full lips.

When she came off the phone, she said, 'That's another one who wants a pitch. I think not charging them is a definite draw. I still can't believe you managed to get Aled to agree to letting us have his field free of charge.'

'I appealed to his better nature,' Owen said. What had really happened was that he had promised the farmer thirty hours of unpaid work in exchange. Aled had the worse end of the deal, in Owen's opinion. The man was a real tight-fisted git, though.

Everyone else in Foxmore was pitching in with enthusiasm, willing to give up their time to make a success of the Fayre, but Aled had wanted payment.

'I didn't think Aled had a better nature,' Harriet joked, then became serious. 'With this latest caller, we should have more than a hundred stalls, plus the food outlets and the craft displays. There should be something for everyone.'

'I quite like the idea of giving edibles as gifts,' Owen said, nicking a slice of carrot and popping it in his mouth before Harriet could object. 'I don't mean boxes of supermarket chocolates,' he clarified. 'I'm talking about local, home-grown, home-prepared produce. People have got to eat and drink, so a present like that should never go to waste.'

'Is that what I'm getting?' she teased. 'A jar of chutney from the deli stall?'

'Don't knock it. I like chutney.'

'That's your present sorted, then.' She tossed a piece of carrot at him and he caught it in his mouth. 'Show off.'

'Seriously, we don't have to get each other anything. Christmas is supposed to be for kids,' he said, swallowing the carrot.

'Who says?' Harriet was indignant. 'And on that note, can you help me get the tree down from the attic? It's the first of December today and we always put it up on the first; it's a tradition. I won't decorate it until after tea, but we can get everything down ready.'

'Point me in the right direction,' he said.

'Um, the attic is upstairs?' she teased, and he rolled his eyes, exaggerating the gesture.

'You think you're so funny,' he drawled.

'That's because I am.' She simpered at him, and he worked hard to restrain himself. He wanted nothing more than to take her upstairs and have his wicked way with her, but the children would be home from school any minute.

Owen loved their banter and flirting. She was so easy to be with. 'You're not as funny as you think you are,' he argued, with pretend haughtiness. 'However, you are adorable.'

'I am?' She dropped the last slice of carrot into the saucepan and swilled her hands under the tap. 'What else am I?'

'Are you fishing for compliments?'

'What if I am?'

'OK, then… you're thoughtful, and loving, and cute…' He opened his arms and she stepped into his embrace. 'You're also incredibly beautiful and very sexy.' He punctuated each word with a kiss.

'Ew! Owen and Mammy are kissing!' Bobby charged into the kitchen at warp factor nine and skidded to a halt.

Laughing, Harriet pushed Owen away. Owen didn't mind. At least Harriet was no longer hiding her affection for him from the children, although he had yet to stay the night.

All in good time, he told himself. There was no rush. He was perfectly happy with the rate at which their relationship was developing. They were building it on mutual respect and friendship, as well as stolen passionate encounters and lots of snuggles in front of the telly.

'Did you win?' Harriet asked as Bobby flung his school bag on the floor. 'He had a match this afternoon,' she explained. 'They've been playing on the floodlit pitch at Sara's school. Talking about Sara – where is your sister? I thought you were supposed to be catching the same bus home?'

'We won 7–3 and I scored a goal,' Bobby announced, opening the fridge and peering into it hopefully. 'Can I have a piece of cheese and a cracker? I'm—'

'Starving!' Owen and Harriet chorused, exchanging smiles, and Owen could feel a lump in his throat. He was beginning to feel part of this little family, and it gave him a warm glow deep in his heart. Not since he had been a child had he felt such a sense of belonging, and he revelled in it.

'Sara?' Harriet reminded her son.

'She was behind me.' Bobby looked over his shoulder, as though he expected to see Sara standing there. 'She must have gone upstairs. She was crying on the bus.'

'What?' Harriet's heart sank. 'Why didn't you tell me straight away?'

Bobby had a hand to his mouth and he looked worried. 'She said I wasn't to say anything.'

'I'll be back in a minute,' Harriet said, and hurried out of the kitchen.

'Why was she crying, sprout?' Owen asked, cutting the boy a slice of cheese and fetching the crackers out of the cupboard.

'Some girls were laughing at her.'

'What girls?'

'Dunno.' Bobby shrugged.

Owen put the cheese and crackers on a plate and handed it to him. 'Would you like a drink to wash that down?'

'Yes, please. Apple juice.'

'Well done on scoring a goal,' Owen said.

'Thanks.'

'Your mum is pleased too, but she's worried about Sara at the moment.'

'I know.' Bobby took a bite of his snack. 'Are you going to be our new dad?'

Owen blinked. 'I hadn't thought about it.' It was far too soon to be having that kind of conversation. Romance was one thing: weddings and stepfatherhood were quite another. Harriet mightn't want to get married again, for a start.

'I'd like you to be my dad. My real dad doesn't care about us,' Bobby said over his shoulder, wandering out of the kitchen with a plate in one hand and a glass in the other, leaving Owen with a mind full of reeling thoughts and a heart full of swirling emotions.

Wondering if the little boy had said anything similar to his mum, Owen barely had a chance to compose himself before Harriet appeared. Her expression was sombre.

'Is Sara OK?' he asked.

'I'm not sure. She was doing her homework when I poked my head around the door and she wouldn't speak to me. I think she had been crying, though, because her face was blotchy.'

'Do you think she might open up if we put the decorations up? If you don't mind me helping, that is? I can always go, if you want.'

'Stay, please. You've got to help me eat the stew.'

Owen found he was spending more time at Harriet's house lately than he was in his van, and so far this week he had eaten three out of four evening meals at hers. Harriet joked that it was payment for him walking Etta every afternoon, saving her from having to drag the children out after school when it was cold and starting to get dark, but he knew it was deeper than that. She seemed to enjoy having him there at mealtimes, and she especially enjoyed the frantic kisses they shared in the brief window between her arriving home from work and the children coming home from school, like today.

Tingling at the memory, he said, 'I'm glad you want me to stay,' and the look she gave him sent every one of his senses into orbit.

'On Saturday the kids are going to my parents' for a few hours. Dad will pick them up at eleven, so I'll have the house to myself.' She leant in close and whispered, 'Can you be here at twelve?'

His heart pounding and his mouth dry, he said, 'I most certainly can. Now, shall I fetch the Christmas decorations down and try to cheer your daughter up, before I do something I regret?'

–

The house looks lovely, Harriet thought, even if she did say so herself. After they'd eaten the stew, which had been delicious, she had made an occasion out of decorating the tree and putting the trimmings up. With Christmas songs playing in the background and a scented candle filling the air with the smell of cinnamon and berries, she had made mulled wine for the grown-ups, which added to the wonderfully festive aroma in the house, and the children were also given their own special drink.

'Who wants pink fizz?' she cried.

'Me! Me!' Bobby leapt up and down, waving his arm in the air. Harriet could imagine him doing the very same thing at school, and she smiled.

'Would you like some, Sara?' she asked.

'Yes, please. Can I have ice in mine?'

'Coming right up.' Harriet winked at Owen.

'What's in it?' he asked her quietly, after she had poured the children their drinks.

'Fizzy apple juice with a shot of cranberry,' she whispered. 'They have it every year when we decorate the tree. They think they're so grown-up because they're drinking it out of a proper wine glass – Bobby especially.' It made her heart melt to see their little faces as they sipped their drinks. 'Right!' She clapped her hands. 'Where do we start?'

'With the base of the tree, Mam,' Sara giggled. 'She always pretends she doesn't know how it goes together, but she does, really.'

Sara had been quieter than usual during tea, but Harriet was pleased to see her perk up now that the tree was about to be decorated. Some of the tension had leaked from her thin shoulders and she smiled more frequently. Harriet's own smile was less false cheeriness and more natural, and she was starting to enjoy herself. From the grin on Owen's face, she thought he might be enjoying himself, too.

As Owen held the base of the tree steady, Harriet slid each portion into place until it stood upright. It wasn't a small tree, almost reaching the ceiling, and it always looked magnificent when it was decorated.

'I expect you're going to say I should have a real tree,' she commented, as Owen sifted through one of the boxes, picking out baubles, examining them and putting them back again.

'On the contrary. It's good that you reuse it year after year. I'd much prefer you do that than cut down a real tree. There is another option, which is to plant one in a pot outside and bring it in for ten days or so each year, but they don't tend to like being indoors much, and sometimes they die.'

'I take it you don't have a tree?'

'Instead of a tree I have a red–deer antler.' He glanced at the children and lowered his voice so they couldn't hear. 'I tell my nephew and niece that it's Rudolph's spare and he's asked me to look after it.'

'Aw, that's sweet. Where did you get it?'

'Scotland. I was on the moors one day a few years back and I found it. It looks great with a couple of acorns and some mistletoe hanging from it. That reminds me, I must pick some mistletoe – I think it's going to come in handy.' He smirked at her and she giggled when he plonked a kiss on her lips.

'Mam and Owen are kissing again,' Bobby told his sister, and the look of disgust on her daughter's face had Harriet in stitches.

She'd had a conversation with both children concerning her burgeoning romance with Owen, not seeking their permission as such, but rather checking that they didn't object. She knew they liked Owen, but liking a man was a different ball game to him dating their mother. Although Declan's contact with them was sporadic, she was conscious that he was still their father, and the last thing she wanted was to upset them, or make them think he was being replaced.

It had made her feel both sad and glad that, apart from both kids expressing childish disgust at the thought of her and Owen kissing, they didn't mind at all. Sara, with a surprising degree of maturity, had observed that Harriet seemed to be happier since she'd met Owen and she wanted her mam to be happy.

It had brought tears to Harriet's eyes, and she'd hugged Sara so hard that her daughter had begged her to stop. Those poor

233

kids – how could Declan not want to be part of their lives? He had no idea what he was missing and it broke her heart that he had discarded them so easily. Thankfully, her children seemed to be coping and coming to terms with it, and she thought that, for Bobby at least, Owen had a big part to play in that.

Her stomach fluttered as she gazed at the man in question, who was hanging baubles on the branches the kids couldn't reach. Sara was bossing him about mercilessly and Bobby was hopping with excitement, and she swallowed as her heart filled with love.

When the tree was finally dressed in all its festive glory and the rest of the trimmings had been put up, including the elf on the shelf, Harriet made smooth, velvety hot chocolate for everyone. She then turned all the lights off, except for the ones on the tree, and the four of them sang along to the haunting words of 'Silent Night'.

And, as she gazed at the glowing faces of her children and her eyes came to rest on an equally glowing Owen, Harriet realised Sara was right: she did feel happier than she had been for a very long time.

–

As far as Team Macbeth was concerned, Owen was now a firmly established member, so he reluctantly said goodnight to Harriet a short while later and made his way to The Jolly Fox. He would have much preferred to stay and cuddle with her on the sofa, but he had promised to be there for tonight's quiz, so be there he would.

The fact that he and Harriet would have a significant chunk of Saturday all to themselves helped to soften the blow of leaving her earlier than he would have liked, so he had a skip in his step as he sauntered into the hop-fragranced warmth of the bar and scanned the tables for his teammates.

He spotted them immediately, hogging the coveted spot to the left of the fireplace. It was the snuggest place to be on a crisp and chilly December evening, and Mrs Moxley eagerly waved him over.

'It's looking very festive, isn't it?' he noted. A pint of his usual tipple sat on the table as he took his seat and he thanked Dee for getting a drink in for him. Gratefully, he lifted the glass to his lips for a long, satisfying swallow.

'Have you trimmed up yet?' Dee asked. 'Or don't you believe in Christmas?'

'Of course I believe in Christmas,' he said, wiping his mouth and hoping he didn't have a foam moustache, or else he'd start to look like Santa. He certainly felt an affinity to the jolly, red-coated man after immersing himself in the decorating frenzy that had taken place in the Parry household. He had been fascinated by all the homemade baubles that had been produced with considerable pride and a great deal of flourish. She'd told him that each year the children made another clutch of decorations to go on the tree, and some of them had been remarkably good, which had led him to believe that Harriet might have given Sara and Bobby a helping hand.

'And in answer to your question,' he continued, 'I haven't put my own trimmings up yet, but I have been helping Harriet put hers up, so I'm all trimmed-out for the time being.'

Pen beamed at him. 'It makes me so glad to see the two of you getting on so well. I could tell from the minute Harriet set eyes on you that she was infatuated, and if I'm not mistaken, you are too.'

'I might be,' he acknowledged coyly.

'She deserves to have some happiness,' Pen carried on.

'She certainly does!' His reply was heartfelt.

Pen studied him, her expression stern. 'I know it's none of my business, but Harriet is very dear to me so I'm going to ask you something. What happens after Christmas? I'm not naïve enough to think you're only staying in Foxmore to make sure Harriet keeps her promise of not buying anything new until then, but will you move on in the New Year or is she enough to keep you here?'

Gosh, that was a personal question. Not even Harriet had been as blunt. 'I'll be spending Christmas with my family in West Wales,' he said. 'But I'm definitely coming back to Foxmore in the New Year.'

'Glad to hear it. I would hate to think Harriet was just a piece of skirt to you,' Mrs Moxley said, in her usual forthright manner.

'I care for Harriet a great deal,' he said.

'Ah, but do you love her? There's a difference.'

Owen debated whether to reply. He hadn't told Harriet he loved her yet, so surely she should be the first to know.

Oh, what the heck! He was planning on telling her how he felt before he left for Narberth, so it wouldn't hurt if these three ladies knew in advance, because they would know soon enough anyway.

'I love her,' he admitted. 'But I'd appreciate it if you kept it to yourselves. I want to tell her myself and I don't want her to hear it second-hand.'

'I thought you were all for second-hand!' Mrs Moxley quipped, inclining her head to the other two ladies to accept their cries of 'nice one!' and 'you tell him!'.

'Does that mean you're going to settle down?' Dee asked when the laughter abated.

'I'm thinking about it.'

'Because of Harriet?'

'Mostly, but also because I feel at home in Foxmore.'

'Will you buy a house?'

'I'm not sure I'd want to do that. I love my van. I've lived in it, or one similar, for twenty years, give or take.'

'You need to put down proper roots, my boy,' Mrs Moxley told him. 'Ones that go deep into the earth. It's too easy to up sticks and leave when all you've got is a set of wheels.'

Owen didn't have any intention of upping sticks and leaving, but the old lady did have a point. If he continued to live in a van, would it constantly be in the back of Harriet's mind that he could leave at any time? The last thing he wanted was for her to feel insecure.

But he didn't have any other option. Unless… he sold his van.

Camper vans like the one he owned were worth a fair bit of money, and if he sold it, he would probably realise enough to put a deposit on a house. Although he was self-employed, his income was steady, so he hoped he would be able to persuade a building society to give him a mortgage, and after he'd done that – and had those firm roots in Foxmore that Mrs Moxley said he should have – maybe he could ask Harriet to marry him.

Chapter 19

Blast! Harriet's heart sank when she saw the phone number of Sara's school flash up on her mobile. Receiving texts from the school was an almost daily occurrence – who knew there was so much information to be imparted to parents – but this was the first time anyone had rung her.

Sara had been reluctant to go to school that morning, but no more than usual for a Monday (or any other day, for that matter), and as far as Harriet could remember, her daughter hadn't shown any signs of being unwell, although she had complained of feeling sick. But as she claimed to feel sick most mornings before school these days, Harriet had chivvied her along and ignored it. If she kept Sara home every time she said she felt ill, the child would never be in school. She hoped Sara wasn't faking illness so that Harriet would fetch her home, because she would have stern words with her daughter if that was the case. She had no intention of going down that particular road with her. However, if Sara was genuinely ill, that was a different matter, and a wave of guilt washed over her. If she had sent Sara to school when she was truly unwell, what kind of mother did that make her?

Harriet therefore answered the phone with a considerable degree of sheepishness.

'Hello, is that Mrs Parry? Sara's mum?'

'It is. Has she been sick? I'm so sorry, I thought she was trying it on. You know what kids are like… Silly me, of course you do, you work in a school. Ha ha.'

239

'Um, no, Sara hasn't been sick and she's not ill. I'm Mrs Cooke, the headteacher, and the reason I'm calling is because Sara has been involved in an altercation.'

'What? Oh, my God! Is she all right? What happened?' Fear tore through her, leaving her breathless and trembling.

'She's fine. A little shaken, perhaps, but unharmed. We are, however, going to need you to collect her as soon as possible. She has been excluded from school for three days for fighting.'

'*Fighting?* I don't believe it! I thought you said there's been an altercation?'

'There has. Sara attacked another child, and as you are probably aware, the school does not tolerate violence.'

'But Sara's not like that!' Harriet was almost in tears. Her daughter might be finding her feet and becoming a little more belligerent, but she had never been aggressive. If anything, she tended to walk away from confrontation – unless it was with Harriet herself, or Bobby. But even then, she had never been violent. They must have it wrong.

'Are you sure you're talking about *my* daughter? I'm Sara Parry's mam. Sara without an "h",' she added, in case there happened to be two Sara Parrys in the school.

'We *are* talking about your daughter, Mrs Parry.'

'What about the other child?'

'Can you collect Sara now? I'll explain further when I see you.'

–

Harriet didn't know whether or not to be furious, and if so, who with. Sara? Or the school? Clearly something had gone seriously awry. If Sara *had* attacked another child, her daughter was going to be grounded for the rest of her life. There was no way Harriet was prepared to put up with that kind of behaviour and Sara had to learn that her actions had consequences. However, she was convinced the school must have got Sara mixed up with another child, and if that was the case, she wasn't going to be happy at being dragged out of work.

After telling Pen that she needed to leave and apologising profusely, Harriet had removed her apron, grabbed her bag and coat, and hurried home to collect the car, hoping there would be a simple explanation. She would be seriously cross if the school had made a mistake – Pen's Pantry was busy enough at this time of year, without her dashing off – but she would be even more annoyed if Sara had done what she was being accused of.

And underneath her ire was her very real fear that it was true.

When Harriet arrived at the school, the receptionist smiled pleasantly and asked her to take a seat, informing her that Mrs Cooke would be with her shortly. Harriet was left to cool her heels and worry.

'Mrs Parry?' A short woman in her mid-fifties, with a severely cut blond bob and a no-nonsense attitude, marched towards her, holding out her hand. 'I'm the headteacher, Mrs Cooke.'

Harriet took it, wincing at the overly firm grip.

'Would you like to follow me?' the woman ordered.

'Where's my daughter?'

'In my office, reflecting on her actions. As I said on the phone, we do not condone physical violence and we will not tolerate it.'

Harriet nodded, her eyes prickling. If Sara was being scolded by this formidable woman, she must be terrified. Harriet certainly was. The headteacher made her feel about twelve, as though it were Harriet who had misbehaved. Or maybe she was being reprimanded for being such a poor parent that she had a child who hit other children.

'Can you tell me what happened?' Harriet asked, trotting after the woman, who was striding ahead down the corridor. Harriet hurried to keep up.

'Apparently, there was a bit of name-calling and Sara reacted inappropriately. She slapped the other child. Here she is.' Mrs Cooke stopped outside an open door and gestured for Harriet to go ahead of her.

The office was a large one, and Sara looked very small and very frightened. Her daughter was huddled in a seat near an impressively clean and tidy desk, her bag by her feet and her coat resting on her knees. She was holding it up to her face so only her eyes could be seen, and they were red and swollen, and glistened with tears. As soon as Sara saw her mother, she pulled her coat over her head and began to sob.

Harriet hurried over to her and knelt by her side, wrapping her arms around her and holding her close. Whatever Sara had done, however badly she'd behaved, she was her daughter and Harriet loved her. She would help her get through this (after suitable punishment, of course), and hopefully, given time, they could put it behind them.

Mrs Cooke sat behind her desk, opened a drawer and took out a box of tissues, which she slid across the polished surface.

Harriet gave the woman a weak smile, took a handful and gave them to Sara, who reluctantly pulled her coat away from her face to wipe her eyes.

'I'm sorry, Mam, I'm sorry,' was all she said, as she sobbed bitterly.

'Is the other child OK?' Harriet asked Mrs Cooke.

'She's fine. She's gone back to class.'

That was a relief. 'What happens now?'

'Sara will remain off school until Friday, when she'll be expected to return. Sara, look at me.' Sara turned fearful eyes to the headteacher. 'You will be expected to apologise to Darlene.'

Harriet drew in a sharp breath. The other child was *Darlene*?

'Is that a problem, Mrs Parry?' the headteacher wanted to know, noticing her reaction.

Harriet shook her head. 'No. I'll make sure Sara apologises, but I don't think we've got to the bottom of what really happened. You see, there's history between—'

'That's as may be,' Mrs Cooke interjected, 'but violence is not the answer. Sara, do you understand?'

'Yes, Miss,' Sara hiccupped.

Harriet got to her feet. 'Come on,' she said to Sara, seeing that her explanation for Sara's behaviour would fall on deaf ears. 'Let's get you home.'

Mrs Cooke gave Harriet a penetrating stare. 'Mrs Parry, Sara knows what she did was wrong. I hope you will support the school in this matter?'

'Don't worry, I'll make sure she is punished.'

'Exclusion is punishment enough,' the woman said, her stern expression softening.

'That's where you're wrong, Mrs Cooke. You see, my daughter hasn't wanted to come to school for a number of weeks now, for some reason that I've yet to get to the bottom of, so being excluded for three days is probably music to her ears.'

And with that, she whisked Sara's bag up off the floor, grabbed hold of her daughter's hand and marched her out of the office.

Harriet waited until they were in the car before she said, 'Do you want to tell me what happened?'

'I'm sorry, Mam, I didn't mean to slap her, but she was being so horrid.' Sara hiccupped.

'In what way was she being horrid?'

'She's been picking on me ever since I started at this stupid school.'

Harriet's heart broke. Her daughter's pain was palpable. 'Is that why you don't want to go to school?'

Sara nodded.

'Why didn't you tell me?' God, she must be the worst mother in the world if her child didn't think she could tell her about something as awful as this.

Sara shrugged.

'Have you told anyone? A teacher?'

243

'Catrin knows but she's scared of Darlene, too. Everyone is.' Sara turned her stricken gaze to her mother. 'She's awful, Mammy. We all hate her, but…' Her chin wobbled.

'You're scared she'll make your life miserable if you say anything or stand up to her?' Harriet could feel tears trickling down her own face, but she made no move to wipe them away.

'I suppose. Mammy, is it true that I don't have to go to school tomorrow?' Her little face was so hopeful that Harriet's heart twisted in pain.

'No, cariad, you don't have to go to school until Friday.'

Sara's face fell. 'I don't want to go at all.'

'You can't stay home. You have to go to school. I'm so sorry, but you do.'

'I'll run away,' she threatened. 'I'll ask Owen if he'll take me with him when he leaves.'

'He's not leaving. Well, he *is*, but only to spend Christmas with his mam and dad. He'll be back afterwards.'

'Oh.' Sara's face crumpled.

Harriet was at a loss to know what to do for the best. She'd have a chat with her parents, see if they had any ideas, and she'd talk it over with Owen. He mightn't have any children of his own, but he had a sensible head on his shoulders and maybe he could bring a more detached viewpoint to the table. She had better inform Declan, too – and that wasn't something she was looking forward to, so she may as well do it as soon as she was home and get it over with.

Before the three-day exclusion period was up, she also intended to make an appointment to see the headteacher again. Although Sara was to blame for lashing out and should never have resorted to violence, Mrs Cooke needed to be made aware that there was a bullying issue in her school. Physical violence was unacceptable, and Sara would be punished for it, but so was emotional abuse and that shouldn't be tolerated either.

If Sara needed to apologise, so did Darlene.

After settling Sara on the sofa with a glass of milk and a snack, Harriet hurried upstairs to her bedroom and closed the door.

244

She didn't want Sara to overhear the conversation, just in case Declan went off on one. There had been enough upset for one day.

Harriet listened to the long beeping noise on her phone and frowned. The sound she was hearing wasn't the familiar dialling tone and it took her a moment to realise why – it was the sound of an international call.

When he answered, he didn't sound pleased to hear from her. 'Harriet? What do you want?'

Harriet tensed. 'Hi, Declan, I thought I'd better let you know that Sara has been excluded from school, for assaulting another pupil.' She kept her tone neutral.

He didn't say anything for a second or two, but she could hear laughter, music and splashing noises in the background.

'You rang me just for that?' he said eventually, and she could tell he was annoyed.

'You *are* her father,' Harriet pointed out, her own ire rising. 'I thought you might like to know.'

'I'm on holiday. What do you want me to do about it?'

Harriet sucked in a sharp breath. 'Nothing. Not a thing. Like you usually do.' On holiday indeed! How nice for him. *She* would like to be on holiday right now.

'Is that it? My pint's getting warm.'

'Don't you want to speak to her? Ask her how she is? Why she did it?'

'Nah, you can sort it.'

Like I always bloody do, she thought. 'Have a nice ti—' He had rung off and she was left holding a dead phone.

Breathing deeply as she tried not to lose her temper completely, Harriet splashed water on her face before she went downstairs. Once more, Declan had abdicated his parental responsibility, and she felt like crying when she realised she was on her own with this – again.

But she wasn't on her own – not completely. She had her parents and she had Owen, who cared about her children more than their own father did. And who also cared about *her*.

'I'm so looking forward to the Christmas Fayre,' Rowena announced as Harriet entered the zero-waste shop on the hunt for toothpaste tablets on Friday morning.

She had seen them in Owen's tiny shower room, and when he'd told her what they were for, she thought they were a good idea, especially for the children. Because each tablet contained only enough toothpaste for one brushing, it meant that Bobby, who was partial to squirting normal toothpaste so liberally that the family went through a large tube every week, would only use what was needed. And there was also the environmental factor of keeping the tablets in a reusable container.

'So am I.' Harriet's reply was heartfelt. She had loved organising the Fayre, but if she had realised how much work it would be, she might have passed. Thank goodness for Owen and Kelly – she would be lost without their help. However, if it wasn't for them, the Fayre wouldn't be happening, so it was only right they did their fair share, she mused dryly.

Thinking of Owen brought a smile to her lips. He had been a godsend these past three days, taking care of Sara while Harriet went to work, and she didn't know what she would have done without him. Thankfully, Sara had returned to school today, so everything was back to normal. However, Harriet was worried how her daughter would cope; she had tried to arrange a meeting with Mrs Cooke to advise her of the bullying situation, but the headteacher was 'off site' and would be for the next few days, which meant that Harriet was forced to wait until the woman was available.

Rowena asked, 'How is Owen? I haven't seen him for a while.' She sent Harriet a knowing look.

'He's great. He's been such a help with the Fayre and… other things.' Harriet winced. She wasn't keeping it a secret that Sara had been excluded from school, but neither was she broadcasting it.

'I bet he has!'

Harriet blushed. 'That's not what I meant.'

'But you're more than just Fayre-planner buddies.' Rowena was laughing at her, but in a kindly way.

'We might be,' Harriet hedged.

'Aw, look at you. You've gone all coy. Are you and Owen getting serious?'

'I can't possibly say,' Harriet replied primly.

'I'll take that as a yes. I'm so pleased for you. You deserve some happiness.'

That highlighted both the diamond and the lump of coal that was Foxmore – everyone knew everyone else's business. It was both a blessing and a curse, but she wouldn't want it any other way.

Rowena said, 'I must thank him again for that piece he did about Sero. We've set up an online shop on the back of it and it's really taking off. It's early days, but the figures look promising.'

Harriet was about to congratulate Rowena, but something the shopkeeper had said caught her attention. '*That piece?*' she asked. What did Rowena mean by 'piece'?

'The article he wrote, the one that was published in… I forget the name of it. He did a great job. Here, I'll show you.'

Harriet watched, perplexed, as Rowena hooked her phone out of the back pocket of her jeans. She had no idea what the woman was talking about.

Rowena handed her the phone and Harriet took it, frowning.

Her frown deepened as she read a skilfully written article in an online magazine, which extolled the virtues of zero-waste shops and combined it with a compelling story about how the one in Foxmore had been set up via a co-operative.

'*Owen* wrote this?' she asked.

'It's good, isn't it? And he didn't want any payment for it either, bless him. He said he'd earned enough from selling the article and by the redirects to his blog. But I expect you

know that already. Owen is a gem – but you know that too…'
Rowena stopped. Her eyebrows shot up and she stared at
Harriet, horrified.

Harriet stared back, guessing that the expression on her face
must be giving the game away that she didn't have a clue about
any of this.

'Oh, blast. You didn't know?' Rowena looked mortified.
'Damn, I shouldn't have said anything – and Owen did ask me
not to, but because you're together I assumed you must know all
about it. Look, forget I said anything.' She bit her lip. 'I'm sorry,
I truly am, but it's not as though he's doing anything wrong, is
it? I did wonder at the time why he didn't want anyone to know
that he's the person behind *Planet B*, but I'm sure he's got his
reasons.'

'*Planet B?*' Harriet echoed. She had no idea what *that* was,
either.

Rowena groaned. 'I've really put my foot in it, haven't I? Me
and my big mouth.'

Harriet pursed her lips and said frostily, 'What is *Planet B*?'

Rowena's smile was faint and apologetic as she said gently,
'Don't you think you should ask Owen?'

'I'm asking *you*.'

'I hate breaking a confidence.'

'You already have. I'll find out eventually, so you may as well
tell me now and save me some time.'

Rowena inhaled deeply. '*Planet B* is the name Owen writes
under, but I don't know any more than that, sorry.'

Harriet gave Rowena her phone back. 'Thank you. I won't
drop you in it.'

She was conscious of Rowena's eyes following her as she left
the shop and hurried home. She was supposed to be on her
way to work, but something was going on and she needed to
find out what. It mightn't be anything to worry about, but if
that was the case, why hadn't Owen told her about this article
he'd written? And there was also the implication that he had

written others. Why was it such a secret? Why hide behind a pseudonym? And why had he led her and everyone else in Foxmore to believe he was an odd-job man?

As she scurried down the road, Harriet phoned Pen. 'Do you mind if I'm a bit late this morning? Something's come up.'

'Oh dear, it's not Sara, is it?'

'No, nothing like that.'

'Anything I can help with?'

'Thanks for the offer, but no. I'll be in later; I'll tell you about it then.'

'OK, lovely, take as long as you need. I can manage.'

Harriet knew that Pen probably wouldn't manage, so she would try to be as quick as she could. She didn't like leaving her boss in the lurch, especially not at this time of year, when the cafe would be crowded with shoppers wanting a spiced latte and a slice of Christmas cake or a mince pie. But she simply had to find out what was going on.

Harriet flew in through the front door and almost fell into the sitting room in her haste to reach the laptop. It was old and slow, but it was better than trying to squint at her mobile's small screen.

Briefly, Rowena's words popped into her head, and she vowed that she would ask Owen what was going on, but first she wanted to see if she could find anything about *Planet B* online, just in case there was something she needed to know before she spoke to him. Hiding one's identity like this wasn't normal behaviour as far as she was concerned, unless there was something he was ashamed of or he had done something illegal – and if so, she wanted to be in full possession of as many facts as possible before she confronted him.

Maybe 'confront' was too harsh a word, but goddammit, she had entrusted him with her kids and if there was anything dodgy about him, she had a right to know.

Typing in the name Owen Loxton didn't bring up any hits that were relevant to him, but neither had she expected it to.

She had already idly looked for him on social media not long after he'd issued his challenge, and hadn't found him on any of the sites, which hadn't bothered her, considering his attitude towards consumerism.

However, when she entered *Planet B* into the search bar, so many pages popped up that she didn't know which one to read first. Top of the page was some kind of computer game, and below it was a site selling board games, and then a couple more things she didn't think were relevant... and then she spotted it.

There was a blog called *Planet B,* and as soon as she clicked on it, she knew she had found Owen.

She also knew why he hadn't told her about it: front and centre was a photo of someone she immediately recognised, even though their back was to the camera.

It was a photo of Harriet herself!

Chapter 20

In disbelief, Harriet scanned the site quickly, scrolling through the blog posts, her anger mounting with every word she read and every photo she saw.

Owen mightn't have used her real name, or that of her children (if he had, she would have totally lost the plot), and he had been very careful not to post any images which showed her face or theirs. He hadn't even mentioned Foxmore by name, just referred to it as a picturesque village in rural mid-Wales. *But that wasn't the point!*

She wasn't sure what angered her the most: him not asking her, or him writing the damned thing in the first place. And beneath her anger was a growing well of despair, with undercurrents of heartbreak bubbling to the surface.

Owen had used her.

Harriet meant nothing more to him than a series of blog posts on the internet, and the acclaim and approval of those readers who had commented.

An experiment, that's all she was. A way to convince others that not buying new was the way to save the planet.

Stuff the sodding planet! She'd had a gutful of it. The planet could take a hike as far as she was concerned, and so could Owen.

How dare he post things about her online! Every man and his dog could see what she'd bought, including that stupid designer dress!

Furious and heartbroken, Harriet slammed the lid of the laptop shut.

She didn't want to read any more. She'd read enough. Too much. And for a second, she wished she had never seen the damned blog posts, wished she hadn't set foot in Sero earlier. She also wished she hadn't accepted a stupid challenge from someone she'd only just met, wished she had told him to mind his own business, and wished she hadn't been at work that morning.

But most of all, Harriet wished she'd never set eyes on Owen Loxton, because if she hadn't, her heart wouldn't be shattering into a million pieces.

–

Owen was at a loose end this morning. For the past three days he had kept Sara entertained while Harriet was at work, and he was surprised to find that he was missing the child's company.

He felt he'd got to know her better, and she him, and although Sara was technically being punished by being excluded from school, the two of them had had a whale of a time. He had shown her how to make chocolate hazelnut cookies (vegan, naturally) and gingerbread stained-glass biscuits (also vegan), which they'd packaged up ready to give to Harriet's parents for Christmas. Sara had been chuffed to be able to give a gift that her mother hadn't chosen or bought, and Owen had made a note to do something similar with Bobby.

They'd also gone for long walks along the riverbank with Etta – Sara complained so much about having to go out in the cold and tramp along a muddy path that her mother had been convinced her daughter had hated every step of it. At one point, the girl had over-egged her pretend dislike so much that Owen had been sure Harriet would twig.

Owen had also introduced her to a series of books called *Just William*, which he had enjoyed as a child, and he'd encouraged her to read them aloud so he could legitimately tell Harriet that Sara had been practising her reading, when in fact he had been howling with laughter at her impersonation of Violet Elizabeth, one of the characters.

He wondered how she was getting on. He knew how anxious she had been about going to school today, despite his assurances that she would be fine. Over the past three days he had tried to tell Sara that she should hold her head up high and not worry what others might think, and he had used himself as an example, explaining how he used to be ridiculed because of his way of life and his beliefs. Twenty years ago, neither van-life nor being deeply passionate about the environment had been quite so trendy. He'd told her he could very easily have given in, but he hadn't – and was very glad that he hadn't.

However, Owen wasn't an eleven-year-old girl, with an eleven-year-old girl's outlook or pressures. He could only guess what she was going through and try to bolster her confidence. Harriet tried, too, but he suspected Sara might listen to him more, purely because he wasn't related to her.

Thinking about Harriet gave him the idea to pop into the cafe. He was due to see her immediately after she finished work, and he was looking forward to it. His pulse raced at the thought of what they might get up to in those precious few minutes, and he told himself to behave. But he wanted to see her *now*. If he was honest, he wanted to see her all the time. She was on his mind constantly, invading every thought he had, and he loved it.

Owen didn't know how he would manage not being with her over Christmas. For the first time in his life he wasn't looking forward to spending it with his family. He would much prefer to spend it with Harriet. But he couldn't let his parents down: he knew they were looking forward to seeing him, and so was his brother. Maybe he could take Harriet and the kids to meet them in the New Year. He would take them in the van – Sara and Bobby might enjoy the experience. It might be the only chance they'd have before he sold it. Just before Christmas was not the best time to put a camper van on the market, but as soon as winter was out of the way, and people's thoughts started turning to summer holidays and being outdoors once more, he'd sell it.

The smell of cinnamon and spices, mingling with those of coffee and vanilla, hit him as he walked into Pen's Pantry, and his mouth watered. Bless her, Pen had put a few more vegan dishes on the menu over the past few weeks, and he felt duty-bound to try them all. He'd not long had breakfast and it was far too early for lunch, but there was nothing wrong with indulging in a hot chocolate and a Christmas cookie, especially if it gave him a chance to ogle Harriet.

She had her back to him and didn't see him enter, and he was tempted to creep up behind her and tickle her, but he thought he'd better not. Pen was a very tolerant and understanding boss, but Harriet was at work after all, and he didn't want to make her feel awkward.

Instead, he chose a table and sat down, waiting to catch her attention.

Feeling eyes on him, he glanced towards the counter and realised Pen was staring. Owen smiled and gave her a little wave, but his smile turned to a frown of confusion when she glared at him.

'What's wrong?' he mouthed, but all Pen did was shake her head, her lips set in a thin straight line. 'What?' he asked again.

Pen jerked her head towards Harriet, and Owen's heart sank. *Oh no, please don't let there be something wrong at school*, he thought. But when Harriet turned around and caught sight of him, he drew in a sharp breath. Her gaze was flinty, her eyes narrowed when she noticed him, and she didn't look at all pleased to see him.

Pen hurried over to her and he heard the cafe owner say something to Harriet in a warning tone. She then placed a hand on her arm, but Harriet shook her off.

'It may as well be now,' Harriet said. 'The sooner I tell him, the sooner he can bugger off.'

Pen said, 'Don't. Not here. Take him out the back if you have to.'

'You're right.' Harriet beckoned him over and Owen got to his feet, his stomach churning. Something was going on, but he had no idea what.

He followed her straight, stiff back as she pushed her way through the door leading to the staff area, with dread in his heart.

'What's going on?' he asked as soon as the door swung shut behind them.

Harriet whirled on her heel, her hands on her hips. She looked furious. 'I could ask you the same thing,' she said, 'but I won't, because I know. I've seen it.'

'Seen what—?' Owen began, then his blood ran cold. He knew without being told what it was that she had seen. 'If it's about the blog, I can explain.'

'Don't bother!' Harriet spat. 'I know exactly what's been going on and why. Is that all I am to you? An experiment? Let me tell you: this experiment is over. It's near enough to Christmas so I think I've won your stupid challenge, don't you? There's no need for you to hang around in Foxmore any more.'

'But—'

'And I'll tell you what else is over – *us*. To think I believed you cared for me! Ha! More fool me. I want you to leave now. Go!' she commanded.

Owen was having difficulty gathering his thoughts. For Harriet to find out in this way was unthinkable. He had been planning on telling her eventually – he hadn't intended to keep it from her forever, because he knew that sooner or later he would have to tell her what he did for a living – but he was going to explain everything after Christmas, once the experiment was over and the final blog posts on the subject were done and dusted. He had even rehearsed in his head what he was going to say. How had she found out?

He was about to ask when he realised it didn't matter. He didn't care how she'd found out. All he cared about was that she had told him to leave.

'Please let me explain,' he begged, his heart an uncomfortable lump in his chest.

Harriet refused to look at him, lifting her chin and staring at a point over his shoulder.

'Harriet, please.'

'Get out. I never want to see you again. I wish I'd never seen you at all. We were fine until you came along, with your don't-buy-anything-new ideas. It's done nothing but cause trouble. My daughter is in bits because of you.'

'Hang on a minute...' he began, thinking that she wasn't being entirely fair, but he ground to a halt. In a small voice he said, 'This can't be the end of us.'

'Oh yes, it can.' She was resolute. He could hear it in her voice and see it in her eyes. They were over.

He took a shuddering breath and held it for a moment, before letting it out slowly. 'If that's what you want...'

'It is.'

So Owen did the only thing he could – he left.

–

Harriet fought hard to hold back her tears. There would be plenty of time for crying later, when she was alone. Right now, there was Pen and a cafe full of customers to think about. She might want to go home and bawl her eyes out, but she couldn't.

While trying to compose herself, she jumped when the door opened, and for a second her heart leapt, thinking Owen had returned, but quickly plummeted again when she saw it was Pen. Harriet didn't want him to come back anyway. When she'd told him to leave, she'd meant it. But that didn't stop her wanting desperately to see him again, to feel his lips on hers, his arms holding her tight. He might have acted despicably, and she might be unable to forgive him for what he had done, but it didn't stop her from loving him. Emotions couldn't be turned off like a light switch, and she knew she would feel the pain of this for a long time to come.

'Are you all right, my lovely?' Pen asked.

'Not really.'

'He's gone,' Pen continued.

'Good.'

'He looked awful,' Pen added.

'Good,' Harriet repeated.

'He looked as though he was crying.'

'Join the club.' Harriet sniffed, wiping her eyes. Holding back the tears wasn't working, was it?

'Do you want to go home?' Pen offered.

'Thank you, but no. I'll be better off keeping busy.'

Pen said, 'Your face is enough to scare small children.'

Harriet tried for a smile and failed. 'I promise I'll be more cheerful.'

Pen continued to stare at her. 'Are you sure you don't want to go home? I can manage.'

That was what Harriet was worried about. That Pen *would* be able to manage without her – permanently. She was also worried about what she was going to tell the children. Sara and Bobby idolised Owen, and they would be devastated to learn they wouldn't be seeing him again. At least she hoped they wouldn't. When she had told him to go, she didn't just mean out of the cafe: she meant out of Foxmore. Life would be impossible if he stayed. She would be terrified of bumping into him around every corner, and then there was the Christmas Fayre... Oh God, the *Fayre*!

It's all right, she told herself, *everything is under control*. There was hardly anything more to be done, and what was left could be split between her and Kelly. The two of them could do this on their own. They didn't need Owen.

She waited for Pen to go back out into the cafe, then Harriet went to the loo to splash some water on her face. The expression in the eyes looking back at her from the tiny mirror above the sink made her want to weep. She looked broken.

Which was exactly how she felt.

-

Owen stumbled back to the field, tripping over his own feet in his haste to return to his van, stow everything away and get on the road.

He had to leave Foxmore *now* – he didn't want to stay there a second longer than he needed to.

With shaking hands, he unlocked the van door and fell inside, dropping heavily to his knees. This couldn't be happening. He'd thought Harriet loved him, but she hadn't even wanted to hear his side of the story.

Who was he kidding? He didn't have a leg to stand on. Because of his actions, he had lost her trust and her love.

This was his fault – he shouldn't expect her to hear him out. Why should she? Because in a way she was right. He *had* used her. But only at the very beginning, when she hadn't meant any more to him than a blog post and a boost in readership. That he had written it with the best intentions was neither here nor there. He had known at the time that not asking her permission, or at least not telling her about it, was underhand, but it hadn't mattered then because he hadn't been in love with her.

He should never have fallen in love. He wasn't cut out for it. He had lived a perfectly happy and contented life without the complications that being in love brought.

And now look at him – he didn't know if he would ever recover from this. His heart was broken and he'd never felt pain like it. He wanted to wail his anguish, howl his loss and rage at his stupidity. But he did none of those things.

With grim despair, he steadily gathered up and packed away everything that couldn't be unsecured when he was on the road, going through the familiar motions on autopilot. He wished he could gather up his memories of Harriet as easily and stow them in a box in his mind, so he would never have to think of her again. Because he had an awful feeling that his hurt would take a long time to fade, and his broken heart would take a long time to heal. If it ever did.

But the worst thing was – he only had himself to blame.

Chapter 21

'You've lost weight.' Pen wasn't being complimentary. Her gaze was disapproving as she scanned Harriet from neck to knees.

'At least something good has come out of this last week.' Harriet hastily popped her apron over her head and tied it at the waist. 'I need to lose some ballast before the stuff-your-face season starts. My mam cooks enough veg and roasties to feed the street, and expects *me* to eat most of it because she's "watching her figure".'

Pen said, 'If you're not careful, you'll fade away.'

'I highly doubt that.'

'Have you heard from him?'

'No, Pen, I haven't. I keep telling you that it's over, so there's no need to ask me the same question every single day.'

'Sorry,' Pen muttered.

Harriet's mouth twisted. 'It's me who should be sorry. I shouldn't take my bad mood out on you.'

'You're suffering from more than a bad mood. You've got a broken heart.'

'That's as may be, but there's nothing I can do about it.'

'You could try talking to him. I know Owen was a tit for doing what he did, but I've read his blog – he started writing about your challenge before you and he got jiggy.'

'Got *jiggy*?' Harriet rolled her sore, red eyes. At least Pen hadn't suggested she wore dark glasses to hide them. 'OK, let's say I forgive him for that *oversight*,' she exaggerated the word. 'He should have told me when it became clear we were becoming more than friends. There is only one reason I can

261

think of for him not saying anything – he didn't care about me. I was just a blog post and a pair of willing arms.'

'Tosh! Anyone could see he was head over heels about you. And *I* can think of a reason – he left it too late. I reckon that by the time he realised he should have told you about the blog, he was in too deep to explain it away.'

'Huh! The more likely explanation is that he thought I'd never find out. Why else would he ask Rowena not to say anything?'

'I still think you should speak to him. Look at you! You're a mess.'

'Gee, thanks.'

'Admit it, you love him.'

'What if I do? It doesn't make any difference.' Harriet changed the subject. 'Is it still OK for me to leave early today?'

'Of course it is! You've been waiting all week for this meeting. You have to go. Let's hope the headteacher can sort it out. You can't go on having Sara bullied, the poor little mite. Is she still refusing to go to school?'

'She can refuse all she likes, but she's got to go and that's that. It doesn't help that she's missing he-who-shall-not-be-named.'

'Owen?' Pen's voice was louder than it needed to be.

'Shhh!' Harriet glanced around to see if any of the Pantry's customers had heard. 'It's been hard on both kids.'

'You're going to have to tell them at some point that he's gone for good.'

'Not until after Christmas,' Harriet insisted. 'And by then they'll have hopefully forgotten about him.'

'Don't be so sure.'

Harriet wasn't sure at all; she was just trying to convince herself. Telling them that Owen was visiting his parents for the festive season would only work for so long. She was sure Sara smelled a rat, because her daughter kept on about Owen being at the Christmas Fayre on Sunday. She was adamant that he wouldn't miss it, no matter how many times Harriet told her that he wouldn't be there.

Bobby, on the other hand, had gone quiet after the initial seemingly endless questions, and Harriet was worried about him.

Great – that meant she was concerned about both of her children. Some Christmas this was going to be.

–

Christmas decorations were on display in the school's foyer, Harriet noticed, as she perched primly on a hard plastic chair to await the headteacher. As she studied the acrylic paintings dotted around the walls, with the caption 'Contenders in our Christmas Card Competition' emblazoned above, she wondered where Sara was. She had asked that her daughter be in the meeting, and she hoped Sara would be brave enough to tell Mrs Cooke what was going on. It would be much better coming from her than from Harriet.

Harriet heard the click of high heels coming down the corridor and she sat up straighter as Mrs Cooke hoved into view.

'Mrs Parry? Would you like to follow me? Is it still bitterly cold outside?'

'Um, yes, it's freezing.'

'I think we might be in for some snow,' the headteacher said. 'I know there's none forecast, but I can smell it in the air.'

All Harriet could smell was a faint aroma of boiled cabbage, presumably from the canteen, floor polish and the headteacher's perfume. It made for an unpleasant combination.

To Harriet's relief, Sara was already waiting in Mrs Cooke's office. She looked petrified; her eyes were huge, with dark circles beneath them, and her face was thin and pale. On seeing her daughter, Harriet was even more determined to put an end to Darlene's bullying ways. And if nothing was done, Harriet was prepared to take Sara out of this school and move her to another.

'I'm pleased to hear Sara has been behaving herself,' Mrs Cooke began. 'She's settled back into school after her exclusion and I don't have any concerns at this moment in time.'

'*You* mightn't, but *I* have,' Harriet retorted. 'I wanted to have a meeting with you because I know why Sara lashed out at Darlene. And before you say anything, I don't condone what my daughter did, but neither do I condone Darlene's behaviour. She has been bullying Sara ever since term started, and she bullies many of the other children, too. They are scared of her, and Sara is terrified.'

Mrs Cooke cocked an eyebrow. 'She didn't seem terrified when she slapped her across the face.'

Harriet felt Sara's hand slip into hers and she squeezed it tightly. It had taken her a long time to persuade her daughter to tell her why she had snapped and hit Darlene, and she knew Sara was scared of reprisals, but this had to be said.

'Darlene was saying some horrid things to her. And while I know that's not an excuse, I'll try to put it into context.' Harriet hurried on when she saw the headteacher's expression, proceeding to tell her all about the challenge, the dress and the party. The only thing she didn't mention was the family's financial situation, which had been the main driving force behind buying second-hand items in the first place, figuring that it was no one else's business but her own. Instead, she focused on the environmental benefits.

'Is this true?' Mrs Cooke asked Sara when Harriet had finished.

Sara nodded miserably.

'Tell Mrs Cooke what Darlene said when she realised you were wearing one of her old dresses,' Harriet urged.

'She laughed at me and said she didn't like the dress anyway and it looked stupid on me.'

'What else?' Harriet said.

'She kept saying that only poor people wore other people's clothes, and she kept laughing and saying she didn't want to be friends any more. I didn't care, Miss, honest, but she told everyone else that they couldn't be friends with me either. I hate her.'

'So I see.' The headteacher's tone was dry. 'Is that any reason to hit her, though?'

'No...' Sara hung her head and began to cry.

Harriet said, 'I know children fall out all the time, one minute they are best friends and the next they're not speaking to each other, but this is different. Sara is genuinely scared of her. I don't think it's acceptable to taunt people because they don't have as much money as her family does.'

'It's *not* acceptable,' Mrs Cooke agreed, thoughtfully. 'How is the challenge going?'

'Some days it's harder than others,' Harriet admitted. 'Birthdays and Christmas especially.' She told her about the Fayre on Holly Field on Sunday.

'What a marvellous idea. Do you mind if I come along?'

'Not at all. The more the merrier. But can we get back to the problem of my daughter being bullied?'

'Let me look into it. I'll have a chat with Sara's form tutor and teachers to see if they can shed any more light on what's going on. I'll also have a discreet word with some of the other children. As you can appreciate, I have to be sure of my facts before I speak to Darlene. Please be assured that I will deal with her firmly if she has been bullying your daughter.'

Harriet recognised that this was the best she would get for now, and she fully appreciated that the headteacher needed to investigate first. 'Thank you for taking the time to meet with me,' she said politely.

'It's almost the end of last lesson, so would you like to take Sara home with you now? I don't think she's in any fit state to go back to class,' Mrs Cooke added, kindly. 'Good luck with the Fayre. I'm sure it will be brilliant.'

I hope so, Harriet thought, but her heart wasn't in it any more. She couldn't wait for it to be over so she could try to forget that Owen Loxton existed.

It's strange being in my childhood home again, Owen thought, as he ran his hand down the banister of the old former rectory, remembering how he and his brother used to incur their mum's wrath when they tried to slide down it. He'd been just a kid, but his dad hadn't had any such excuse, and he used to join them in their antics, hitching his backside up onto the polished wood and laughing like a loon when he almost fell off at the bottom.

Those were the days, when playing in the large overgrown garden behind the house was the only thing that mattered. Or sometimes they would venture into the grounds of the ruined castle which sat on the outskirts of Narberth, and pretend to be knights and kings.

It had been a magical place to grow up, and it was a magical place to return to. But right now, Owen wasn't feeling any magic at all. He alternately felt numb or in pain, and neither feeling was pleasant, although the numbness was marginally more preferable.

The pain was more acute late at night when he was lying in bed, sleepless and with memories circling around in his head like the red kites which rode the thermals in the fields beyond the garden. And in the morning, when he opened his eyes, for a blissful second he forgot his heart was in pieces, only for it all to come crashing back. The parts in between were a little better, but not much.

He couldn't believe how much being in love hurt. It tore at him, red-clawed and insistent, and he was so miserable that he didn't know what to do with himself. There was work enough to keep him occupied but he couldn't face it. He had been commissioned to write a piece on wild boars in British woodland, but for once in his life he couldn't summon up the energy to care. Plus, he also had to write a final post to wrap up the 'Dawn' series, but the last thing he wanted to do was to immerse himself in that world again.

Maybe he would be able to face it after Christmas.

His phone trilled with an incoming call and his heart almost leapt out of his ribcage, but when he looked at the screen and saw that it wasn't Harriet's number, he dropped the phone on a cushion and flopped onto the sofa.

'Are you going to answer that?' his mother demanded, bustling into the snug with a mug of cocoa in her hand. 'Drink up,' she said, shoving it at him. 'It'll do you good.'

He highly doubted a hot drink would make any difference, but he duly took it from her and sipped it, aware she was only trying to help.

The phone continued to ring and Owen continued to ignore it. 'It isn't anyone important,' he said. He didn't recognise the number, and if it was important, the caller could always leave a message.

His mother huffed and Owen smiled sadly. She was the type of person who could never ignore a ringing phone or a knock on the door, and he knew that him not answering was driving her crazy. Thankfully, it soon stopped and he returned to his morose thoughts.

'When are you going to stop moping around?' his mother asked, plopping onto the sofa next to him, the cushions bouncing, almost making him spill his cocoa. 'You've been here a week and all you've done is loaf around, looking sorry for yourself. I understand you're hurting but you're not doing yourself any favours.'

'Is that code for you wanting me to do something?' he asked.

'Now you come to mention it, you couldn't split some of those logs in the log store, could you?' she asked. 'Your father has been meaning to do it, but you know what he's like.'

Owen's dad was a procrastinator, always putting off until tomorrow what he should be doing today, especially when it came to something he didn't like. Splitting logs wasn't his dad's favourite job in the world. Not only that, he wasn't getting any younger, so the job was probably harder than it used to be.

'Why didn't you say? I'm happy to help, you know that.'

His mum snorted. 'Happy, my bum,' she said. 'There's nothing happy about you. Are you going to tell me what's going on? You said it was to do with a woman, but you haven't told me what. Is she married? Is this unrequited love?'

'No, and I don't think so.'

'You've got to do better than that. That's not an answer. You know I'll keep on at you until you tell me.'

Owen knew, but all he needed to do was to hold out for another two weeks, and then Christmas would all be over and he could get back on the road again. He was tempted to hop in his van and drive off now, but that would be churlish. Besides, he had nowhere he wanted to be – aside from Foxmore, and that was impossible – and he had already told his parents he was staying with them until the New Year, so it wouldn't be fair to change his mind now.

Owen squared his jaw. He might as well tell her now, before she eventually wore him down with her nagging.

'Her name is Harriet, and I did something silly,' he began.

Before he could continue, his mother jumped in with, 'Owen, you didn't cheat on her, did you?'

'No, I did not. I did betray her trust, though…' And he went on to explain how the two of them had met, and how he had decided to write a series of blog posts on the back of a challenge he had set her, and how he had kept it from her. To the sound of the fire crackling in the hearth, and with the afternoon darkening around them, he told his mother that he had fallen in love, and that he'd believed Harriet loved him, although neither of them had said it in so many words. His mother's face was full of sympathy when he told her how his world had come crashing down around his ears when Harriet had found out what he had done.

'She told me to leave,' he said. 'She doesn't want to see me ever again and I don't blame her.'

'I'm sure she'll come round when she's had a chance to think about it,' his mother said. 'I'm assuming you didn't post anything horrible or derogatory about her?'

Owen was shocked. 'I'd never do that to anyone, especially someone I love.'

'There you go, then,' she said. 'She probably needs a bit of time. It's been a week; why don't you give her a call?'

'She's got my number if she wants me,' he said. 'I'm not going to make a nuisance of myself by phoning her.'

His mother tutted. 'Young love,' she muttered.

'We're hardly young,' Owen objected. 'I'm forty-one, and she's only four years younger.'

'When you've been together as long as me and your father, any relationship that has been going for less than twenty years is young love. It takes that long to break them in.'

Owen was bemused. 'Break what in?'

'Not what, *who*. I'm talking about husbands. But I dare say, it applies to wives, too. Me and your father had some ding-dongs, I can tell you. I left him once, you know.'

'No, I didn't. What happened?'

'I felt unloved and unappreciated,' his mother declared.

'But Dad loves you to bits! Anyone can see that.'

'I couldn't. He needed to tell me. Perhaps that's what you need to do with your young lady. Think about it.' She got up and patted him on the shoulder as she left. 'Don't forget that wood,' she reminded him. 'You can chop it in the morning.'

'I won't forget,' he called after her, then he thought about what she'd said. Perhaps he should have told Harriet he loved her. But would it have made any difference?

He didn't know, and it was too late now. He had burnt his bridges and there was no way he was ever going to be able to rebuild them.

—

Harriet gazed out of the window on Saturday evening and her heart sank. Oh shoot, that was all they needed – blimmin' snow! The children were ecstatic as they watched the fat flakes drift lazily down from a laden sky, and they were already hunting around for wellies, hats and scarves, even though the white stuff wasn't sticking yet. But Harriet wasn't as pleased to see it.

'Have we got any carrots?' Bobby wanted to know.

Harriet guessed he wasn't asking because he was hungry. 'We have,' she said, 'but don't get your hopes up, it's not sticking. See?' She pointed out of the window, and the children hurried over to it and peered outside.

'It's all over the cars and there's some on the grass,' Bobby said.

'Not enough to make a snowman,' Harriet told him, hoping it would stay that way. 'Anyway, it's getting dark, so you won't be able to go out and play in it until tomorrow.'

She found her phone and dialled Kelly's number. 'Have you seen the weather?' she asked. 'I hope it doesn't stick.'

'It isn't at the moment,' Kelly said, 'but it might once the temperature drops later on.'

'Great, that's all we need.'

'It's not the best, is it?' her friend agreed. 'It would be a shame if the Fayre couldn't go ahead after all the planning we've done. I do hope we don't get much, and if we do that it doesn't put people off.'

In some ways, Harriet would be relieved if it did. She wasn't looking forward to tomorrow one little bit, even though she didn't need to do anything. There was no more organisation to be done, apart from turning up and showing her face. There was no money to be taken on the gate, and she'd already had a word with Aled who, although disgruntled that Owen had left without telling him, had agreed to marshal the parking, so that was one less thing Harriet had to worry about.

Fretfully, she switched the TV on and brought up the news channel.

Mrs Cooke had been right in her hunch that it would snow, but Harriet was relieved when the forecasters said that South Wales would bear the brunt of it, with as much as seven to eight centimetres falling overnight in that area. Mid and North Wales would get off more lightly, with only a smattering of snow, although there would be more on higher ground. Thankfully, although Foxmore was surrounded on three sides by mountains, none of them were particularly high, and the village itself lay at the bottom of the valley; also, the river running through it helped to keep the temperature above those of the surrounding hillsides. Foxmore wasn't likely to see enough snow to make a snowman. The children would be disappointed, but no doubt more of the white stuff would fall before the end of the winter.

Not sure whether she was relieved or disappointed that the Fayre would go ahead tomorrow, Harriet returned to her task of writing Christmas cards. She wasn't in the mood for doing that either, but at least it kept her busy and kept her mind off Owen. Because no matter how often she told herself she shouldn't think about him, since he had left last Friday, thinking about him was all she'd been able to do.

–

That damn number was calling him again, Owen saw, and he was tempted to turn his phone off. Whoever it was obviously wanted to contact him, but not badly enough to leave a message. This was the third time today. Couldn't they take the hint? If he wanted to speak to them, he would have answered the phone.

He got up from his spot on the sofa and arched his back, putting his hands to his spine as he eased out the kinks. No wonder his father didn't like chopping wood; it was hard work. But at least there were now plenty of suitably sized logs stacked neatly in the log store to keep his parents going for a while. He had been at it most of the afternoon, until the drop in temperature had driven him inside. That had been about an hour ago and he hadn't warmed up yet.

Dear God, his phone was ringing *again*.

Cross now, he grabbed it and pressed the answer icon. He was going to give whoever it was a piece of his mind. Talk about persistent. It was probably only a scam call anyway, or market research.

'Look,' he said, as soon as the call connected, 'I don't know who you are or what you want, and I don't care. Stop phoning me.'

'Don't you dare hang up on me, Owen Loxton!' a familiar voice yelled down the phone.

'*Pen?* Is that you?'

'Who else did you think it would be?'

'I didn't know, did I? I don't have your number.'

'I got yours from Kelly. She didn't want to give it to me, but I didn't give her a lot of choice, so don't you go taking it out on her.'

'I wouldn't dream of it.'

'Good. Now, listen. You need to get back here, pronto.'

'Oh God, what's wrong?'

'Harriet is wasting away, that's what's wrong,' Pen said. 'I know the two of you have fallen out and I know why, but if you ask me, it's a stupid reason for you to split up. The pair of you need your heads knocking together. I know you love her, and she loves you, so stop fannying around and come back here and tell her. I can't have her in my cafe with a face like a wet weekend in January. It's enough to curdle the milk.'

'Pen, she doesn't want to see me again. She made that abund-antly clear.'

'Tosh! She was annoyed, that's all. Admittedly, what you did wasn't the best, but it's not as though you've killed anyone.'

When Pen put it like that… 'What do you mean, wasting away?'

'She's pining. Lost too much weight, if you ask me. It doesn't suit her. And like I said, she's as miserable as sin.'

As am I, Owen thought. He hesitated. 'I'm not sure she does love me,' he said.

'Believe me, she does. She told me. And anyone can see that you love her.'

'I do.'

'Well, then. Get your arse back to Foxmore and sort it out.'

'But what if she refuses to see me?'

'She can't refuse if you're in a public place, can she? And she's not going to make a scene, either, not in front of a shedload of people and the kids.'

'Are you talking about the Christmas Fayre tomorrow?' he realised.

'Blimey, give the man a gold star. What did you think I was talking about? You deserve to be there as much as Harriet and Kelly. This Fayre is only taking place because of you, so you should be there anyway, if you ask me. What do you say?'

'I'm not sure.'

'Let me put it another way: if you don't come back and tell Harriet you love her, you'll regret it for the rest of your life.'

Yes, Owen thought, *I probably will*, and with that, he made a decision. He would return to Foxmore tonight, to be there in the morning when the Fayre began.

However, when he hurried to tell his mother he was leaving, she wordlessly pointed to the window and his spirits sank. There was already a thick covering of snow on the ground, and more was falling. He would be lucky if he made it out of Narberth at this rate, and his chances of getting to Foxmore in time for the Fayre were next to nothing.

Chapter 22

It's a nice day for it, Harriet thought, as she opened the curtains and gazed out into the street. It was still dark at seven a.m. on this December Sunday morning, but there was no wind and the stars were visible in a cloudless sky. It promised to be cold and bright, a perfect day for a Christmas Fayre. A light smattering of snow lay on the grass, but not enough to construct a snowman, and the road and pavements were clear.

As they always did, her thoughts turned to Owen, and she wondered what he was doing right now. Would he remember that today was the day of the Christmas Fayre? Or would he have already forgotten all about Foxmore, and her?

Last night as she'd lain in bed, restless and sleepless, she had looked at his website and had been surprised there were no further posts. She had expected him to publish at least another one to end the challenge, but he'd written nothing new.

She'd told herself she shouldn't look, that it wasn't doing her any good, but she couldn't help herself. Neither could she help scrolling through the photos on her phone, and as she did so, she ignored the irony. She had been just as guilty of taking photos of him without his permission, but the difference was that she'd not posted them online for the whole world to see. She had also taken several with his knowledge, both on his own and with the kids, and she studied each one in turn, tears welling up to spill down her face, her heart aching.

'Stop this!' she groaned out loud, and felt a wet nose on her leg. 'Not you, Etta; as far as I know, you've not done anything wrong.'

Harriet had taken to letting the dog sleep on her bed, needing the comfort of Etta's unconditional love – and more than once over the past week, she had woken to find her nose buried in the sleek fur of the dog's neck and tears on her cheeks.

With a sigh, she closed the curtains again and headed for the shower. Pen was right: she *did* look a fright, so she had better try to make herself more presentable, or less like the walking dead at least, so a hair wash and a liberal layer of makeup were called for.

–

Holly Field was already busy when Harriet arrived, and she did a double-take. It was only nine thirty, and the Fayre wasn't due to kick off until eleven. On Kelly's advice, they had deliberately timed it not to open earlier. She had suggested that if people arrived mid- to late morning, they would be more likely to be hungry, so the food stalls and stands should do well. Besides, who wanted to get up at the crack of dawn to tramp around a cold field? Better to let people have a leisurely morning, then they would be more inclined to bundle up and leave their houses.

Stallholders were already setting up, and there was a heady scent of coffee and roasting chestnuts in the air, along with a mouth-watering smell of pulled pork and fried onions.

'Harriet! Over here!' Kelly was standing in front of a trailer called The Coffee Hut, and she was waving frantically.

As Harriet grew nearer, she saw that her friend was clutching two steaming cups and she increased her pace. Coffee would be very welcome right now, although despite the wonderful foody smells and not having bothered with breakfast this morning, she didn't feel hungry in the slightest. Maybe Pen was right, and she was wasting away.

Telling herself there would be plenty of opportunities to pile on the pounds when the Fayre was over, Harriet wrapped her mittened hands around the cup Kelly was holding out to her and gratefully took a sip. It was spiced with caramel and something else… 'Is there Baileys Irish Cream in this?' she asked.

'Lovely, isn't it?' Kelly said, smacking her lips.

'It's a bit early to start on the booze.'

'Give over, there's hardly enough in there to get a fly tipsy! Wait until the mulled wine starts flowing.'

'I take it you won't be doing much in the way of childcare today?' Harriet laughed. The coffee really was delicious and rather moreish.

'Jon is looking after them, but he'll be bringing them along later. How about you?'

'Mam and Dad are minding Sara and Bobby. They'll bring them later, too.' Harriet stamped her feet to try to bring some warmth into them. Despite wearing chunky boots and two pairs of thick socks, the cold was making its presence felt. The upside was that with the ground being frozen there wouldn't be any risk of tyres getting bogged down in the field, which had been one of her concerns, since Owen was no longer here to use the tractor to drag any stuck vehicles free.

'I feel as though we should be doing something,' Kelly said.

'Like what?'

'I don't know. But the three of us have been running around like headless chickens for so long, I feel at a loose end.' She was silent for a moment, then said, 'Have you heard from Owen?'

'No, and I don't expect to.' That was a fib, if she was honest; she'd been hoping that he thought enough of her to wish her luck today, but her phone had been utterly silent when it came to the man she was in love with.

Once again, pain flared in her chest and she swallowed down the lump in her throat.

Feeling at a bit of a loose end herself, Harriet suggested she and Kelly wander around to make sure there weren't any issues, and that there weren't any traders on site selling brand-new items. She wasn't quite sure what she would do if she found any, but she would probably leave that up to Kelly, who was far more frank than Harriet and would soon tell them to sling their hooks.

There was a definite buzz in the air, a sense of excitement and anticipation, and despite her glum mood, Harriet found herself becoming swept up in it. As the field gradually filled up and punters started arriving, she also felt a sense of achievement.

'You should be right proud of yourself,' Mrs Moxley said, as she came to stand by Harriet while she was looking at a stall set up by Mrs Moxley's granddaughter, Rachel.

'I am,' she said, 'but this isn't just down to me. Kelly did an awful lot of the work.' Harriet picked up a box containing a toy train. It was in pristine condition and if Bobby had been a few years younger she might have bought it for him, but it was more suited to a toddler than a nine-year-old. She had better hurry if she wanted to have a look around and snap up any bargains before her two appeared on the scene.

'I think it's also down to Owen,' Mrs Moxley said. 'He left a bit sharpish, didn't he? I heard you had a bust-up.'

Harriet put the toy train back on the table and picked up a tiny Babygro.

Mrs Moxley's eyes bulged. 'Blimmin' heck! You're not pregnant, are you? Is that why he buggered off?'

'No, I'm not pregnant. I keep forgetting how small they are when they're first born, that's all.' She hastily put the Babygro down.

'This is marvellous,' Bernie Williams said. 'I've bought loads already.' The pensioner held up a carrier bag. 'Can't stop,' he added, his eyes lighting up when he saw the stall next door and he dashed off, using his walking stick to nudge people out of the way.

'Someone's happy,' Mrs Moxley observed. She gave Harriet a keen glance. 'And someone else isn't.'

'I'd better be off, too,' Harriet said. 'I've still got a few more things to get.' If one more person asked her about Owen, she thought she might scream.

'Mammy, Mammy!' Harriet turned around at the sound of her youngest child's voice, and she smiled and held her arms open.

Bobby ran to her full tilt, nearly knocking her over. 'Can I have a hot dog? And some roast chestnuts?'

Harriet said to her mam and dad, who were following along a little more sedately, 'He did have breakfast, honest.'

'He's got hollow legs, that one,' Ginny said. Sara was hanging behind, and Harriet peered around her mam to ask, 'Are you OK, Sara? Would you like a hot dog?' Harriet was sure she could stretch to a couple. After all, Foxmore didn't have a Fayre like this every day of the week.

Sara was concentrating on something behind Harriet, and Harriet turned to see a man on stilts, juggling. *You didn't get to see one of those every day of the week, either,* she thought. This really was becoming rather festive: one of the stalls had Christmas tunes playing, which added to the atmosphere, and another was selling Christmas trees and green garlands, the scent of pine sharp and aromatic.

Harriet turned back to her daughter. 'Sara? Did you hear me? I asked if you wanted a hot dog.'

'I'm not hungry.' Her face was closed and pinched, and she looked worried. Her gaze was still fixed on a point behind Harriet, so Harriet looked again.

Oh dear, that was why, she realised, when she saw who Sara was staring at.

Darlene and her mother, Amanda, were heading their way, and Harriet pursed her lips. This was the last thing she needed, today of all days. She guessed Mrs Cooke hadn't yet had a chance to speak to either her staff or any of the children in Sara's class, so—

And there was Mrs Cooke herself, following a few paces behind Sara's nemesis.

Harriet straightened up and squared her shoulders, preparing to do battle. If that child so much as opened her mouth, Harriet would tell her what for. There was no way she was going to stand by while that horrible little girl intimidated her daughter. And the mother was no better. Fancy allowing her child to make fun of another right in front of her nose. Harriet would put her straight, as well.

She caught hold of Sara's hand. 'Leave this to me,' she hissed. 'If this isn't sorted out, I'm taking you out of that school.'

'I don't want to go to another school,' Sara muttered forlornly. 'All my friends are in this one.'

'You're right. If anyone should be going to another school, it should be Darlene. Shh, here they come.'

'Sara's mum, isn't it?' Amanda asked. 'I was hoping to see you. When Mrs Cooke phoned to tell me that your daughter had hit mine, I was appalled.'

'Just you hang on a minute,' Harriet snapped. 'I don't approve of what she did, and I certainly didn't encourage it, but she did have her reasons.'

'And what might they be?' Darlene's mother tilted her head to one side and looked at Harriet expectantly.

'You do know that Darlene has been bullying Sara, and quite a few of the other children? Physical violence might be unacceptable, but emotional abuse shouldn't be tolerated, either.'

'I totally agree.'

'Pardon?' Harriet must have misheard.

Amanda said, 'I admit I believed Darlene when she told me she had done nothing to provoke your daughter, and I also admit that I was pushing for a permanent exclusion. I didn't think three days was nearly enough. But then I found out the truth, didn't I, Darlene? I was hoping to bump into you today because Darlene owes your daughter an apology.' There was silence for a second, then Amanda nudged her daughter. 'Go on,' she urged.

Harriet turned her attention to the child and waited, hardly daring to believe what she was hearing.

'Sor-reee,' Darlene sang, a cocky expression on her face and a sneering twist to her lips.

Huh, Harriet thought – some apology that was.

Darlene's mother looked startled. 'Darlene! Say it as though you mean it.'

'But I don't. I'm not sorry,' Darlene said. 'She wore my cast-offs.' Her tone left no one in any doubt as to how she felt about that.

Harriet felt Sara shrink back at the girl's venomous words, and she pulled her daughter into her side, holding her close. That was it! She was definitely going to demand something be done about that child. If she was this openly nasty in front of adults, what must she be like when she was on her own with her peers? It didn't bear thinking about.

Harriet noticed Mrs Cooke drawing closer to listen and she shot the headteacher an I-told-you-so look.

'I'm so sorry,' Amanda said. 'I don't know what's got into her. She never used to be like this. It's since her dad walked out on us. I've been trying my best to keep things as normal as possible, but it hasn't been easy.' She gulped and her chin wobbled. She had tears in her eyes as she continued, 'I've been struggling to make ends meet—' She laughed bitterly. 'I know what you're thinking: that I can't have been struggling that much to have held Darlene's birthday party in Deri Castle, but her dad's sister is the general manager there, so I didn't have to pay for the hire of the room, and the food was at cost.'

Darlene's eyes were wide and her mouth was open. This was obviously news to her.

Her mother said, 'I had to sell some things to afford the Pandora bracelet she asked for, which was why I was at the boot sale. I'm so sorry you bought that dress. If I'd known what it was for...' She sighed.

To her surprise, Harriet felt sorry for the woman. Hadn't she herself tried to do the same thing in ensuring her own children's lives weren't affected when their father walked out? 'You weren't to know.'

Amanda swallowed. 'Do you know what's truly awful about all this? Apart from Darlene's inexcusable behaviour, that is. I,

281

myself, bought that dress second-hand from one of the boot sales I went to last year, plus the one she was wearing to her party. It's the only way I could afford to keep Darlene in the style to which she'd become accustomed.'

Darlene let out a gasp. 'You liar! You *didn't*!'

'Sorry, my love, I did.'

'I don't believe you!' Darlene cried, but the look in her eyes told Harriet that she did.

'So you see,' Amanda said to her daughter, 'you can get down off your high horse and apologise properly, because you've been wearing second-hand clothes, too. And not because of any noble reason like saving the planet, but because I couldn't afford to buy you all the things you wanted otherwise.'

Darlene was close to tears, and pity stirred in Harriet's chest. Hadn't Sara had the same reaction about wearing pre-loved items? And hadn't Harriet also kept details of her family's financial situation from her own children?

Harriet had more in common with Darlene's mother than she would ever have thought possible.

'Darlene!' Amanda cried. 'Apologise and mean it, or you'll be grounded from now until the New Year.'

'Mam!'

'I'm serious.'

Darlene began to cry. Great big sobs that shook her thin frame. 'I'm sorry, I really am.'

'Don't apologise to *me*, apologise to the person you humiliated and made fun of.'

Darlene's voice was small and hiccupping. 'Sorry, Sara.'

Sara looked up at Harriet, who nodded, smiling her encouragement.

'It's OK,' Sara said. She was sombre and uncertain, and Harriet didn't think the two girls would ever be bosom buddies, but at least hopefully the bullying would now stop.

'Good,' Mrs Cooke said, coming to stand next to Darlene. She put a hand on the child's shoulder. 'I think you've learnt a valuable lesson today. I've been hearing some disturbing things about you, young lady, but I hope your behaviour will improve after this.' The headteacher glanced at Harriet and gave her a quick smile. 'Now, shall we put this behind us, and enjoy the Fayre? I must say, it's a credit to you, Mrs Parry, as is your daughter.' She turned to Sara. 'Which brings me to the reason I'm here today – besides picking up a few bits and pieces for Christmas, of course. Sara, how would you like to be the school's Eco Advisor? I think you'll be perfect for the job.'

Sara was dumbstruck, and Harriet had to give her a nudge to remind her to speak.

'Yes, please,' she said shyly. 'Thank you, Miss. Did you hear that, Mam? I'm to be the Eco Advisor.' She was beaming with pride.

Harriet was beaming, too, and she swelled with love for her gorgeous little girl.

But she was soon brought back down to earth when Sara said, 'I wish Owen was here. He'd be so pleased. Can I phone him and tell him?'

Oh, poo…

Owen spotted Harriet as soon as he'd driven onto Holly Field, his eyes drawn to her like iron filings to a magnet, and he had hurried to park the van. But by the time he'd reached her, she had been deep in conversation with another woman, and a small crowd had gathered around her.

As tempted as he had been to butt in, he'd hung back, sensing that something significant was happening. Kelly was with her, looking serious, and so were Harriet's parents, so he edged closer to listen.

At first he was appalled, but as the story unfolded, he began to feel some sympathy for Darlene and her mother.

When he heard Darlene apologise to Sara and then Mrs Cooke ask Sara if she wanted to be the Eco Advisor, his pride had almost matched Harriet's, and his heart clenched when Sara said she wished she could phone him to tell him her good news.

Owen was unable to hold back any longer. 'You can tell me to my face,' he said, and he choked up when Sara yelled, 'Owen!' and threw herself at him.

'Oof!' Her head caught him in the solar plexus and he almost toppled backwards. His arms automatically came around her to give her a hug, and when Bobby, not to be outdone, hurried to his side, Owen gave him a cuddle too. With a child under each arm, he stared at Harriet.

She stared back. Kelly leant into her and whispered something in her ear. He wished he knew what she'd said, but was reassured when Kelly gave him a brief wave and wandered off.

Harriet continued to stare.

Inanely, he said, 'You've not had much snow here.'

Harriet blinked. 'Um, no.' The proud smile on her face from a moment ago had vanished, leaving her looking pale and subdued.

Reluctantly, he released her children, and Sara and Bobby began talking at once, but Owen's attention was fixed on their mother.

'I had a devil of a job getting here,' he told her.

'Did you?'

'The roads around Narberth were almost impassable last night. I got stuck a few times on the A40.'

'Did you?' she repeated. Her tone gave nothing away.

Owen pushed on, his mouth chuntering as his brain tried to catch up. 'I drove into a drift once and a police SUV had to pull me out. I'm glad it's not as bad here.' He glanced around the field. 'It's a good turnout.'

'It is.'

The children had stopped talking and were looking concerned, sensing something was up.

Ginny said to them, 'Come on, you two, let's leave your mam and Owen to chat. I'm sure they've got plenty to talk about.'

And as she pushed past him, she hissed in his ear, 'If you break her heart again, you'll have me to answer to.'

Bemused, scared and hopeful at the same time, Owen watched Harriet's parents lead the children away. Darlene and her mother had also disappeared, and everyone was going about their own business. No one was taking the slightest notice of him. Except for Harriet: she hadn't taken her eyes off his face, her expression unfathomable.

'Why are you here?' she asked, just as the silence was becoming unbearable. 'Is it to finish off your blog?'

'My blog is the last thing on my mind.'

'It shouldn't be, it's good.'

'It's not important. I'm here to beg you to forgive me. What I did was stupid. I should have asked you.'

'Yes, you should.'

'I can delete it, and I will if you want me to, but thousands have already read it.'

'I don't want you to. As I said, it's good.'

More silence. The sounds of the Fayre ebbed and flowed around them, but he and Harriet might as well have been in a soundproof box for all the notice he took of the rest of the world. The only thing he could concentrate on was her.

He said, 'You might not want to hear this, and if you want me to leave afterwards, I'll leave. But I've got to tell you, so...'

'What?'

Gosh, she wasn't making this easy for him. 'I love you.'

'I know. Pen told me.'

'Your boss is a force to be reckoned with,' he said. 'She ordered me to get my backside to Foxmore because she was worried you were fading away.'

'Do I look as though I'm fading away?'

'You look beautiful. You *are* beautiful. I meant it when I said I love you.'

'I know,' she repeated, and he felt like crying.

Pen had got it wrong; Harriet didn't love him after all.

'And I love you.' Harriet whispered it, and it took Owen a heartbeat to realise what she had said.

He closed his eyes, relief sweeping through him, followed by the most exquisite happiness he had ever felt. He opened them again slowly, hoping he hadn't dreamt it.

She was still there, love in her eyes and a smile on her gorgeous, luscious, kissable lips.

'Come here,' he said, his voice thick with emotion, and he held out his arms.

When Harriet stepped into them and he wrapped her in his embrace, he knew he was the luckiest man on the planet.

Chapter 23

Owen would have loved to have woken up in Harriet's bed on Christmas morning, but they hadn't quite got to the stage where he spent the night with her. It would be soon, he knew, but Christmas Eve wasn't the ideal time for such a momentous event. For one thing, he suspected the kids would be up at the crack of dawn, bounding into their mother's bedroom, eager to open their presents and get the day started. The last thing they needed was to see a big hairy bloke in their mum's bed. Instead, Owen had spent most of the evening with them, staying until after the children had gone to bed, bleary-eyed and filled with overtired excitement (the children, not him). He and Harriet had shared a long, passionate kiss before he had turned the collar of his coat up against the cold, shoved his hands into his pockets and headed off into the darkness.

Even before he'd swung his feet out of bed and slid down the ladder this morning, he could hear his phone trilling with a message. Several messages, in fact: two from Harriet, one from Sara, via Harriet, one from Bobby – not via Harriet, because the boy must have stolen her phone and typed the message himself – one from his parents and one from his brother.

His brother had sent him a photo of the whole family sitting in the living room, with the children on the floor in front of the Christmas tree, and for a second he felt quite homesick, until he saw the time the photo had been sent. Four thirty-seven a.m. Perhaps he wasn't quite as homesick after all… Anyway, he had a whole day in Harriet's company to look forward to, and he wouldn't swap that for anything.

Sorry guys, he thought, as he studied the picture. His parents had been disappointed when he had told them that he wasn't going to be spending Christmas with them, but his mum and dad fully understood his decision, and were totally behind him. His mum had been relieved and thrilled when Owen had phoned to say that he had arrived in Foxmore (he hadn't mentioned the hairy driving conditions) and that he and Harriet were an item once more. She had been excitedly prattling on about meeting her two new grandchildren, and the possibility of more on the way – commenting that he and Harriet should get a move on if they wanted to try for a baby together, because neither of them was getting any younger – when he had hung up on her. Having a baby was not something he and Harriet had talked about, and they might never do. He was perfectly happy with being a stepdad to Harriet's two, without feeling the need to have a biological child of his own. His family was already complete.

He hadn't left his presents for Harriet or the children under their tree, because he wanted to be there to see their faces when they opened his gifts, so he had the quickest shower in the world, hastily got dressed and hurried out of the door. Although he had slept like a yule log last night, he had missed Harriet and he couldn't wait to see her again. Ten hours was far too long to be without her.

He scuffed through the remains of the snow (Foxmore might have got away lightly the day of the Christmas Fayre, but later that night there had been a heavy snowfall) as he skidded along the road, earning himself some smiles and quizzical looks from those people already out and about, and soon he was on her step.

Before he had a chance to ring the doorbell, Sara flung the door open and dragged him inside.

'Owen, Owen!' she cried.

Shucking off his coat and hanging it on the peg behind the door, he followed the excited girl into the living room to see

288

Harriet and Bobby crouched over an intricate train set that Harriet was trying to put together. Etta was looking on intently, with a new toy between her paws. The scene was so perfectly Christmassy that it made his heart swell with love.

Harriet looked up. 'You're a sight for sore eyes,' she said. 'Can you finish this off, while I get the children some breakfast? Honestly, you need a degree in mechanics to put this thing together.'

Owen knelt on the floor and studied the train set. Wow, it did look complicated.

'Would you like some breakfast, or have you eaten?' Harriet asked.

'I'd love some, please. But before you make it, come here, all of you. I want to take a photo.'

'I hope this isn't for your blog?' Harriet chided. 'I thought you were done with that.'

Owen was. Before the Fayre had ended, he had taken a couple of quick snaps and had posted them online to wrap up his blog on the subject of not buying anything new. He was now considering how to help schools champion their own Eco Advisors – with Sara's help and Harriet's permission.

'I want to send it to my parents and my brother,' he said, showing her the photo that he had received earlier. 'I've got my own family now.'

'Do you mean that?'

'I've never meant anything more in my life. Now, gather round and say cheese.'

'*Cheese!*'

–

'What a day!' Harriet collapsed onto her sofa with a deep sigh, stretched out her legs and wiggled her toes. They were clad in a pair of snuggly Nordic socks that she had bought at the Christmas Fayre. Their previous owner had never worn them, disliking their colourful cheeriness; however, Harriet thought they reflected her bright mood perfectly.

She yawned. 'I'm shattered. It's been fun, though, hasn't it? I can't believe how much food my mam cooked. My parents are going to be eating bubble and squeak for the next week.'

Etta scrambled onto the sofa and cuddled into her, and Harriet absently stroked the dog's floppy ears. Etta let out a contented groan. The dog should be happy after the amount of turkey she'd eaten. It was a wonder the little creature hadn't burst.

'I love a bit of bubble and squeak,' Owen declared. He handed her a glass of mulled wine, sat down next to her and put his arm around her shoulders. She curled up and snuggled into him, feeling the solidity of his chest on her cheek and the strength of his arm as he held her close.

On the other side of her, Etta opened one eye, wagged her tail at Owen and then went back to her snoozing.

'Comfy?' Owen burrowed his face into Harriet's hair, seeking the sensitive delicate skin just behind her ear, and when he found it, he kissed her, making her squirm with delighted ticklishness. He was very good at walking that thin line between making her shriek with laughter and making her gasp with desire.

'It was nice of your mum to make me a nut roast and vegetarian gravy,' Owen said.

'You are a member of the family now. But I've got to warn you, you'll probably be sick of nut roast by the time next Christmas comes around.'

'You think I'll still be here next Christmas?' he teased.

'You'd better be,' Harriet warned. 'You don't want Pen hunting you down again.'

'I'm so glad she did.' Owen put his glass down on the floor by his feet and took hers out of her hand, putting that on the floor too.

'Oi, I hadn't finished!' she protested.

'I thought you might want me to kiss you, but if you prefer to drink wine—'

'Kiss me, kiss me,' she urged, anxious to feel his lips on hers now that he had put the idea into her head. They could drink the wine later. Much later, if she had her way...

'Before I do,' he said, 'there's something I want to tell you. I've decided to sell the van.'

Harriet sucked in a breath. 'Why?' She hadn't been expecting him to say anything like that, and she wondered what had made him decide.

'Because I want to buy a house. I told you that I'm serious about settling down in Foxmore, so I think it's time I put down roots here.'

Over my dead body, she thought. 'I don't think you should sell it. The van has been a part of your life for so long that you'll only regret it. I've got a better idea. Why don't you move in with us?'

'Pardon?'

'I'm serious. Why don't you move in with me and the children?'

When he didn't say anything, Harriet wondered whether it had been too soon to mention something so momentous. He probably wasn't ready for such a commitment and—

'I'd love to.' He was gazing at her with such adoration that she was finding it difficult to breathe. 'But what about the van?' he asked. 'There's no point in keeping it, if we're living together.'

'There is – we're going to need something to take our holidays in,' she said. 'And the first one should be in the New Year, to Narberth. You've met my parents, it's only fair I meet yours. I want to see where you grew up.'

'They'll love you,' he said. 'And the children.' He squirmed around on the sofa so he was facing her. 'What a brilliant idea!' He drew her close and bent his head.

Harriet lifted her chin, closing her eyes, ready to be kissed. But before his lips met hers, she said, 'We might as well begin as we mean to go on. Stay the night... Please?'

'I thought you'd never ask.'

Harriet disentangled herself from his embrace and got to her feet. She held out her hand to him and he rose slowly, his gaze locking onto hers as she wrapped her arms around his neck. She nibbled his lips, her tongue finding its way into his mouth to kiss him deeply.

'Mmm,' she murmured, coming up for air after several delicious minutes. 'Shall we go upstairs?'

'We'd better, unless you want me to ravish you under the Christmas tree.'

'I don't think that's a good—' she began, when a loud huff interrupted her.

Etta was staring at them. But instead of pretending she had an injured paw, she got up, scrabbled at the cushion, turned in a circle and then lay back down.

Harriet laughed. 'Do you know what that means?' When Owen shook his head, she said, 'It looks like you have Etta's seal of approval. She knows you are part of the family, too.'

And when Harriet looked at the little dog's face, Etta was smiling.

Acknowledgements

I am thankful to so many people in my life. Here's a handful…

Emily – my enthusiastic and supportive editor.

The rest of the Canelo team – because they're just as fab.

Catherine Mills – no relation, unless being my soul-sister counts.

My mum – who prefers crime novels but reads my books regardless.

My daughter – I am so immensely proud of her.

My husband – the hero in my very own romance.

Poppy – the sweetest, most loving dog in the world. She makes me smile every day.

You, my readers – because you chose to read this book. You have my heartfelt thanks and gratitude xxx